Sara Lewis was born in New York City but she has lived in many places, including Santa Barbara, San Francisco, Boston, Holland, and London where she was at acting school for a year. When her ambition to act fizzled, she turned to clinical psychology, but she soon realised that what she really wanted to do was write. With a job as a textbook editor to pay the rent, she started writing short stories. Her stories have been widely published in the States and after her collection *Trying to Smile and Other Stories* was published, she wrote her first novel, *Heart Conditions*.

Sara Lewis now lives in California with her husband and two children. *But I Love You Anyway* is her second novel.

Also by Sara Lewis

HEART CONDITIONS

Sara Lewis

But I Love You Anyway

ABACUS

An *Abacus* Book

First published in the United States
by Harcourt Brace and Company in 1996
First published in Great Britain by Abacus in 1996

A CIP catalogue record for this book
is available from the British Library.

ISBN 0 349 10717 3

Printed and bound in Great Britain
by Clays Ltd, St Ives plc

Abacus
A Division of
Little, Brown and Company (UK)
Brettenham House
Lancaster Place
London WC2E 7EN

Contents

1 Nice to Meet You   1

2 Downpour   4

3 "I Don't Remember You"   19

4 Someone Else's Date   34

5 Creative Business Solutions   55

6 Nice Family   74

7 Brake Lights   94

8 The Meaning of Skunks   116

9 The Henry Thing   138

10 The Money Thing   158

11 Merry Christmas   168

12 Oldies   187

13 Emergency   205

14 Good Things, Bad Things   214

15 Sorry, We're Closed   231

16 Things Work Out   238

17 Now, This Moment   247

But I Love
You Anyway

CHAPTER 1

Nice to Meet You

My sister, Eve, was late. We were meeting for coffee. I took one of the empty tables and sat there for a minute or two, waiting. Eve had been very distracted lately because she had just fallen in love. The week before, she went to one of her self-help workshops, called Meditate to Find Your True Mate. Sure enough, it happened right there at the workshop. His name was John, and already she was spending every spare minute with him. When she wasn't with him, she was thinking about him. A couple of days after they met, I had found her spaced-out next to the big photocopy machine in our store, smiling to herself and making a hundred copies of someone's water bill, instead of just one. She kept taking phone calls from John in the back room of our store, closing the door and leaving me stranded with a growing line of customers in a hurry. Twice, she had arrived at work in the morning directly from his house, looking dazed and rumpled in her clothes from the day before.

This morning she had called me just as I was about to leave to take my children to school, and said, "Let's get together before work. I want to show you something. I'm on my way out now. I'll meet you at the good coffee place as soon as you're done at school." And now she was late. I wondered how long it was going to take before the effects of falling in love wore off.

I had my bank statement in my purse, so I took it out and started going over it. As I went down the columns checking off the ATM withdrawals, I had the feeling that someone was looking over my shoulder. I looked up and glared at a man who had sat down right beside me with his cup of black coffee. Instead of looking away when I caught him scanning my bank statement, he looked me straight in the face and smiled. He said, "Good morning. Perfect day, isn't it? Way too nice to be balancing the books. And you look like the kind of person who always comes out in the black anyway."

I gave the slightest grunt of an acknowledgment to let him know that I did not feel like chatting, nor did I appreciate his peering over my shoulder. I went back to marking off the checks I'd written.

"Where's your coffee?" he said. "Can I buy you one?"

"No," I said without looking up. "Thank you." I could feel him still looking at what I was doing, like warm breath on the back of my neck. I folded up my papers and looked around for another table. Now the place was full and there wasn't one.

"That's a pretty necklace," he said. "What is that?" He reached forward to touch the heart I wear on a chain around my neck. I drew away from his hand, leaving it stranded in midair. He smiled again. "Hey," he said. "I just wanted to know if that's onyx. I wasn't going to bite you."

I looked out the front of the place to see if my sister was coming. "Yeah," I said. "Onyx."

"Late again, huh?" he said, following my gaze to the parking lot. "I'm going to get you some coffee." He stood up. "We'll have our coffee together. No sense in us both sitting here alone. Cappuccino? Latte? Café au lait? Am I close? It's something with milk in it, right? And you don't look like the low-fat or skim type to me. Tell me if I'm on the right track."

Firmly, I said, "I don't want you to buy me coffee. Thank you anyway."

He smiled at me, stood up, and got in line.

My sister came in then. I stood up. "Eve," I said. "Let's sit outside. This creepy guy sat down next to me and wouldn't leave me alone. Or better yet, let's get our coffee to go and take it to the store. I want to get out of here."

She said, "But we still have an hour before we open, and I wanted to show you something."

"Show me at the store. Let's go."

"Wait," she said. "Take it easy. What did he do that was so creepy?"

I said, "I don't know. He said he liked my necklace, and he wanted to buy me coffee."

"I see what you mean," she said sarcastically. "Disgusting."

Just then, the guy walked up with a cardboard cup in his hand. "I decided on café au lait," he said, trying to hand me the cup. When I wouldn't take it, he put it on the table. Then he kissed my sister on the mouth. They looked deeply into each other's eyes for what seemed like the longest time.

My sister said to me, "This is John. John, this is my sister, Mary. She's called Mimi. This is what I wanted to show you, Mimi: the love of my life."

"Oh," I said. "Nice to meet you."

CHAPTER 2

Downpour

Eight months later, Eve and John were getting married at the edge of a cliff.

It was a two-hour drive to the wedding site. I drove with my mother and my two children. We didn't want to get our wedding clothes messed up on the long drive, so we all wore our everyday clothes until just before we got there. There would be no place to change at the spot where the ceremony was to be, my sister had warned me. A few miles short of our destination, I pulled over and parked at the side of the road so that we could all take turns changing in the car. "Grandma first," I said. My daugher, Melanie, who was eleven-and-a-half, and my son, Daniel, who was nine-and-a-half, waited with me up the road, while my mother wiggled out of her velour walking suit and into her mother-of-the-bride outfit.

It had been sunny and warm when we left our house in San Diego. Now Melanie and Daniel were hugging themselves to keep warm in a strong, cool wind. There were big, dark clouds overhead. "It's going to rain," Melanie said. "When I get married, I'm doing it inside, in a church with stained-glass windows."

I said, "It's not going to rain. You just wait and see. The sky will clear just before the wedding. The sun will come out. It will be perfect. The weather has a way of cooperating for weddings. Your turn to change." My mother came to join us. "You look nice," I said.

She tugged at her skirt. "Well," she said, looking down at herself skeptically. "It's the best I could do."

Melanie put on her dress, peach colored with big white flowers on it, chosen by my sister because Melanie was a bridesmaid. Then she put on eyeshadow and brushed her hair several times. I tried not to look too much and managed not to call to her to hurry up.

My mother said, "This wind! I don't know why I even bothered with my hair." She put her hands to the sides of her head. Then she looked up at the sky. "It's going to rain."

"No, it's not," I said. "It's going to be beautiful."

My mother held her hair down and looked at me sideways. Melanie got out of the car.

Daniel was fast, getting into his khaki pants and button-down shirt in about two minutes flat. His father—we were divorced—had taken him to get a navy blue blazer. A tie was out of the question.

I was even faster than Daniel. As matron of honor, I had a peach dress just like Melanie's, only bigger. The color was not good on me, but I didn't care about that. I was just grateful that I hadn't had to shop for anything, except shoes. When I was finished dressing, I called them all to get back in the car. "Let's go," I said. "We don't want to be late."

We continued uphill until we came to the place where the wedding was to be and pulled into a paved parking lot, where, so far, there were only two other cars.

We were early. The only other people there when we arrived were a photographer and John's friend Dave, an ordained minister without a parish, who was going to perform the ceremony. The wedding was to take place on a grassy flat place with a sweeping view all the way to the ocean. There were a lot of white folding chairs set up in rows. A strong wind pushed against us, parting our hair in the wrong places, flattening it across our heads. My dress pressed tight against my legs. The photographer took pictures of us being windblown, and I thought about how I would have to look at them for the rest of my life. Or maybe not; you couldn't tell how things would turn out.

My sister arrived. A friend brought her. Someone else was bringing the groom. Eve wanted her dress to be a surprise for John. She joined us behind a clump of bushes, where she tried to hide as well as stay out of the wind.

"You look beautiful," I said, and she did. She had on a long white dress with a tight beaded bodice, a cinched waist, and a full skirt. She had her hair down and wore a veil made from the lace overskirt of the dress our mother had worn forty-three years before.

The other guests—about a hundred of them—began arriving in a caravan of all kinds of cars. Shiny new vans with telephone antennas, beat-up hatchbacks, station wagons, and a couple of motorcycles pulled up and parked. Dressed-up people found seats. My mother sat in the front row, across the aisle from John's mother, father, and brother, who had come all the way from Minnesota, and his sister, who lived in Orange County. Melanie, Daniel, Eve, and I waited behind the bushes. Eve's veil was blowing wildly to one side. I caught it and held on to it. It was so old and fragile, I was afraid the lace would tear.

"Don't," Eve snapped at me. "Leave it alone." I let the veil go and didn't say anything. I knew she was just nervous. She stood for a few minutes frowning at the clouds. "It's going to rain," she said.

"No, it isn't," I said. "If it rains at all today, it will be much later, after dark. Tonight."

"It better be," she snarled, folding her arms.

The car arrived with John in it. My stomach shriveled. I thought I was doing such a good job of acting happy for the wedding, but now I could feel my face dropping and had to work hard to pull it back up the way I wanted it. There was something about John that always made me feel I should zip my purse shut when he was near me and try not to say too much. I decided to admire the view for a minute until I got myself organized again. It was all clouds now; you couldn't see down to the ocean anymore because of a deep layer of light gray and a new underlayer of dark gray, rolling toward us on the strong wind.

"Let's start," Eve said. Melanie went to tell the minister it was time.

I put my arm around Eve's shoulders. "You look perfect," I said. "Everything will be just the way you want it."

She smiled at me, and we hugged.

A woman started playing her acoustic guitar and singing "Imagine." Melanie and I made our slow walk between the two rows of chairs and took our place in front of the minister. Then Daniel came up the aisle with Eve on his arm. I could see my mother rummaging for Kleenex in her bag. I knew what got to her. It was seeing Daniel offer his arm to Eve, that John Lennon song and all the hope and sorrow that always came with it. Eve and Daniel seemed so vulnerable, so exposed, standing there in the wind.

My mother had cried when I got married too. Both times. I was still in college the first time. We were divorced when Daniel was two. My children saw their dad every other weekend. Three years after our divorce, I remarried. Then, two years later, my second husband, Bill, died of cancer just three months after he became ill.

All day, I had been thinking about how much had happened since Bill died. My kids had gotten a lot bigger and smarter. My mother had earned a state achievement award for teaching. Eve had become my business partner, taking Bill's place at the mail-and-parcel center he and I had started. I didn't want to run it by myself. For years, Eve had been a doll maker, selling her work at craft fairs all over the country. The traveling had worn her down. After she came to work with me full-time, I built her a dollhouse with real panes in the windows and a skylight that opened and shut. Eve was working on making a family for it. If I could give Bill a tour of my life as it was now, that tiny skylight would have been one of the things I would want him to see. Today Eve was marrying someone Bill had never met.

I looked at the groom, standing beside my sister. John was nice-looking enough, clean shaven with a good haircut and straight white teeth. I was not sure what it was about him that put me off. He bought me presents; maybe that was it. Expensive French perfume, a Walkman cassette player with auto-reverse, and a silk scarf all appeared gift wrapped with my name on them within a few months of his meeting my sister, nice presents that I would never use, no matter what. Or it may have been the way he was so kind to my children that gave me the creeps, offering to pick up Daniel from soccer or Melanie from the library when we got busy in the store. It could have been the way he asked to help out in the store and didn't expect to be paid that got under my skin. Or it might have been the way he was so positive and encouraging every time anything went wrong. I was working on making myself like him. I had never seen him do anything bad. And my own sister loved him and claimed she was going to spend the rest of her life with him. Despite my efforts, so far I had not been successful at changing my feelings about John.

Now I didn't dare look at my mother, who had told me that the first time she saw John, the back of her neck prickled and she got goose bumps on her arms. We had had several secret discussions about him. "I want to know where his money comes from," my mother had whispered. "And then again, I'm not sure I do."

My sister was thirty-eight and had never been married. She'd had plenty of boyfriends, some serious, but due to one disaster or another, she had not married any of them. After all those years of trying to work things out with one guy after another, Eve had decided right away that she wanted to be with John forever. She had been planning this wedding most of the eight months since she met him.

By this time, I was sure my mother would be really blubbering. One thing I was not going to do was cry. I had absolutely decided against it. Under normal circumstances, I cried easily. And weddings were crying traps, with all the promises about love and trust and happiness, about two people becoming joined as one. I knew it would be work, but I was up to it. I could be very tough and unemotional when I put my mind to it.

The minister was saying, "Please turn to face one another." They did. "Do you, John, promise to love, honor, and cherish Eve forever?" John promised. The minister said, "Do you, Eve, promise to love, honor, and cherish John forever?" Eve promised. The sky grew darker.

Eve handed me her flowers so she and John could look into each other's eyes and slide rings over one another's fingers. I didn't shed a single tear, didn't even get the slightest clenching in my throat. My chin did not tremble, and my eyes did not blur with tears. I congratulated myself on my strength.

It started to rain, just a few giant spatters for several seconds. One landed on my wrist, then three big plops of water made the bouquet shudder in my hands. Eve and John kissed, and suddenly we were all standing in a downpour. There was no cover, not even a tent or a big tree to run for. It got noisy with the rain and everyone jumping up out of chairs and telling each other what to do. I handed the flowers back to my sister. She looked at me, momentarily frozen in panic.

Quickly, I said, "Rain at a wedding is good luck! Did you know that? This means you'll have children and always be happy together!"

"It does?" she said. The rain flattened her bangs into wet strings. John took her hand, and they ran between the chairs to a waiting car and drove off to the hotel where the reception was going to be.

My mother, my children, and I ran to our car. My mother was still crying. "She looked so pretty before the rain started," she said. I handed her a tissue. She wiped her eyes. "Such a shame to have the weather spoil everything." She sobbed quietly.

"Rain at a wedding is good luck," I said, patting her.

"I'm sure it is," she said. She wiped her face with the tissue and looked at herself in the rearview mirror. "But look at my hair! That wind was just unbelievable. Now that it's wet, there's not a thing I can do." She turned the mirror so she could see herself better and went to work with a hairbrush, fixing herself up. "You wait. You'll cry just as hard at Melanie's wedding."

"No, she won't," Melanie said from the backseat. "I'm not getting married."

"Oh, I think you'll change your mind about that someday, sweetheart," said my mother.

"I won't. But if I do, I'm not inviting anybody. I'm going

to get married on a beach in Hawaii and not tell anyone until after it's over."

"That sounds very nice," I said, looking through the little rivers running down the rear window as I backed up the car. "Very peaceful."

"What happened to the church?" Daniel said. "The stained-glass windows?"

"I changed my mind," Melanie said.

"I'll invite you to my wedding, Mom," Daniel said.

"Thank you," I said.

"Nobody will marry you," Melanie said. "No one on the face of this earth."

"Shut up," he said.

"Guys," I said, putting the car into first and falling in behind a van in a line of cars on its way to the reception. "Let's all just be happy for Aunt Eve today. No fighting or whining for the rest of the day. How about that?" The two of them were quiet, looking out their windows at the rain.

At the hotel, I stood in front of the hand dryer in the women's room, hitting the button over and over again, twirling around, bending my knees, standing on my toes, trying to get my dress dry. Melanie patted her dress and hair with paper towels. My mother was flapping her skirt trying to get the wrinkles out. Despite our efforts, we looked bedraggled.

When we came out, Daniel was waiting for us, leaning against a wall nearby. He had changed back into his jeans and T-shirt. "What's this?" I said. "You can't wear that here. This is a wedding reception."

"You look like a slob," Melanie said.

"A dry slob," said Daniel. "Mom, I'm starving. Do we get to eat now?"

My mother said, "Are you going to let him look like that at your sister's wedding reception?"

"I guess so," I said.

Melanie said, "If I did that, you'd kill me."

I said, "Do you want to change into your dry clothes? You can if you want to."

"And look like a jerk?" Melanie said. "No thank you!"

We all followed Daniel into the dining room.

There were tables set up for a sit-down lunch, but first everyone was supposed to stand around, drink champagne, and talk. Melanie and Daniel sank into a big white couch, and I went to the bar to get them sodas. While I was waiting, I looked around at the other guests. A few of my sister's friends from high school were there, women a couple of years younger than me with husbands or boyfriends I'd never seen before. There were also several of her more current friends, a couple of them customers from our store. Friends and family of John's were around, though not as many as from Eve's side. Then there were some people who seemed to be connected to both of them, people they had met at the meditation workshop and kept in touch with.

Just a couple more hours, I told myself, then I could go home, put on loose clothes, play loud music, and start sketching out a desk I was planning to build in my garage.

It seemed a little too quiet for a wedding reception. Most of the people didn't know each other. There was music playing, a tape of Eve and John's favorite songs. Their songs were like their guests: I could tell which ones were Eve's, which ones were John's, and which had become important to both of them over the last several months. Eve's songs were the alternative rock ones, dating back no further than three or four years. John had chosen a lot of oldies from the sixties and even the fifties. My sister and I had always disliked oldies. Even as girls, we scorned out-of-date music. "If you listen to oldies, you might as well be dead," my sister used to say. As "Going to the Chapel" was finishing, I asked myself for the hundredth time how Eve could marry someone who would choose to have oldies at their wedding. What about him could have changed her mind about something so fundamental as music?

My heart leapt at the introduction to a song Melanie and I liked. It was "Sometimes" by James. I hurried with the drinks back to the couch so I could get there before the vocals started. I made it, just barely, sliding a little on the smooth wood floor in my new shoes, before I squeezed in between my two kids and began to sing with Melanie.

> *There's a storm outside*
> *and the gap between crack and thunder*
> *crack and thunder*
> *is closing in. It's closing in.*

Melanie and I kept singing together all the way to the chorus—the part that Melanie liked best that went "Sometimes when I look deep into your eyes, I swear I can see your soul"—through to the end, the same way that, since we were teenagers, Eve and I had sung hundreds of songs memorized from the radio.

My sister probably put the song on the tape for Melanie and me, not knowing how appropriate the lyrics about rain would be. Hearing it was like unexpectedly running into an old friend after a bad day. Until it came on and suddenly made me feel better, I hadn't realized that the wedding had reminded me of a funeral. It was the wind and the gray sky and standing on grass with a group of close family and friends, listening to a minister. I kept thinking of Bill. And I felt that today I was losing someone else close to me forever. Marrying John, Eve seemed to be leaving me, if she hadn't departed already, to be in a faraway place where I couldn't reach her.

People could become annoyed by our family habit of sing-

ing along. Either they liked the song themselves and our am-
ateur voices ruined it for them, or they didn't know the song
and felt excluded. Today it didn't seem to bother anyone, because at the reception, the guests all seemed to belong to separate, disconnected groups anyway. When the song ended, a
couple of guests clapped, smiling indulgently at us. I felt myself turn red to the roots of my hair.

I stood up and tried to find someone to talk to so that
later my sister wouldn't have anything to complain about con-
cerning my behavior at her wedding reception. "Isn't it beautiful that they found each other?" said a thin blond woman in
an early sixties thrift-store suit and a blue pillbox hat, most
likely one of the meditation workshop crowd. "I just love them
both so much. I think they're perfect together."

I said, "Yes."

There was a blank pause with me smiling stupidly into it,
then the woman in the pillbox hat said, "Are you a friend of
theirs?"

I said, "I'm Eve's sister."

"Oh," said the woman. "Now I see it. You look alike." She
drifted away.

Daniel laughed. Eve and I didn't look at all alike. She was
fair, and I was dark. She had blue eyes, and I had brown. I
was five feet eleven inches tall, and she was five seven. She
had a long, thin face, and I had a round face. You could hardly
tell that we came from the same family, except for our feet.
We both wore size eleven shoes and had extra-long second
toes. This was one of the ways we knew for sure that we were
really sisters; our feet were the feet of twins.

It was time to sit down for lunch. I hoped I wasn't going
to feel pressured into making a toast. I tried to think what I
would say if I had to and my mind went blank. I found my
place card and sat down. I was at a long table with the bride
and groom, my mother, and other family and friends. Melanie

and Daniel were at another table with three younger kids and some adults who were not the parents of the other kids. I wanted to sit with my children, but my sister had strong ideas about the way she wanted things on her wedding day, and I knew better than to ask for changes.

Eve and John were sitting at the center of the table, and I was across from them. Now they were smiling at me over the flower arrangement between us. I smiled back. "Everything looks so nice," I said, my voice sounding hollow.

I was sitting next to John's brother, Frank, whose wife couldn't come because they lived in Minnesota and she had just had a baby. "When I left home," Frank was saying, "there was snow on the ground and more expected. Where I live, you couldn't have considered an outdoor wedding this time of year. You've got to be grateful that it was just rain today. I hope you people appreciate the weather out here."

"We don't," I said. "We've lived in San Diego all our lives. When Eve and I were little, we used to wish it would snow. We made sleds for our dolls out of cardboard boxes and tried to make them slide down grassy hills in parks and sloped cement driveways. It never quite worked."

Frank laughed. Food came. I looked over at Melanie and Daniel, worried that they wouldn't eat it. They were talking conspiratorially to each other. I hoped they were going to talk to the other kids and the man and woman at their table. My mother was concentrating on her food, and I tried to do the same.

"Nice ceremony," Frank said.

"Very nice," I said. "They put it together themselves."

"I hear you're going to Mexico for your honeymoon," Frank said to Eve and John. They weren't listening. Eve finished saying something to John. He laughed.

"Cancún," I said. "They're going to Cancún."

The pillbox-hat woman said she and her husband went to

Europe. "We started off in Paris and traveled all over for three months. It was a blast," she said. "I'll never forget it." I wondered where he was today.

My mother said, "We went to Niagara Falls. It seems so silly now. But we were very young at the time—way too young when I look back on it—and it was exciting and beautiful." For a moment, a dreamy glow came over her face.

I looked at the children again. Daniel was saying something to the woman they were sitting with, and it was more than three syllables; that was good. Melanie was chewing something; also good.

Next to me, Frank said, "We went to Portugal, and it was cold and rainy. The food was terrible. Even the tea was bad. How can you make bad tea? But it didn't matter. We stayed in the hotel the whole time, reading. We had fun. It was nice. We were so happy to be married and it seemed such an adventure to be in a foreign country." He looked at me. It was my turn to say where I had gone on my honeymoon. I ate some rice.

The conversation moved on to someone else, John's cousin Barbara, two flower arrangements away. She said, "My sister eloped. They went to Fiji and got married there. They stayed for two years. Kind of a two-year honeymoon."

"That sounds nice," I said.

John's cousin went on, "She didn't want to deal with the dress and the food and the family and all. She never liked being the center of attention, so this was better for her."

"You have to do what feels right," I said.

Eve said, "Personally, I always wanted to wear a long white dress and a veil. I had to wait a little longer than I expected, but I finally got my chance." She put her arm around John's shoulders. He tipped his head so that it was against hers. "I was afraid the veil was going to drop off and fly away in the middle of everything. I forgot to worry about a downpour."

"You looked absolutely radiant," our mother said. To the rest of us, she said, "I saved my wedding dress all these years, and Eve used some of my lace for her veil. Those buttons were on my mother's dress as well as mine, and now here they are again on Eve's."

Without meaning to, I saw myself at my second wedding, wearing a pale blue, tea-length silk dress and believing I was all finished forever with feeling lonely.

"Pretty," said John's cousin. She leaned forward to make eye contact with me from her end of the table. "Did you use parts of your mom's dress for your wedding too?"

"No," I said. "I didn't. The first time I got married, I wore jeans. We were in college. We didn't have any money, so we didn't go anywhere on a honeymoon. The second time, I had two kids. And even though I wanted to wear a traditional white dress, I didn't even consider it. I thought it wasn't allowed or something. Wasn't that dumb? As if anybody cares what you do. As if it matters if they do care." I didn't mean to go on like this. Just a simple short answer was all that was called for. But I was talking fast, as if I had to hurry to get out what I wanted to say before something happened. "I didn't go on a honeymoon that time, either. And now look at me: I'm forty years old, I've been married twice, and I've never had a white dress or a honeymoon." My voice broke on the last word, and I started to cry. It happened too quickly for me to brace myself against it or to quickly think of something funny to say to shift the conversation in another direction. Everyone else at the table was still for a minute.

Then my sister said, "Uh-oh."

My mother said, "Sweetheart—"

I didn't just get a little misty-eyed or choked up; a deep sadness bubbled up into my throat and then out through my eyes so that tears as big as the raindrops at the wedding splashed onto the tablecloth. I tried to laugh at how ridiculous this was and more tears came out. I tried to swallow the tears away, but I felt as though I was going to strangle. I had to take a deep breath. More tears came and a sob. This was followed by the thought that my sister had just married someone who made my skin crawl; that we would never be as close as we used to be; that the hopefulness built into a wedding was false because the ceremony was just the beginning of a long journey to deepening isolation and disappointment. Tears dripped down my cheeks. Now I was glad the children were at another table.

"*Mimi*," my mother said. She was doing everything she could with her face to beg me to stop.

Eve put her fork down and looked at the tablecloth.

"Sorry," I said. I bit my lower lip and cried some more. It seemed as though the lid to a central part of me that had been twisted tightly shut for a long time was suddenly loosened. I found that this unexpected release of sadness into the atmosphere was not something in my control. Now that I knew I had no choice, it didn't feel bad to let it go.

My mother said, "Take a drink of water, dear. Shall we go to the ladies' room a minute?" But I was too far gone now. My face contorted with grief and I gave in to it.

"Here," someone said. A handkerchief came.

"Thank you," I said, unfolding the handkerchief and putting it to my face. I wiped my eyes. Mascara came off on the handkerchief. I didn't care; someone would wash it. I lifted my head and smiled, blinking into the light, looking around the table at the faces staring at me or looking away. I felt like a toddler just finishing up a long, strenuous temper tantrum: I had behaved poorly, and I knew I would have to pay for it somehow, but for the moment I felt a lot better.

CHAPTER 3

"I Don't Remember You"

"Why were you crying at Aunt Eve's wedding reception?" Melanie wanted to know.

She had waited until the Friday night after the wedding to ask, so the question took me by surprise. We were about to watch a movie we had rented. I didn't know that Daniel and Melanie had seen me cry. While I considered possible answers, I listened to the gentle roar of the microwave fan and the tiny explosions of popcorn inside it. Daniel looked up at me from the TV and waited for what I was going to say. "Everybody cries at weddings," I said. "It's traditional."

Bending over the VCR, Daniel said, "People cry during the wedding part, Mom, not the eating part. Somebody didn't rewind this." He pushed the rewind button.

I said, "OK, I was a little late. The whole thing was very emotional. I was just, I don't know, happy for Aunt Eve. She's my *sister*."

Daniel straightened up and looked at me. Melanie put a hand on her hip. "Sure, Mom," she said. "You were happy. That's a good one." The microwave beeped ready. She took the popcorn bag out, straightened her arms to hold it away from her, squeezed her eyes shut, and, ever so slowly, pulled the bag open. Once I had warned them about the dangerously hot steam from microwave popcorn bags; maybe I overdid it.

I said, "I mean it. Aunt Eve has wanted to get married for the longest time. For a while, she was afraid she might not be able to find the right person. Now she's with someone she loves, who loves her too." I went to the cupboard for a bowl and handed it to Melanie.

Daniel came to the kitchen. He got out three glasses and opened the fridge. He said, "You should find someone too, Mom."

Melanie said, "You *should*. You should get married again."

I didn't say anything. I planned to be single for the rest of my life, like my mother, who never remarried after her divorce from our father when Eve and I were little. Everyone liked our father. You couldn't help it. He was handsome and funny and a good storyteller. Meeting him, people wanted him to know as soon as possible how much they cared about him. "Let me call my brother-in-law," someone would say fifteen minutes after meeting our father for the first time. "He owes me a favor. He'll do your taxes for you for nothing." A seamstress he knew once sewed Eve and me beautiful matching party dresses. Restaurant owners he met let us all eat for free, as if we were famous or members of their own families. But something went wrong between my parents early on, something they couldn't get past, and they split up. We hadn't seen him in years. My mother never wanted to try again with anyone else, and now, after my own two marriages, I felt the same way.

"Daniel, you can start the movie," I said. He pushed the button on his way to the couch. We had lost our remote control about a month before. We all sat down to watch.

The phone rang. Both kids said "Grandma" at the same

time. Daniel got up to stop the movie. He sat down on the rug in front of the machine and waited there so he could restart it as soon as I hung up.

"Hi, dear." It was my mother. "Have you heard from Eve?"

I nodded to the kids, letting them know it was my mother. "No," I said. "She's on her honeymoon. She might not call us at all, you know."

"Well," my mother said. "I just thought since you girls are so close—"

"I'll let you know if she calls," I said. "We're just about to watch a movie. You can come over and watch it with us if you want." Both kids shook their heads no. My mother always talked during movies, making comments as it went along about all the things that were wrong with it.

She didn't want to come over anyway. "Oh, no," she said. "I'm fine here. I have my book."

"All right then. I'll talk to you tomorrow." We hung up. Daniel pushed the start button on the VCR and came back to the couch. I handed him the popcorn, and he took some and put his feet up on the coffee table. I handed the bowl to Melanie, and she kept it on her lap.

The phone rang again. Melanie said, "I bet she changed her mind." She picked it up this time. Daniel got up to stop the movie. "Hello?" Melanie said. "Oh, hi, Dad. Are you better yet?" It was my ex-husband, Richard. "Just a minute. Here's Mom."

Richard said, "I'm all stuffed up. Everything hurts. I've been sleeping almost all day, having these weird nightmares. I just called to find out if anyone is still out there."

"You have the flu," I said. "Take some Tylenol."

"Tylenol?" he said, as if I had suggested some odd home remedy he had never heard of. "Do you think that would help? Do I have any?"

"Does Dad have Tylenol?" I said to Melanie.

"In his medicine cabinet, top shelf," she said.

I told him where it was and got off the phone.

"What a baby," Melanie said.

I said, "He's lonely because he hasn't seen or talked to anyone all day. Tomorrow maybe you guys can ride over on your bikes with some groceries."

"OK," Daniel said. "Did he say he had juice?"

"I didn't ask," I said.

Daniel called his father back. "You're supposed to drink plenty of fluids, Dad," he said. "We're going to come over tomorrow and bring you some stuff. What do you need?"

Richard was always like this, getting us to help when things went wrong. I fixed his towel bars when they fell off the wall and repaired his broken sprinklers for him. He called me one day from a roadside, where his long-suffering old Honda had just conked out. I don't think he had ever changed the oil. I had to lend him my car for a month. The kids and I used the pickup that had belonged to Bill, until Richard got organized enough to buy another car.

There were a lot of areas in which he was just not practical, but Richard had plenty of good qualities too. He was kind and truthful and an attentive father. He was good in a crisis—an emotional disaster, not a plumbing emergency. He was a junior high guidance counselor, so he got a lot of practice sorting out trouble.

The way we became friends again after our divorce was that, first of all, a lot of time passed. I married Bill. Richard had a girlfriend who lived with him for a couple of years. Our children went to Richard's place on weekends, but apart from that, the two of us didn't have much to do with each other. Richard's girlfriend moved away. Then Bill died, and it was hard for me to restart afterward. I stayed in bed a lot and didn't want to have anything to do with food. I could remember standing in front of the bathroom sink, wondering how water could still flow from a faucet, splash around, and go down the drain in that bizarrely normal way when Bill was dead, when the entire universe had changed forever. My mother and sister tried to help me, but I lashed out angrily at them, as if I held them responsible for what had happened.

One night Richard came over to pick up Melanie and Daniel for the weekend. They both cried and told him they didn't want to go. They were afraid to leave me alone. Richard stayed with us for three weeks. He cooked and did our most urgent housework. At night he put the kids to bed, which I couldn't do then without squeezing them in painful embraces that went on too long. Then he came into my room and sat with me while I clung to his shirt and stared at a wall until we both fell asleep.

After a few weeks of this, I started to walk around a little bit during the day; I could eat something now and then. I knew I was going to recover when it came time to buy a Christmas tree. Bill had been dead for three months. Richard said, "Let's all go and pick out a tree together."

I knew what he was thinking: This isn't so bad, all of us in one house again. Maybe we should just keep going. Maybe enough had happened to us that now it was possible to live together again and get along; he was back to that. I didn't think so. From out of my dark, sad fog, I said, "No, Richard." He looked at me, startled by the sudden crack of static in my voice. "You go get a tree with the kids for your house, and I'll go get one with them for my house, the way we usually do. I appreciate your help, and I feel better," I said. "I'm going to be fine now."

That night, Richard went home, and I started doing my own laundry again. I could talk to my mother and sister in an even tone of voice. I went back to work, and Eve came into the business with me. My mother helped us in the store sometimes and often watched the kids for me. Richard went back to being my ex-husband full-time.

During the next several months, I started doing projects at home. I didn't want to have too much free time. At first, I chose small tasks—refinishing a dresser for Daniel, hanging curtains for Melanie. Then the dishwasher broke down and I looked in one of Bill's home-repair books and figured out how to fix it. I reorganized the garage with new shelves I installed myself. I took over Bill's tools and bought some new ones of my own, a belt sander, a new set of wrenches.

I built a wall unit that covered one whole side of our family room. It had a space for the television with a roll-down door; a VCR shelf with a drawer under it for tapes; another place for the tape deck and CD player with a drawer for cassettes and CDs; bookshelves; and cupboards for the kids' games. While I was making it, I became obsessed with using every spare minute on it, getting the quieter tasks done at night and very early in the morning while the kids were asleep and doing the noisier parts during the day on Sundays, when our store was closed. I bought a lot of take-out food and paper plates so I didn't have to waste time cooking and cleaning up. If there was something else we had to do, a concert at school or a family party, I would sit through the event with hot waves of anxiety crashing against the inside of my chest as I thought about the time it was taking away from my project. The whole job took five months. When my mother saw the finished wall unit, she said, "Mimi, look what you've done! Bill couldn't have done anything like this."

"Of course he could," I said quickly. "Some of these pieces came precut; all I had to do was assemble them." I didn't want to do anything better than Bill could have. I just wanted to take over some of his steadiness, his calm competence, and keep it for my own. To fill the void left by the finished wall unit, I found another project to do, rebuilding the shelves in the store. I let Eve wait on all the customers for a week while I cut shelves and mounted them on the walls.

Each time I finished a project, I felt a little let down, a little sad. Then I scrambled to find something else to work on right away. The tools, the wood, the glue, and the hardware were my buddies, pals of mine who would always be there and never leave me. My mother urged me to join a grieving group. I said I would look into it, but I never did. I just couldn't bring myself to sit down with a whole roomful of people as sad as I was.

Now Daniel, still on the phone, told his father not to use nose drops; they were bad for you, he said. Then he said, "I love you, Dad. See you tomorrow." He hung up, crawled across the rug, and started the movie. We watched for a full eight minutes before the phone rang again.

Daniel pushed the button on the VCR. He picked up the phone. "Hi," he said. "This is Daniel. We can't come to the phone right now because we're watching a movie. Please leave a message after the beep and we'll call you later. Beep." Then he listened for a few seconds. "Just a sec." He handed me the phone. "Mom, it's for you."

"Hello?" I said.

"Hi," said an unfamiliar man's voice. "Is this Mimi? My name is Henry. I met you at John and Eve's wedding." *Henry, Henry, Henry,* I was thinking. No face came to mind. "I was at your table. I was with John's cousin Barbara." Which one was Barbara? I tried to picture the table, the seating arrangement. The nice one in her late thirties who had never been married? No, that was a sister, Louise. Barbara must have been the one with the sister who went to Fiji. But I couldn't remember who had been with her. He went on, "It wasn't a date, really. I mean, I know her from work, and she didn't want to go alone. I was just doing her a favor, you know? I was wearing a purple tie?"

"I'm sorry," I said. "I don't remember you."

"Oh," he said. "Really? That's too bad, because I thought we kind of— You remember you said the cake came from that bakery downtown? And we talked about popovers."

"Popovers?" I said. "No. I don't remember saying anything about popovers."

"I was the one who brought up popovers."

"*Mom,*" Daniel said.

"I'm sorry," I said. "My kids are waiting to watch a movie with me. Could you give me your number and I'll call you back?"

"I didn't know you had kids," he said. "You're not married, are you?"

"No," I said. "Is there something I can help you with, some reason you called?"

"Well, yeah. Sorry. I thought that was obvious," he said. "I wanted to ask you out. I was wondering if you were free to go to dinner tomorrow night?"

"Dinner?" I said. "I—"

"Or if tomorrow's no good, we could try Sunday night. Is that bad for you too?"

"No, it's just that—"

"Or a movie, maybe. In a theater, I mean."

"I'm sorry. I don't remember you. Not at all."

"So, you don't want to go out with me?" he said.

"It's not that I don't want to go out with you." Melanie and Daniel pricked up their ears. I thought a minute. I was planning to replace a small counter in my mother's kitchen with a desk where she could talk on the phone and pay bills or grade papers. I was all set to buy the wood tomorrow and start cutting it in the evening. I didn't know how to tell this person that I didn't go on dates.

He took advantage of the pause. "Good, then is tomorrow OK?"

"I didn't say—"

"Seven? I can pick you up. Where do you live?"

"I'm sorry, I didn't mean—"

"I know, you don't remember me, and you don't want to go out with someone you don't remember. But trust me, we talked. We liked each other. I don't mean to be pushy. I don't want you to think I'm that way all the time. But it's just going to be dinner; then if I'm a dud, you never have to see me again. I'll pay and everything. Before tomorrow night, you can call people who know me to check me out. I'll even give you a few numbers."

I laughed. The kids were staring at me, and I took the phone to the kitchen. "That's all right," I said. "I can come up with my own numbers."

"So you'll go, you mean? You will have dinner with me?"

"Sure," I said. "I mean, I guess." What was I doing? But he sounded nice, and he was funny too. I gave him our address.

I hung up. The kids were looking at me, waiting to hear the story. "I'm going out tomorrow night. Grandma will come over and stay with you. I think. I mean, I haven't asked her, but she probably will."

"Fine," said Melanie.

"OK," said Daniel.

They kept looking at me. I said, "Are we going to watch this movie, or what?" Daniel pushed the button. I turned off the ringer on the phone.

The next day on the way to my mother's to drop off Melanie and Daniel, I had a little talk with myself. I said, *There's no need to tell Mom about the date with Henry.* Once I told her the story, I knew it was going to turn into a big deal, with my mother getting all excited for me, telling me to have a good time, asking me afterward how it went. I didn't want to go through all that. I wasn't even going to mention Henry. My plan was to stop in the driveway just long enough for my kids to get out of the car, then wave at my mother while I was backing out. I could call her from the store later and say quickly that I was really busy and couldn't talk, but I had to go out, and would she mind coming over this evening?

My mother lived in a townhouse condo a mile and a half from my house. I got there too early. Before I knew it, she was standing at my car door, saying, "You've got a few minutes, honey. Why don't you come in and have some coffee and a chat before you get crazy down there."

She never had half-and-half or sugar, and I couldn't stand coffee that had been sitting around the way it always did at my mother's house. But I said, "OK," and then I was opening the car door and stepping out. *Chat,* she said, and I knew what that meant. If I wasn't careful, if I didn't watch myself, I was going to tell her about my date. And it wouldn't be her fault if I said more than I wanted to. I would simply have to use a little self-restraint. I could be very tough.

I went inside with my mother and the kids.

"Grandma," Melanie said. "Is it OK if we use your computer?"

"Absolutely," she said.

"See you later, Mom," Daniel said.

"Have fun," I said. They went into my mother's extra bedroom.

"Now I won't see them again for hours," my mother said to me.

I said, "Give them a time limit. They don't have to sit in front of that thing all day."

"Oh, I don't mind," she said. "That's more or less the reason I bought it."

In the kitchen, she poured some coffee into a cup, and I reached for it. She said, "I just made this an hour ago. So what's going on with you?"

I added skim milk to the coffee, which turned it gray, and tore open a packet of Equal. I said, "I have a date with someone I met at Eve's wedding." I was like someone hypnotized, taking a bite of raw onion every time a bell rang.

"You *do?*" she said.

"Yes. Can you watch the kids tonight too? I know it's a lot after having them all day. I promise you I'll make it up to you somehow." I was going to move on fast to telling her about the desk I was going to build, but she jumped in right away.

She said, "Of course I will. They're no trouble. Tell me all about the new man in your life."

"I'm not sure who he is, but I met him at Eve's wedding," I said again, as if trying to convince myself. "His name is Henry. He called last night." I smiled and wanted to slap myself for it.

"Henry?" my mother said, frowning. "I don't recall a Henry." She closed her eyes. "Oh, wait, yes, maybe I do." She opened her eyes and pointed at me. "Tall, balding, about forty-five, recently divorced. Was he the one? I think I saw him looking at you. Now he was a little on the heavy side, but he seemed very sweet. Kind."

"Maybe," I said, doubtfully. "There were a lot of people there. I don't remember him."

My mother made a disbelieving O with her mouth. "You don't remember him? You're going out with someone, and you don't even know who he is?"

"He sounded nice on the phone," I said weakly.

"Mimi," she said. I thought she was going to warn me

about how dangerous this could be. But she clasped her hands together and said, "It will be an adventure!"

I said, "Do you remember seeing anyone who looked sleazy at the wedding?"

"Now let me think," she said. "Well, yes, a few shady characters from John's side. But you said he sounded nice, and I'm sure he is. Anyway, it's just one date."

I said, "What are the chances that something bad could happen?"

She looked at me. "Just about zero."

"I'm going to work," I said, standing up and dumping the coffee in the sink.

"You didn't even get to finish your coffee," said my mother. "Want to take some with you?"

"No thanks. But listen." I rummaged in my purse for my wallet. "Melanie and Daniel are supposed to bring some groceries over to Richard's because he's sick. Let's see, he probably needs Kleenex, orange juice, maybe some English muffins, um—" I handed her some money.

"I've got some chicken soup in my freezer he can have."

"Perfect," I said.

"We'll take care of it. See you later."

Driving to the store, I tried to communicate telepathically with my sister. "Eve, call me," I whispered while stopped at a traffic light. "Eve, call Mimi." I closed my eyes and tried to visualize my sister picking up a Mexican telephone, putting it to her ear, pressing the numbers for the store. Behind me, someone honked; the light was green.

At the store, there was a woman waiting for me to open up. "I'll be just a minute," I said, unlocking the door, turning off the alarm.

I turned on the lights, the big photocopy machine. "All right," I said to my customer. I copied some recipes she had cut out of a magazine. When she left, I turned on the radio.

They were playing the new Elvis Costello record. On this one, he was reunited with the original Attractions. With some people, even breaking up was no more than a temporary phase. I sang along with the ones I had already memorized and missed having Eve here to sing with me.

I called one of Eve's friends who had been at the wedding, told her about my date, and asked about Henry. "Henry?" she said. "Uh, now let me think. Was he the fat guy who just got a divorce? Kind of bald?"

"I don't know," I said. "That's the problem. I don't remember meeting any Henry."

"I think that was him," she said. "He looked a little, I don't know, serious, but he didn't seem like a serial killer or anything."

"OK, great, that's all I wanted to know," I said.

"Of course, I guess serial killers don't *look* like serial killers or how would they get any victims?"

A man came in with a form he wanted notarized. "I'll let you know what happens," I said into the phone as I got out my seal. "Thanks."

I made some copies of a résumé, discounted because the woman had a coupon from the newspaper, which reminded me to run that promotion again. No one came in for a while, and I made a call to John's sister. I barely knew her. I told her about the date. I said, "He was with your cousin Barbara."

"Barbara?" she said. "She brought someone? I didn't talk to her much, but honestly, I thought she came alone. I wasn't at your table, remember? Sorry, can't help you. Have you heard from Eve? I wonder if they're having a good time."

I said, "She hasn't called. I'm sure they're having fun, though. She usually calls me right away if things aren't going well."

"If she does call, say hi for me."

"I will." We hung up.

I packed and sent some toys to a woman's grandchildren in Canada. I faxed a one-page love letter to a number in Chicago. There were some long gaps between customers. Was business falling off lately? I wondered. I tried to think back over the past few weeks to decide whether this was a significant trend to worry about or just a normal preholiday slump. I didn't reach any solid conclusion. I ate a piece of the candy we kept in a jar on the counter and started sketching the desk I was going to build.

The phone rang. It was Eve. I said, "I was just thinking about you."

"It occurred to me that I should give you our phone number here. How's the store?"

"Slow. But don't think about work when you're on your honeymoon. How is it?"

"Hot. Nice. You know, sand, bathing suits, fancy drinks, that kind of thing."

"Sounds good. Listen, I have a question. A guy named Henry that I apparently met at your wedding called me up and asked me out."

"Great. Is he cute?" Eve said.

"That's the thing. I don't remember meeting him."

"Not at all?"

"No. He says he was there with John's cousin Barbara. They know each other from work. So I was wondering if you guys knew him or at least remembered him from the wedding, so I could get some idea of what I'm getting into here."

"Are you kidding? I was in a complete daze. I hardly remember being there myself, let alone John's cousin's date. Hold on a minute. Let me get John. Honey?" There was a long pause. "Oh, there you are. My sister has a date with a guy named Henry? She met him at the wedding. He came with Barbara?"

I heard John say, "Who's Barbara?"

"Your cousin."

"Oh, yeah."

"But Mimi doesn't remember him. She's wondering if we do, so she'll know if she should get out of it or what."

I waited while John thought about it. Then he said, "Henry?"

"Yeah?" Eve said.

"Henry, huh. I don't remember a Henry."

I said, "I'm starting to get nervous. Who is this guy?"

"The Mystery Man," said my sister. "Just go out and have fun."

"I'll try."

"See you in a few days," she said.

The store wasn't busy enough to keep me from thinking about my date. I asked myself, How bad could he be? Terrible, of course. I regretted agreeing to go. But even though I was getting nauseous just thinking about it, I had said I would go, so I had to, on principle. I had a personal rule about not backing out of things. Besides, I didn't even have his phone number to call and cancel.

CHAPTER 4

Someone Else's Date

Melanie was watching me get dressed. So far, she had not made any comments about what I was wearing, and I was grateful. "I'm sorry I have to go out," I said. "Are you guys tired of Grandma after being with her all day?"

"No," Melanie said. "Grandma doesn't bug us the way she bugs you and Aunt Eve."

"That's good."

"Mom, can I say something, even if it might hurt your feelings?"

"No," I said. "Not if it might hurt my feelings. Of course not."

"When you wear that shirt tucked in with those pants, your butt looks huge."

"Melanie, I said no. Didn't you hear me?"

She held up both hands. "Sorry, sorry, sorry. But it's a *date*. You want to look *good*. I'm trying to help you."

"Now listen to me—," I began, but the doorbell rang.

Melanie gasped. "He's *here!*" She jumped up off my bed, ran to the bedroom door, ran back. "Oh my god!" she said.

I spoke slowly and clearly, as if talking her through an emergency. "Go to the door," I said. "Let him in and be polite. Do *not* talk about me. I'll be right there." She took a deep breath and walked out. Quickly I untucked my shirt and put on a long sweater.

I could hear Melanie talking to Henry in the living room. Daniel came out of his room to check out Henry. In the bathroom, I put on lipstick again and fussed around for a while to delay. After a minute or two, I could hear them all talking together, interrupting each other and laughing, as if they had been friends for a long time. Finally I forced myself to go out and join them.

As soon as he saw me, Henry looked startled, then confused. Maybe I didn't look the way he had remembered me over the past week; maybe I looked different when I wasn't wearing the peach dress. As it turned out, he was not the heavy, bald, newly divorced forty-five-year-old that, by now, I expected to see. This was a different person altogether. Henry appeared to be about twenty years old. I looked carefully at his face. He had the kind of eyebrows that didn't arch, dark horizontal strokes above his eyes, which were brown without any creases around them. He had a nice, straight nose, not too pointed or flat or round, and a sweet mouth that came to two points in the middle, as if it wanted to make a pink bow. And he was short. There may have been the faintest trace of a memory of this face in my brain, but I wasn't sure. Maybe he remembered connecting with me, but I was positive I had never felt the same way about him. I could tell right away that the two of us had nothing in common, no overlap whatsoever.

He reached forward to shake my hand. "Hi," he said quietly. All the laughter and chatter from a few moments before was emptying out of the room like a cooled bubble bath draining from a tub.

"Hello," I said. "Nice to meet you. I mean, see you again."

"Likewise," he said. He let go of my hand, put his hands in his pockets, cleared his throat, and looked at the door.

"So did you find the house OK from my directions? A lot of people get lost in this area. If they're not used to it."

"Uh," he said. "I found it fine."

"Good," I said. "We just have to wait until my mother gets here to stay with the kids, then we can go." I didn't want to go anywhere with him. I didn't want to sit in his car and then a restaurant and then his car again and try to think of things to say. I wanted to watch television with the kids, then work in the garage for a couple of hours after they went to bed. I could hear my mother's car in the driveway. I was dreading the moment she saw Henry. For some reason, I was afraid she would laugh.

She opened the door without knocking. "Hello, everybody," she said loudly, as if calling up a long flight of stairs to see if we were home. But we were all right there. "Hi," she said to Henry. "I'm Joyce, Mimi's mom. Are you—let's see—" She looked at him, then at me. She didn't get it.

"Mom," I said, "this is Henry. My date."

"Goodness me!" she said. "I am so sorry. I was thinking maybe you were a neighbor or something. I know there's a young man across the street, who—well, anyway, so nice to meet you."

I grabbed my purse before my mother said anything more. "Kids, be good, and don't stay up late." I hurried out the front door with Henry trailing behind.

"Nice meeting all of you," he said. I closed the door almost before the words were out of his mouth.

We drove downtown to a new restaurant I had never been to, a favorite of his, he told me. In the car, he said, "You're tall."

I said, "Yes, I am. I'm five eleven."

"That's tall," he said, shaking his head. "That's really tall."

This kind of comment had already become tiresome when I was about eleven. By now, it barely registered. "How tall are you?" I said.

"Five-six," he said. I nodded. "Is that a problem for you?" he said. "That I'm shorter than you are?"

"No," I said quickly, "not at all."

"Good," he said. "Your height is not a problem for me either."

Why should my height be a problem for him? I found this irritating, but managed not to say anything. I wanted this date to be over. I planned the way I would make the evening as short as possible: I wouldn't order an appetizer and wouldn't have dessert or coffee. The kids might still be up when I got back.

"Have you lived in this area long?" he said

"No," I told him. "This area didn't exist five years ago. It was dirt and tumbleweeds. We bought a house here in one of the first developments that opened. Then my mother bought a townhouse nearby. Nobody has lived here long. It's all new."

"Oh," Henry said. "Really."

When we got to the restaurant, we found that the wait would be forty-five minutes to an hour. "It's worth it," Henry assured me. We went to the bar. I smiled politely at him whenever he looked at me, trying to be pleasant. We ordered glasses of white wine from the bartender.

Henry said, "So, what kind of work do you do?"

"My sister and I own a store called Wrap It Up. We do packaging, copying, mailing, faxing. Office services for people with no offices or small offices without all the equipment."

"Yeah," he said. "A mail-and-parcel center. And how's business?"

"Pretty good," I said. "We're in a good location. We started out when the shopping center was brand-new and the only one in the area. For four years the big supermarket in our center was the only one in about a five-mile radius. There's another one now, not too far away. But we've built up a solid clientele."

"That's good. You're in a very competitive market. You've got some big chains to deal with. Mailboxes, Etc.; Postal Annex Plus; and—what's that new one you see all over the place now?—Send It, Inc."

"But none of those has outlets in our area," I told him.

Henry said, "Not yet. What you need is something that distinguishes you from those stores. You have to offer something unique that the chain stores don't have."

"We do. We ship large items, like single pieces of antique furniture," I said. "Hardly anybody does that. And Eve and I are friendly and knowledgeable. People like us." I looked down at my hands and found them busy tearing a cocktail napkin into small pieces. "Our business makes a nice profit. It has since we opened."

"Hm," Henry said. He leaned toward me, thinking for a few seconds. "That's good. But I don't think it's enough. You need more services or products that the other stores don't have." He wrinkled his forehead, concentrating.

"What do you mean, it's not enough? We have a lot of good customers who come in several times a week, who are very happy with us," I said. "And new people discover us all the time. I'm telling you, there are no other stores like ours in our area."

Henry backed off. "Great," he said, and smiled at me. "Then you're doing fine. You don't need my input at all. Sorry."

I gathered all the napkin pieces I'd made, put them into a pile, and dropped them into an ashtray. I sipped my wine. Though I knew that this was my moment to do it, I didn't feel like asking him what he did for a living.

"I'm a marketing consultant for a software company," he told me anyway.

"Wow," I said, trying to be polite. "Interesting."

"Not at all. I hate it," he said, and shrugged. "I went to graduate school to get an MBA and specialized in marketing. It got me a great job I can't stand." He laughed. "What I like, what interests me, are big multinationals and the ways they sell to a complex world market. That's what I did my thesis on. I read a pretty good book on small businesses once. The idea is that you have to find a unique niche in your specific market area and make it pay. Small businesses are not my specialty, though. I mean, it's interesting, finding a unique way to fill a need. That's fun. But I really like big things; big is good."

"I see. So why didn't you get a job working for a multinational? If that's what you like so much?"

"Couldn't find one. Couldn't find my niche." He laughed. "I needed a job, and this one was available. So I took it."

We sat there for a while, not saying anything. There was music on loud and other people were talking around us. The song was "Linger" by the Cranberries, something Eve liked a lot. I knew all the words and was fighting myself not to sing. I put more napkin pieces into the ashtray. Beside me, I had the feeling Henry was busy racking his brain for a new topic.

Next, a Morrissey song came on, "The More You Ignore Me, the Closer I Get." I sat up straight and said, "I love this song."

"You do?" Henry said, amazement sparkling in his voice. "I do *too*. I love this! I have the tape in the car. I listen to it all the time. Over and over. I'll play it for you later. I would have played it on the way, but I didn't think you— I mean, you can never tell what— I don't know your musical taste." What he meant was he didn't expect someone as old as I was to like this kind of music.

I nodded and sang along by mistake.

"Your kids are nice," Henry said after I'd started to think he had given up on finding something to talk about. "I like kids. Have you been divorced a long time?"

"Yes. Then I remarried, and my second husband died." Of course I knew that this wasn't a good topic. But if I didn't mention it, and it came up later on, he would want to know why I hadn't talked about it earlier.

"I'm sorry," he said, looking straight into my face.

"It was three years ago," I said, and then when he kept looking at me, I felt I had to say something more about Bill, just a descriptive detail or two about his personality to make him seem real. Then I would ask Henry about his family. I said, "Music didn't mean anything to him. Sometimes I wonder how I could have chosen someone like that." Henry swallowed, looking at me, his eyes wide. Not knowing quite where I was going, I continued. "It wasn't that we had different taste or anything. It was just that he had no use for music. At all. Not interested. If he were here right now, he might not even notice that there was music playing. Can you imagine that? I thought I could teach him. I would play him a song I liked and say, 'Listen.'" I pointed my finger up in the air, showing Henry the way I had acted with Bill, trying to make him appreciate a brilliant lyric or an ardent, burning guitar solo. "'Listen to this,' I kept saying. And Bill would always say, 'Yeah.'" I imitated Bill's impassive face as he nodded and didn't get it.

Henry smiled.

"I don't know why, but I thought he would like the same music I did if I instructed him about what the good parts were, if I could somehow get him to understand what was good. Eventually, I gave up, long after I should have. He probably found it irritating the way I tried to make him listen to what, to him, wasn't even there. I took it personally. I felt there was an essential part of *me* that he just didn't get."

Henry was quiet. I had gone on longer than necessary about Bill, and now I could stop. I drank some wine, put my glass down, and found I wasn't finished talking. I still hadn't given a full picture of Bill. "He laughed at my jokes," I said. "He was always so calm. He knew how to do everything. I remember him repairing our kitchen drawers, which, even though our house was new, fell apart as soon as we moved in. I sat on the floor, watching him put the pieces back together with wood glue and screws that were longer than the ones the drawers came with. I wouldn't have thought of that. 'Let the tool do the work,' he told me. I liked that: 'Let the tool do the work,' as if he didn't have to do anything.

"When he didn't know how to fix something, he looked it up in one of his home-repair books. It had never occurred to me to look in a book to find out how to fix a toilet or install a deadbolt lock. I liked watching him do these projects and listening to him describe each step as he went along. It was so comforting the way, to Bill, everything was possible. You know what I mean?" I looked at Henry, listening, wrinkling his brow, trying to understand. "Whatever fell apart or broke, he never freaked out or panicked. He would just kind of look at it for a while, study it from different angles, and then quietly figure out a way to get it going again. Nothing was ever too far gone to be salvaged, as far as Bill was concerned.

"Anyway, whether he was trying to teach me or just thinking out loud, more of his home-repair training rubbed off on me than my musical instruction did on him. Several months after he died, I started watching how-to shows on public television. I missed seeing Bill fix things. As I sat in front of the TV, I would find myself thinking, *That's going to have to set overnight,* just before the guy on television straightened up and said exactly the same thing in the same words. *A power screwdriver would help there,* I would think; then the host picked one up and demonstrated it. I found that I knew things I hadn't been aware of learning." I smiled at Henry. "He never did come around about music."

"There were obviously a lot of other good things about him that made the marriage worth it," he filled in for me.

"I loved him," I said.

He nodded. "Do the kids see their dad?"

"Every other weekend. He was supposed to have them this weekend, but he's got the flu."

"So he lives close by?"

"Yes," I said. "Just a couple of miles from me. Listen to me: Yak, yak, yak." I took another sip of wine. My mouth was dry from talking so much. "Do you mind if I ask you a personal question?"

"Uh, no. Go ahead." He drank from his glass.

"How old are you?"

"Me? I'm twenty-eight. How old are you?"

"Forty."

He nodded.

"Do you always go out with older women?" I said.

"No," he said. "I don't think I ever have before. I guess this is the first time."

There was a table ready for us. We went to it and started looking at menus. We ordered. The food came and we began to eat it, murmuring to one another about how good it was, offering to share, declining food from each other's plate. A waiter cleared the table. We turned down dessert. Without meaning to, I sighed, relieved that it was almost over.

"I have to tell you something," Henry said.

I had an urge to hold up my hands and say "Don't." I was

sure this was going to be like Melanie leveling with me about my pants. Reluctantly, I looked up from the dinner napkin I had, for some reason, refolded into a fan.

He said, "I thought you were someone else."

"Pardon me?"

"At the wedding, I met this woman. I asked Barbara—you know, my friend from work—to get her number. Barbara called her mother, and her mother called someone else. I got your number. I called you. I was thinking of another woman. I don't remember you from the wedding." He was blushing.

My face burned. "I was the matron of honor. The bride was my sister."

He nodded without seeming to recall this.

"I was the one who cried at lunch," I said.

"Cried?"

"We were talking about honeymoons and wedding dresses and all of a sudden, I burst into tears. I couldn't stop myself."

He said, "What were you crying about? Happy or sad?"

"Sad."

"That's too bad. Sad about what?"

"Because I never wore a white dress or went on a honeymoon," I said. I laughed. "There was more to it than that, I guess. My sister's new husband, John, and I haven't hit it off very well." This last comment slipped out before I could stop it, but as we would never see each other again, and considering how much I had said already, it didn't seem to matter much.

"So then what happened?" he said, interested.

"I stopped crying," I said. "We ate cake and went home." I picked up my water glass. "And now here I am on someone else's date."

"I guess," he said. "But listen. I really like you. I think it worked out fine. I'd like to see you again. If that's OK. I'm going to call you again, all right? And I know we've finished dinner, but could we spend a little more time together? Go for a walk, maybe, and talk some more?"

He was being generous, reaching out to me. I couldn't bring myself to accept the gesture. I said, "I've got a lot of things to do tomorrow. I need to get home." This was exactly the kind of behavior I had worked hard for years to train out of my children. "When someone shows kindness to you, accept graciously," I had said a thousand times when they were little. "If you don't like the present, take it anyway and say thank you."

"Some other time, then," he said. He borrowed my pen and wrote his home number on one of his business cards. He gave his credit card to the waiter without looking at the check, without looking at me. The waiter came back, and Henry signed the bill. He started to put the pen in his pocket, but pulled it out again, looked at it. "Sorry. That's yours." I put the pen back in my purse, and we got up to go. On the way home, we listened to the Morrissey tape and hardly spoke.

My sister was back at work, tan and smiling. She was wearing new earrings. She lifted her hair to show me: brightly colored parrots on perches swung from her ears. "These were about fifty cents. I feel kind of guilty, but I really like them. I got a whole bunch more, if you want any—palm trees, parasols. I know they're not really your kind of thing, but if you want some, just say." She checked to see if the green light was on to start copying on our big, high-speed machine. "We took a scuba-diving class, and it was great. If the equipment weren't so expensive, I'd do it here."

"The water is way colder here," I said.

"Yeah. What's this pile?" she said about a thick stack of paper on the counter. She picked up the order paper-clipped to the front. "Bridget's new book? Already?"

"First draft. That's due by two this afternoon." Bridget wrote historical romance novels and had been one of our customers since we opened.

"OK, I see that." Eve skimmed the first page and shook her head. "Where does she get her ideas?" She put it down and picked up the next order. "And what's this? Oh, another thesis. Is this one of Ajit's friends?"

"Yeah, he sent us a couple more people."

The phone rang, and Eve got it. "Wrap It Up, Eve speaking. . . . Brochures?" she said. "Hold on and I'll see." She pushed the hold button. "Brochures for the Rumpelstiltskin Preschool?"

"Ready," I said.

She pushed the button on the phone. "Yes, you can pick them up anytime. . . . And thank *you*." As soon as she hung up, the phone rang again. "Yes, we gift wrap. Or you can save by wrapping it yourself with our supplies. . . . We're open until six. . . . And thank *you* for calling." After she hung up, she said, "Did you finish those menus?"

"Here," I said, pointing to a box of take-out menus for a deli a few stores down.

"I'll take them down there," Eve said. "I need a bagel. These aren't supposed to be folded, are they?"

"No, the cashier does that."

"OK. You want anything?" she asked.

"No, thanks."

While she was gone, John called. It was just the first of many times he would call during the day. I said, "I hear you had a nice time."

"Exquisite," he said. "Absolute perfection. Is your beautiful sister there?" he said.

"My beautiful sister is making a delivery and getting herself a bagel. But I'll tell her you called."

A woman came in holding a baby on her hip with one

arm and a shopping bag on her other arm; a preschooler and a toddler were hanging on to her sweatshirt. She said, "I have to send a package to Vermont. It has to go out today, or it won't make it on time."

I said, "No problem." I looked in the bag: kids' clothes and toys with the price tags still on. "Shall I gift wrap these for you?" I showed her the price list.

"Oh, *would* you? These are for the girl, and these are for the boy. My sister has twins who'll be two this Saturday."

"All right," I said. "Is this paper all right for the boy? And how about this for the girl?"

"Cute," she said. "Yes."

"I'll do this right now," I said. "We have some toys and crayons for the kids while you wait."

Eve came back as I was wrapping the presents. She started on the photocopying. The phone rang again. "That's probably John," I said. "He called while you were gone."

Eve answered the phone. "Wrap It Up. This is Eve speaking. Yes, she is. Just a minute." Eve pushed the hold button. "It's Henry."

"Who's Henry?" I said, pretending I didn't remember.

"Henry. You know, from the wedding. The mystery guy you went out with. How was that anyway?" She checked her copies, put another stack on the feeder.

"Shoot," I said. "He called me by mistake. He thought he was calling someone else. He probably liked that woman in the sixties outfit, but he got me. Anyway, whoever he wanted to go out with, he got my number by accident." Eve laughed. "He's twelve years younger than I am and five inches shorter. You should have seen his face when he saw me." The woman with the kids looked up from where she was sitting on the floor, smiling, amused at the story of my date with Henry. Eve put her hand on her stomach and laughed some more. "It's not that funny." I pushed the hold button. "Hello?"

"Hi, Mimi. This is Henry. How are you?"

"Fine, thank you. You?"

"Fine. Are you busy Sunday night?"

"Uh . . ." The phone had a long cord. I pulled it around the corner into the little back room we used as our office. "Yes, I am pretty busy."

"I thought you might want to go with me to a concert. I got you a ticket."

"It was nice of you to think of me," I said. I could feel my sister listening. I closed the door as far as I could with the cord in it and tried to speak quietly. "You know, I don't think it's such a good idea to go out again. Maybe the other night worked out a little better than we expected, but I don't think we should make a habit of it. Thank you, though." He didn't say anything. Silences on the phone always make me talk more. I worried suddenly that he would think I was turning him down because of his height. I said, "It's not that I didn't, you know, find you attractive. But I just don't think it would work out. I'm really too old for you."

He didn't speak right away. I took a breath to start again. Then he said, "I like you and find you attractive too. That's why I called. Our ages aren't important. But it is important that we had fun together, that we really *talked*. Maybe it's different for you. Maybe you go out with men you like all the time. But for me, this is unusual, finding someone I click with. It hardly ever happens. And when it does, it usually turns out that the woman is married or about to move to Seattle or something. So I think we should go out again. I really do."

"Thank you. I'm flattered." I was. I just didn't know how to explain that I didn't want to click with anybody. Nice as it was in the beginning, clicking was just the first intoxicating stage of something that would most likely lead to a lot of anguish later on. I decided to stay with the age difference as a way out. "I agree that usually age shouldn't be a barrier to seeing someone. But in this case, for me, the gap is too big. I don't think I could overlook it. I'm sorry."

There was another pause. This time I pressed my lips tightly together and waited for what seemed like a long time. Then Henry said, "I don't agree."

"Sorry," I said again.

"Me too," he said. "I'm really sorry."

"But thanks for asking. Really."

"So long."

"Bye."

My sister was filling a box with Styrofoam chips when I came out. I put the presents in it, weighed it, put it in the UPS corner, and took money from the woman with the three children.

"Thank you, thank you, thank you," she said. "You don't know what it's like to wait in line at the post office with these guys."

"Oh, yes I do," I said. "I certainly do."

She laughed and said to the children, "OK, guys, let's put the toys back."

When we were alone again, Eve said, "What did Henry want?"

"He wanted to go out again," I said.

"You're kidding."

"No. I'm not kidding. He tried pretty hard to convince me."

My sister laughed. "So what did you say?"

"I don't see anything funny about it. I turned him down."

"God, I should hope so."

"What does that mean?" I said.

"You said he was twelve years younger than you!" she said.

"He is."

"I think that's a huge difference," Eve said. "And so do you." She went to the back to get more cartons. When she returned, she said, "I mean, what would you even have to talk about? You would have nothing in common. When you started college, he was six!" I didn't like the way she kept smiling to herself about it while we were putting the cartons away. I could picture her telling John later, the two of them chuckling together about my bad date with Henry and our age and height differences.

I went into the office to make phone calls and order supplies while Eve waited on customers. John called a couple of times. I could hear Eve's side of the conversation. It seemed that he was at home baking. John didn't have a job. He hadn't worked since we had known him, but he always seemed to have plenty of money. My mother and I had still not dared to ask about its source. They were only talking about food—spices and oven temperatures—but she took the phone as far away from the office as the long cord would stretch and hunched around the receiver for privacy. I knew she was a newlywed and everything, but it was annoying the way she made such a big production out of the fact that she and John had their own little world that didn't include me. The kids and I had our own little world too, of course, but that was hardly the same thing.

When she hung up, I said, "What's he doing?"

She smiled. "Making cookies."

"Very domestic."

"I think so too."

"Does he make dinner or anything useful?"

"Of course. He's an excellent cook."

I knew this. I had eaten his cooking.

"Mimi," Eve said in a quiet voice. She glanced at the door to see if anyone was about to come in. She bit her lip and took a breath. "John's in trouble. The restaurant he used to manage, it was, well . . . money disappeared from it while John was working there. It went out of business. Someone

stole a lot of money from the place. They think John did it."
Eve started rearranging things on the counter, straightening
the stapler and the tape dispenser. "Can you believe it? John,
of all people."

I had a watery feeling in my stomach, and my legs wanted
to run. I said, "Why?"

"God," she said, "I don't know." She added a few paper
clips to the jar. "He ran the place, and he had access to the
money. I guess that's why they think he did it. Anyway, I'm
just telling you in case anybody comes in here, whips out a
badge, and starts asking you questions."

"A badge?" I said. I wanted to tell Eve, *You have made a
bad mistake. You can get out of it; I will help you.* But just like
the other times I had wanted to say this, I stopped myself.

She shook her head. "He loved that restaurant. This is
really hurting him, that people would think he would do that.
Anyhow, I just thought you should know about it, in case—
well, in case things get ugly."

I wanted to get away to see if I could get rid of the sour
taste at the back of my throat, get my legs back under me.
"I'm going out for some coffee," I said. "Want some?"

"No thanks," she said. "John makes the best coffee. And
now that I'm used to it, nothing else is good enough." She
smiled to herself.

I said, "I'll be right back."

I didn't just go to the grocery store, where I usually got
my coffee. I needed more time than that. I drove to the other
shopping center to go to the good coffee place. On the way,
I shoved in a Cranberries tape and turned it up, sang along
about how my life was changing. I had it turned up pretty
loud so that my own singing wouldn't ruin the song for me.

The center was busy. I drove around a couple of minutes
until I found a parking space. This group of stores had just
sprouted out of a big, empty dirt-and-tumbleweed lot in a

matter of only a few months. It had been open about six months now, and every time I came over here, some new store had just appeared. Now it seemed the center had almost out-grown its parking lot. If I were opening our store now, I would choose this center instead of ours. I worried again that our business was falling off. No, I told myself, our center was fine, our business was fine. Everything was just fine. For the moment, I tried not to think about Eve and John.

I bought a pound of coffee, had it ground, ordered a coffee to go, then started back to my car. As I was checking out all the new stores, I saw a sign that made my heart stop. It read "Send It, Inc.: Copying! Mailing! Faxing! Mailboxes! Word processing! Your complete office services store. Opening December 1st." I had to stand there a minute until I could breathe again. I had this odd sensation, as if I were standing at the edge of the ocean with a wave receding, a feeling that the world was slipping away, disappearing from beneath my feet where I had counted on it staying put. I looked at the sign again, read every word once more, and went to look into the store. There was paper over the windows, but by standing on my toes, I could see in: a long counter in a medium shade of blue; plasterboard walls, still unpainted; a pegboard on one side, where they were probably going to hang supplies for sale; and hundreds of built-in mailboxes. I gave myself about thirty seconds more to panic, just standing there with my mouth half open, thinking, *I can't do this, we're never going to make it, our store is going to have to go out of business, and then what will we do?* I went back to my car. I turned the key, rewound the tape, pressed play, and backed out of the parking space. This time I just howled it out, no longer concerned about sparing the integrity of the music.

My sister was staring at me, trying to take in the news. I had gone past the staring phase into the hyper-idea phase.

"See, what we need," I was telling her, "is to offer some product or service that the other guys don't have."

"Damn," she said. "I mean, who are these people? And what do they do? I never even heard of Send It, Inc."

"I haven't quite come up with *the* winning idea yet, but I'm sure there's something, something big to give our business a boost, something new and a little different," I said. "Oh, they're a relatively new company that's growing fast. They've opened up a lot of new stores all over California in the past year or so. I thought we could kind of brainstorm and try to come up with something together."

There was a pause while Eve closed her mouth and looked at the rug. "I'll talk to John about it," she said.

"What do you mean, you'll talk to John? He doesn't work here. He doesn't know anything about what we do. Talk to *me* about it. *I'm* your partner!"

"I mean, sometimes he comes up with good ideas about business. What are you so touchy about?"

"Nothing. I'm just saying you don't have to check with John about everything. Just because you're married to him doesn't mean he knows anything about our business," I said.

"He knows a lot. I'm not checking with him. I'm just going to see if he can come up with some good ideas. The more input we have, the more chance we have of solving the problem. Right?" Her nose was peeling.

"I guess," I said. "I mean, right."

I waited on a man who wanted a flyer about a gardening service copied. The phone rang and Eve got it. "Until six," she said. "Thank *you.*" After she hung up, she said to me, "It's not as if business is terrible. Maybe both stores can make it." She looked at my face. "OK, OK, I'm thinking. More advertising?" We were both quiet for a minute. I felt like I was having one of those nightmares where everything goes wildly wrong in all kinds of ways at once: You arrive at a class and find out that there's going to be a big test that you didn't know about; you forgot to buy the textbook; you aren't wearing any clothes. "What about more cards and office supplies?" Eve said.

I had the flyers ready. "OK," I told her absently, putting the pile into a bag. "I'll check the stock after this."

"No," she said. "To expand our market."

"That's five thirty-six," I told my customer. I took his money and made change. "Thank you very much." He took his bag and left. "Oh," I said to Eve. "You mean *offer* more cards and office supplies? We've already got too much competition there. There's that card place at the other end of the center. The grocery store sells that stuff too." I twirled a strand of hair between my fingers. "Maybe a messenger service for delivering local packages?" Eve straightened up, looked hopeful.

I shook my head. "But we would have to hire someone else full-time, just for that. We can't afford it."

"Would we? I don't know. You've been doing this longer than I have," she said, slumping again.

The UPS guy walked in. "Hello, ladies," he said. "And how is the world treating Mimi and Eve today?" Every day, he greeted us exactly the same way.

"Fine, thanks," Eve and I said together like two puppets.

I pulled out two packages. "Not much today, Ron," Eve said.

"I'll take what you've got." Ron winked at us and put the two boxes on his dolly. "See you tomorrow."

When he was gone, I said, "You don't have to apologize to him for our business being slow."

"I wasn't apologizing. I said we didn't have much. Our business isn't slow. Some days he has to make two trips. Why are you snapping at me?"

"I'm not snapping," I said. "Sorry, I guess I was. I just have to think carefully about this and try not to panic. We can figure this out, right? We can handle it. I'll be right back."

I went to the office and closed the door. I pulled a card out of my wallet and picked up the receiver.

He answered on the first ring. "Henry Patterson."

"This is Mimi," I said quickly. "I changed my mind. I would like to go to that concert, after all. You're right about our ages. They don't mean anything."

There was a slight pause while he took in what I had just told him. Then he said, "Is seven-thirty good for you?"

"Seven-thirty is perfect," I said. "Who's playing?"

CHAPTER 5

Creative
Business Solutions

I had been in the garage since four-thirty, in my pajamas, working on an audiocassette organizer for the store. For practice, I had used dovetail joints, to see how difficult they were. I read about how to do them in a book first. The joints were pretty difficult for me but had turned out surprisingly well. I looked at them now, rubbed my hand over the corners feeling for rough spots, sanded again. I had angled the slots for the cassettes so that even in an earthquake, the tapes wouldn't fall out. I was thinking about making another one of these for CDs.

The door to the kitchen opened. "Mom!" Daniel yelled. He was dressed in his bright green soccer uniform.

"I'm right here," I said. "Don't shout. You startled me."

"You're not even dressed! I have a game!"

"What time is it?" I looked at my joints again, examining each corner.

"Seven thirty-nine!" Daniel said.

Warm-up for Daniel's soccer game started at eight. "Why

didn't you come get me earlier?" I said, setting down the organizer and trotting to the door in my bare feet.

"I didn't know where you were," Daniel put up his hands helplessly. "We're never going to make it," he said, following me into my bedroom. I pulled some clothes out of a laundry basket. "It's way too late. You can't take a shower, put on your makeup, get dressed, and drive me over there in twenty minutes." I took my clothes into the bathroom and shut the door. "Maybe we should skip it, Mom," he called through the door. "I think we're just too late today."

I pulled on my pants. "Oh, I see," I said. "And you have a sore throat and a stomachache and you twisted your ankle? We've been over this too many times, Daniel. There is exactly one way to get out of soccer. At the beginning of the year, you don't sign up. You were the one who decided you had changed your mind over the summer, that you liked some of the new guys, that you thought you were getting into running." I got my shirt and socks on and yanked a brush through my hair. "I tried to get you out of soccer gracefully this year, but now that we're in, we're going to keep going until it's over for the season." I opened the door. "Ready."

"You didn't take a shower."

"Where's my purse?"

"Kitchen. Where's your lipstick? God, Mom." He grimaced.

I opened Melanie's door. "Honey, we're going to soccer," I said. She was curled in a ball around her pillow. She didn't move. "We'll be back at ten-thirty. Then your Dad is picking you up."

"I'm asleep. God, Mom. First you wake me up with all that banging around in the garage, then you come slamming in here to tell me a bunch of stuff I already know."

"Excuse me," I said. "I'm sorry." I went to the side of her bed, bent down, put my hand on her hair, and kissed her. "You look so pretty lying there. When you're asleep, you look just like you did when you were a baby." I kissed her again. "Will you be all right here by yourself? Do you want to come with us?"

"Go," she said without moving.

"Going," I said.

"So what about physical contact?" my friend Patty was asking me, standing beside me at the soccer game. Daniel was on the same team as her son Mark. We had known each other since high school. Sometimes when I looked at Patty, I could see her younger self, like a transparent overlay in a biology book: the blond hair that had hung straight down to her waist, the dresses she made herself out of fabric imported from India, her full mouth shining with colorless lip gloss; lift the plastic sheet and there was the Patty of today, short hair that stood up in spikes, darker at the roots with some gray coming in, lips a little creased and freckled from age and too much sun, the color-coordinated exercise outfits she wore all the time because she was always on her way to or coming back from a workout. We were still friends after all this time, not only because we liked each other but also because we had children the same ages who went to the same school. Patty, long divorced, sold real estate. She was the one who convinced me to move to this part of town when it first started being developed. Our area had grown fast in the last few years, and she had made money. She lived in one of the bigger houses in our neighborhood with a pool and canyon and ocean views. She drove a Volvo with a phone in it. Still, sometimes when we were together, it was hard to remember that we were grown-ups now. "What happened when you said good-bye?" she asked me now.

"Hm?" I said. I was rummaging in my purse for lipstick. "I'm trying to think up ways to bring in more business," I said.

Patty said, "Come on, Mimi. Tell me. Eve said you went out with someone you met at her wedding, and then you don't tell me about it. Did you have fun? Did you hit it off? Did he kiss you?"

"No, no, and no," I said. We kept our eyes on the game as we talked.

"He didn't even kiss you?" said Patty. "Why not?"

"I made it pretty clear that I didn't want him to."

We watched a boy run head-on into Mark. "Jeepers!" Patty said. A long time ago, when our children were learning to talk, we had trained ourselves not to swear. Patty put a hand over her mouth, waiting to see if Mark was all right. He didn't fall over from the crash, just staggered off course for a few seconds, then went on. "Phew," Patty said. "That kid ought to be thrown off the team. How many times has he done that this year? No focus! Zero concentration!" I didn't say anything to support her point, because Daniel didn't concentrate on soccer either. He focused on some things, but this was not one of them.

"OK," Patty said, recovering. "Where were we? I want to hear the whole story."

I sighed. "You're going to be disappointed. It's not the kind of story you're after, I'm afraid. He called to ask me out, but I didn't remember him. He sounded nice, so we went out. He was way shorter than I am, twenty-eight years old, and the woman he meant to call from the wedding was someone else. It was all a big mistake."

"How embarrassing." Patty said, "And no chemistry, sounds like. I mean, you can tell right away about that. It's there or it isn't." She put her hand on my shoulder, waited until I turned to look at her. "But listen to me. It wasn't for nothing. The reason you went out with this guy was to clear the path for someone else, someone who is right for you. Clearly, this Henry person is too young. A complete mismatch.

But there is someone else for you. You don't have to settle for a short youngster you have nothing in common with, who doesn't do anything for you physically. So, good. You found that out and you don't have to see him again."

"Actually, I'm going out with Henry again tomorrow night," I said. "We're going to a concert."

She paused for a minute. "On the other hand, he sounds very sweet. And you both like music, so perfect."

"What about chemistry?" I said.

"Give it time," she said. "These things have to build."

The ball was coming straight for Daniel, who, for some reason, was standing all by himself near the other team's goal. He ran toward the ball, prepared to kick, then at the last second, a boy from the other team scooted in close and kicked the ball in the other direction.

"Lizards!" Patty said, clenching her fists and squeezing her eyes shut tight for a second. "Daniel almost had that."

Daniel didn't look at me. He joined the pack of boys, trying to disappear. "This is not Daniel's game," I said to Patty. "I don't think Daniel has a game."

"He'll get better," Patty said.

"Are you sure about that?" I said. "We've been doing this since first grade. I feel sorry for him. It's awful to keep doing something you're lousy at."

"Like me and cooking," Patty said. "But he could improve. You don't know. Does he practice kicking the ball around at home?"

"Never."

"They're supposed to practice. It really helps if they practice."

"He doesn't."

"Maybe he practices with Richard," Patty said.

"Could be," I said. "Maybe they practice a couple of hours every other weekend and no one ever mentions it to me."

Patty was the snack parent this game. As soon as the coach blew the whistle for rest, Patty tore open a big box of granola bars. I helped her pour the juice and hand it out to the boys. "Don't forget to throw away your trash!" I said out of habit, almost without realizing I was saying it.

"Put the wrappers and the cups in the can when you're finished," Patty said, as if we were part of a team too.

When the game resumed, Patty and I picked up the garbage off the grass. When we took our places again to watch the game, I said, "Do you have any ideas about how I could increase my business?"

"Go! Go! Go!" Patty was yelling at Mark, who had the ball. He lost it. "What?" she said. "Did you just ask me something?"

"Too bad," I said. "That was close. He'll make it next time."

"I hope so," she said.

"I was asking if you had any ideas for our store, to bring in more business. You know that empty store next to the frozen yogurt place at Coastal Palms?"

"Yeah," Patty said.

"It's going to be a Send It, Inc."

She looked at me. "No way. That is serious bad news for you guys."

"No kidding."

"What are you going to do?"

"I'm trying to come up with a plan," I said. "I was just wondering if you had any ideas. I'm thinking there must be some market I haven't tapped into, some segment of the community that I'm not reaching. Maybe there's a service we could offer that we just haven't thought of yet. I keep going over and over it in my head. Is there a new kind of equipment I could buy or lease to bring more people in? I don't know. You're a good businesswoman, so I thought I'd ask you for your suggestions."

"Uh," Patty said, watching the boys. "Why doesn't he put

some of those other guys in? Look at Michael Cruz. He's dragging."

"Their store looks like it's going to be nice. And that's becoming a very busy center over there. So right off the bat, we're looking at an uphill battle."

"Yeah," she said. "Oh, good. There he goes. What's that kid's name? I always forget."

"Josh," I said. "There's the new Ralphs there and the work-out place. The parking lot is always full."

We looked at the boys running after the ball for a long time. I thought about Melanie at home by herself. I always worried when I left her alone. I was trying to decide whether or not to call her from Patty's car phone. I didn't like the feeling that she couldn't reach me, even if it was only for an hour or so. But I didn't want to wake her up again. And of course, she would call Richard, my mother, or Eve if there was a problem. Then I wondered if I should call Eve and ask her how business was this morning or just wait and find out when I got there. I decided to wait. Daniel was on the bench.

"How many more minutes?" Patty said.

"Just a few," I said. "So what do you think? About the store. Do you have any ideas, something we could do right away to boost our clientele?"

"What?" she said.

"My store," I said. "I need some ideas."

"Uh," she said. "Advertise?"

I looked at her. "That's *it*? That's your answer? Come on, Patty. I need help. I was counting on you for in-depth, well-thought-out, creative suggestions."

"Sorry," she said. The whistle blew, and the game ended. I had no idea what the score was. We had lost; I could tell that much from the look of despair on the boys' faces. "Snakes!" Patty whispered. "Mark didn't score once all morning. This coach is an idiot."

"Next time," I said. "But could you think about it—the store—and see if you can come up with any ideas?"

"Sure. I'll try," Patty said. She handed Mark his sweatshirt.

I handed Daniel his sweatshirt. "Later," Daniel said to Mark.

In the car on the way home, Daniel said, "I hate soccer, Mom."

"I know, honey," I said. "I hate it too. Next year, don't sign up. OK? We'll make an agreement, put it in writing, and I'll have Aunt Eve notarize it for us." I wondered if there was any way to increase our notary business.

"I just wish I could quit now," Daniel said.

"You made a commitment," I said. "Now you have to follow through."

"Oh, Mom," he said. "Why do you always have to say that?"

"Because it's important," I said.

As soon as Richard had picked up the kids, I put my new tape rack in the car along with my drill, a level, a screwdriver, and some screws. I took off for work, stopping at the good coffee place in Coastal Palms on my way. I got antsy waiting in a long line for coffee for Eve and me. I looked at my watch. I wasn't late, but still I didn't like waiting in line. Finally, with the coffee in a cardboard tray, I headed back to the car, walking by the new mail-and-parcel center on the way. When I was just past it, I decided to turn back to look at it again, to see how it was coming along. Standing on my toes, peering over the paper, I was suddenly face-to-face with a painter on the other side of the glass. He was smoking a cigarette, looking at me. "Help you?" he yelled through the window.

"Just looking," I said.

"Not open yet," he said. "Few weeks."

I nodded and went to my car.

As soon as I got to our store, Eve said, "Thank god you're here. I've been standing around all morning doing nothing. I'm going nuts. Where is everybody today? The whole center is dead."

I said, "Why don't you go get us some lunch, and when you come back, we can talk about what we're going to do with this place."

Eve shook her head. "It's too early for lunch, and I want to go," she said. "I need to get out of here. I miss John. I'll see you later."

"But I got you coffee," I said.

"No, thanks." She put on her jacket and picked up her keys. "See you. I hope it picks up a little bit for you."

After she left, I sat on a stool for a few minutes, waiting for someone I knew to come in so I could have a chat. No one did.

I held the tape rack against the wall near the cash register, checked it with the level, made two pencil marks on the wall. I put the rack down and drilled. I put the scews in, hung up the rack, and put my tapes away. I alphabetized them. Once more I looked at the corners of the rack, rubbed my hand over the joints. After I make something, I keep going back to look at it, to touch it, to see how it all fits together. I turned on the radio. I listened to some commercials, then turned it off.

I called my mother. "What are you doing?" I asked.

"I'm doing my stretching exercises," she said. "I was just getting started. Could I call you back?"

"No, wait. I just wanted to tell you something. You know that empty storefront next to the yogurt place in Coastal Palms?"

"No."

"OK, well there was one. And you know what's going in there, starting in December?"

"No," she said. "What?"

"A Send It, Inc."

"What's that?"

"Oh, Mom," I said. "Come on, you know. It's a big chain of mail-and-parcel centers. It's competition for us. Not two miles from our store."

"Goodness me," she said. I waited, but she didn't go on.

"Is that all you have to say? The bottom is about to drop out of my business and you say, 'Goodness me'?"

"What did you want me to say?"

"I wanted you to help me figure out what to do about it."

"*Do* about it? What could you possibly do about it? You can't keep them from opening a store where they want one."

"I don't mean that," I said. "I mean, help me think up ways to make our store stronger so we can compete, so we won't be blown out of the water."

"Gosh," she said. "I wouldn't know about that. That's not my department." She thought a minute. "Maybe this is a good time to think about getting into something else, some other business. Maybe this little area is getting too crowded."

"Sure," I snapped. "We should just give up. Is that what you're saying? Just hand over our customers to them, all the business we've built up over all these years? Crawl out of here on our hands and knees and start all over from zero?"

"All right, then," she said. "It seems you've already made your decision: You're going to stick with it. You've always been very persistent. I'm sure you'll come up with some way to make it work. You girls are very resourceful." She wanted to get off the subject, off the phone. My mother didn't like talking about problems. "It's getting late," she said. "I don't know where the day goes. I've got to get out and take my walk or I'll never do it."

"Wait," I said. Our store was empty. Outside the sky hung gray and heavy over the parking lot. I was hungry. The coffee in the cardboard cup I was holding had gone cool in my hand. I didn't want my mother to hang up. I tried to think of something good to keep her on the phone. I said, "I'm going out tomorrow night. I have a date. With that guy."

"With what guy?"

"Henry. From Eve's wedding."

"You're not."

"Yes."

"Isn't he a little young for you, dear?"

"Young?" I said. "Not really."

"Fine, then. I hope you have a wonderful evening. What time do you want me?"

"Want you?"

"To stay with Melanie and Daniel. Isn't that why you called?"

"Oh," I said. "Right. They'll be home. Thanks, yeah. Seven?"

"Seven o'clock, then."

"And the kids want to have you over for dinner on your birthday. We'll have Eve and John too. A party."

"Thank you. That sounds very nice."

"Have a good walk."

"I will. Good-bye, dear."

After I hung up, I poured the coffee down the sink in the bathroom. Five customers came in all at once. I took care of them, then I was alone again. Eve had already straightened all the shelves and restocked everything. As I was trying to think of someone I could call, Bridget the novelist came in. For once, she was alone.

"Hi, Bridget," I said. "Where are the kids?"

"I don't know how you recognized me without them. It's Saturday," she said. "My husband's home with them, believe it or not." She put a piece of paper on the counter. "I need this faxed to this number."

"Sure," I said. I put the fax in the machine. "Say listen, I'm trying to figure out how to increase our business. Do you have any ideas? There's a new place opening in the other shopping center and I'm worried that it's going to hurt our business."

"Sure," she said. "Stay open twenty-four hours. Then I could come in at five in the morning while the kids are asleep and my husband is home. Or how about on-site day care? Lower prices?"

"They're about as low as they can get right now."

She nodded. "I know!" she said, pointing her finger upward. She had an idea. "What about advertising?"

"Oh," I said. "Thanks for your input." I stapled the fax confirmation to her letter and handed it back.

"Anytime," she said. She paid me and left.

I asked several other people who came in for their ideas on what we could add to our store. A few seemed interested to learn about the other store that was opening. I could see they were planning to go there. Several suggested that I advertise and offer lower prices. Frances, a freelance graphic designer who had a mailbox at our place, seemed a little panicky about the new store opening. She said, "You're not thinking of going out of business, are you? Because I count on this place. I need you here. Your address is on my letterhead."

I said, "No, we're not going out of business. But we're going to have to think of something pretty quickly."

"Good luck," she said and hurried out.

As soon as Henry and I walked into the stadium for the Elvis Costello concert, I saw Richard at the concession stand. I knew he would be there somewhere, but I had hoped that in a place this big we might miss each other. There were three lines. Not knowing who Richard was, Henry took a place right behind him. "Want a Coke?" Henry said to me. "Want something to eat?"

"No thank you," I said. "Nothing for me."

Hearing my voice, Richard turned around. "Mimi," he said. "I didn't know you were going to be here. Where's your seat?"

"Hi," I said. "I don't know." I turned to Henry beside me, conscious of the way my head had to tip down from looking up at Richard, who was over six feet tall. Richard turned to Henry. For a moment, he paused, a question beginning to form on his face. Then he said, "I'm Richard," and extended his hand.

"Henry."

They shook hands, and Richard turned back to me. "You look nice. Wow, a skirt! This is quite a moment."

Richard looked at Henry again and back at me. "Hey, I need to talk to you, Mimi."

"OK," I said. "What's up?"

"Could we— Do we have to—" He looked around for some place we could talk privately.

"Can't you just call me tomorrow?"

"Over here. Excuse us a sec," he said to Henry. I followed him to a souvenir T-shirt cart. Then Richard was speechless for a few seconds.

"What?" I said. "What did you want to talk to me about?"

He looked at Henry, ordering at the concession stand, and sighed. "My car's making this weird noise," he said, "kind of a screeching every time I start up after stopping."

"You called me over here to talk about your car?" I said, but caught myself. I didn't want to start anything now. "Fan belt. Take it in to that place I told you about. Get it serviced." I started walking away.

"You think so?"

"Yes."

"Could you drive there with me and then drop me off at school?"

I shot him an irritated look and didn't answer.

"All right," he said. "OK, OK."

Henry was standing there, waiting for us to finish. I joined him, and we went to find our seats. Henry said, "What was that all about? Who's he?"

"His car is making a noise," I said. "He thought I might know what it was, what to do. He's my ex-husband."

"He's your—no kidding! He seemed pretty nice."

"Yeah," I said. "He's nice."

"So you guys don't want to kill each other or anything?"

"Not all the time," I said. "I mean, it's been a while."

"Pretty unusual," he said.

"Don't get me wrong," I said. "He can still get under my skin like *that*." I snapped my fingers. "But so can a lot of people I've known for a long time."

He smiled at me and moved in closer. "You smell good."

"Thanks," I said.

It was a long wait for the music to start. It always is, but this seemed longer than usual. I tried to think of things to say to Henry, questions to ask him to get a conversation going. I was trying not to think about the store. "Where do you live?" I said.

"I have an apartment near work. It's nothing much."

"Do you have a roommate or anything?"

He smiled. "No."

I kept thinking. "Have you ever seen Elvis Costello before?"

"No. You?"

"Yes," I said, "several times. Richard, you know, my ex-husband," I waved my hand in the direction of the lobby where we had seen him, "really loves Elvis. We saw him twice in clubs on his first U.S. tour. After that, every time he toured,

Richard would buy us tickets to more than one show. This was way back when we were together, of course." In my head, I figured out how old Henry was at the time of Elvis's first tour: eleven. "A long time ago. Richard is a die-hard fan."

"Oh," he said, flustered. "Maybe I should have chosen something else to do."

"No," I said. "Sorry. I didn't mean that. I'm crazy about Elvis. I could never see him too many times. He's great. It's been years since I saw him live. Really. And it's a treat every time. You'll see what I mean." I never thought that going to see Elvis Costello would make me feel old.

We didn't say anything for a while. Then Henry said, "Why did you call me back? What made you change your mind?"

I watched the sound engineer take his place behind a big console in the middle of the room and start to fiddle with knobs and sliders. I looked at the exit sign. I said, "I like you." Hearing myself say this, my face grew warm.

He took my hand, and the lights went down.

The music was loud, about as loud as the sound of an airplane taking off ten feet away, but with brilliant lyrics and a variety of interesting tempos. It didn't hold my complete attention, though. I couldn't get my mind off the store. Tonight, just before I closed, one of the men from the rental office came by to see me. The shopping center was going to raise our rent by fifty percent in three months, when our current lease expired. They could do that. I checked. Coupons, I was thinking; a big sign, visible from the street. Everything I had already thought of was going around in my head. When the music was over, I felt guilty for not giving Elvis my full attention, for not appreciating how far he had come in seventeen years, for not focusing completely on the way he never stopped moving forward.

Henry held my hand all the way to the car. He had held

it so long that I imagined the skin on my fingers growing puckered, the way it did during a long bath. He took me home. We didn't listen to any music in the car; Henry said he wanted to keep the concert in his head as long as possible.

At my house, we went in the back door. I figured my mother would be asleep on the couch in the living room and I didn't want to disturb her.

"That was fun," I whispered in the kitchen. "Want something to drink?"

"No, thanks," he whispered and sat down at the table. I sat down next to him, then regretted it. "You're so pretty," he said.

"Thanks," I said, standing up again fast. "But wait. Listen, I want to ask you something." I didn't want him to kiss me. I couldn't do this. I had made a mistake, going out with him. I was going to ask him for his ideas about our store, to distract him, but then I stopped myself. He would think this was the reason I went to the concert with him. "Are you hungry?" I said.

"No," Henry said.

He moved his feet, and I worried that he was going to come over to me. I looked in the sink for some dishes to wash, but my mother had done them all and put everything away. I looked around for something else to occupy me, but I couldn't find anything.

Henry didn't get up. He leaned back in his chair and said, "How's business? How are things going with your store?" Then he put his hand over his mouth. "Sorry. I forgot. I wasn't going to talk to you about that. I promised myself. I did pretty well up to then, though, don't you think? I can't help it, nervous habit. Give me a minute and I'll think of something else."

"As a matter of fact," I said, "since you brought it up, maybe we *could* talk about work for a minute. If you don't mind. I keep trying not to think about it, but I'm thinking about it anyway. I'm having some business problems, and I wondered if we could pick up the discussion I didn't want to have the other night. If you mind, just say so, and we can talk about something else."

"Mind?" he said. "Not at all. Go ahead."

"OK, here's the problem. Send It, Inc., you know, the big chain, is opening an outlet in a shopping center near ours. *And* our rent is going way up when our current lease expires in three months."

He smiled, as if I had just told him good news, and rubbed his hands together. "Let's get to work. OK. Now, what have you thought of so far? Is there some paper around and a pen?" I got the paper and pen, while he took off his jacket, getting comfortable.

"Just a few things that probably wouldn't work out," I said.

"Like what?" He held the pen ready.

"A messenger service to deliver packages locally?"

"Yeah?" he said, prompting me.

"But I'm not sure we can afford to get it going," I said.

"Do the other places offer messenger service?"

"No," I said.

"Let's not rule it out then," he said. I sat down next to him again while he wrote "Messenger service." He looked at the pen. It had the name of the store on it. He wrote "Office supplies." He pointed the pen at me. "What about—"

"Office supplies?" I said. "We already offer some. But there's a card store in our center that does too, and so does the grocery store. It's not—"

"Forget that then," he said, crossing out "Office supplies." He tapped the pen against his cheek. "Try to think a little off center, something that might get people in there who haven't come in before now, maybe even something outside of the office-service area that you're sure the chain stores are never going to get into. Come on," he said. "Let's brainstorm here.

Maybe we can hit on a unique, original solution that will save your business. Custom banners? Some kind of office party service? Are you or your sister any good at balloon animals or magic tricks?" He smiled and expected me to laugh at the thought of myself entertaining at an office party. I didn't, and he went on. "There are a lot of things you can try. Of course it's a challenge. I'm not saying it's going to be easy, but you can think of it as a chance to grow in a new direction that you might not have considered otherwise."

"That would be a very positive way of looking at it." I stared at the refrigerator. "I've thought about it a lot and I can't come up with anything. I'm worried that we may have to close our store, that we may go out of business."

"No," he said, shaking his head. "That's not going to happen. We won't let it. It's just a matter of working hard and coming up with some creative solutions. You've got a solid business, and it's not going to disappear overnight." He sounded so sure of this that I let myself feel a little bit relieved. Henry touched the back of my hand with one finger. I didn't pull away because he was being so nice about the store.

We heard my mother stirring in the living room, waking up. Then we heard her footsteps. I put my hand in my lap. My mother walked into the kitchen and seeing us there, jumped and gave a short scream. "Goodness!" she said. "You startled me!" She put a hand over her chest. "I didn't hear you come back."

"We were trying to be quiet," Henry said, standing up. "We were making a big effort."

"The two of you would make excellent burglars," she said, going to the fridge, opening it. "How was Elvis?"

"Great," Henry said. "Elvis is a genius. My ears are still ringing, though. The neurons scream as they die." He put his hands over his ears, listening, then let go.

"How were the kids?" I said, standing. "Anything happen?"

"Daniel didn't finish his book report. I set the alarm for six so he could do it before school."

"Good," I said.

My mother looked at Henry. "Did Mimi invite you to my birthday party a week from Friday? I'm going to be sixty-three."

Henry smiled. "Congratulations. I don't know." He looked at me. I smiled. It had not even crossed my mind to invite him.

My mother said, "Please come. It will be fun. We'd love to have you."

"I'd like that," Henry said. "What time?"

"Seven-thirty. Right here at Mimi's. You don't have to bring anything."

"I can't wait," he said.

"I'll look forward to it too," my mother said. She looked at her watch. "Oh, it's late. Mimi always goes to bed so early. Are you parked right out front, Henry? We can walk out together."

"Oh," Henry said. "Yeah, I—" He looked at me. I wanted to talk about the store some more. I didn't want him to go yet. But I couldn't bring myself to say this in front of my mother. "I guess I'll see you Friday," he said.

"Yeah, Friday," I said.

At the front door, Henry turned around. "Night, Mimi," he said, and opened the door to let my mother out first.

CHAPTER 6

Nice Family

The next day, first thing, I called my mother. "Hi, sweetheart," she said, a happy, oblivious breeze in her voice. "Henry seems very taken with you," she said. "I like him."

"Mom," I said. "I wasn't going to invite him to the birthday party. You shouldn't have done that. I've only been out with him twice. I wasn't even sure I wanted to see him again." Eve and John would be checking out Henry, giving me their assessment of him after the party. I pictured Melanie being sulky and difficult, Daniel saying something embarrassing. I didn't mention the way my mother had made Henry leave too early the night before.

"Goodness me," she said. "What have I done now?"

"It was for me to decide when and if I wanted to see him again."

She said, "You're right. I should have stayed out of it. I'm sorry."

I was expecting an argument. "Yes. Well," I said. "OK, I'll make the best of it, I guess, but next time you invite your own friends."

"I certainly will. I mean, I have. Dot and Helen are coming too."

"Oh, joy. This will be a great evening."

"Now, they're not so bad."

"Hm," I said. "I hope they like burritos."

"That sounds lovely."

I was late getting back from work and had to make the food and get ready in a big rush. Melanie and Daniel had made a banner to tape up in the living room for their grandmother's party. It read: "Goodness me! Goodness me! Grandma Joyce is sixty-three!"

"That looks nice," I said as they were finishing painting it. "But hurry up with it. People are going to be here soon."

"We're going to have to use your blow dryer then," Melanie said, painting some flowers in one corner of the banner. "The paint isn't dry."

"All right, but I'm going to need it soon," I said. "And listen for the timer on the cake. Can you do that for me? Don't forget." I was rushing around the living room, grabbing paintbrushes, sweatshirts, homework papers, and junk mail that I found lying around, and gathering it all into a pile to hide somewhere.

"Mom, whoa," Daniel said. "You're getting all hyper again!" Slowly, carefully, he added green stems and leaves to Melanie's flowers.

"Not like that!" she said. "Daniel!"

"Better than you could do," he said.

"Finish up, you guys," I said. "They'll be here any minute. And when Aunt Eve gets here, just put her rice thing in the other oven. Her salad can go right on the table. Are you listening to me?"

"Mom, he's right," Melanie said to me. "I keep trying to tell you: Most people are always late. That gives you ten, maybe fifteen minutes extra for everything you have to do. If you would just remember that, you wouldn't have to get so frantic all the time." She stood back and looked at her work. "There! Done. I'm going to change." She started for her room.

"Clean up your paint mess first," I said, almost running past her to start my shower. "Don't forget about the cake."

I couldn't stand being late. Even the possibility of it sent me into a panic. This drove my children nuts, as I was always nagging them to hurry. Anyone who knows me at all knows that I can't stand it when other people are late either. I know exactly which childhood experience this hang-up comes from, not that knowing helps.

It was my father's fault that I had this urgent need to be punctual. When Eve and I were growing up, he was always late. On weekends when we visited him, he would drop us off somewhere and tell us to wait for him at a certain place and time. We would rush to get back to the appointed location, only to wait there for ten minutes, fifteen, half an hour. "After thirteen cars, he'll be here," I'd say to Eve, and we'd count the passing cars. "After twenty-nine cars," I'd tell her, and we'd start over again.

He was late to pick us up from other people's houses too. Our father had a lot of friends, and sometimes the people in his neighborhood, people we hardly knew, invited us over to play, or to their children's birthday parties. We brought the presents with us in our suitcases and kept party outfits at our dad's, fancy dresses with puffy slips that made the skirts stick out, and shiny black party shoes. After the parties were over, parents would come to pick up the other kids at the time the invitation said the party would end. Eve and I would sit and wait for a long time with the family who was hosting the party. At one house, we were there so long the parents started to worry. We sat there while the father dialed our father's number over and over, listened to it ring, hung up, and told us each time that he must be on his way. When our father finally did pull up out front, he was happy to see us, enthusiastic about hearing what we had done all afternoon. I mentioned how long we had waited for him, that the other kids had gone home long before. He was so apologetic, so deeply sorry about leaving us there so long, that we were convinced he wouldn't ever do it again.

The day I decided never to be late was when I was ten and Eve was eight. Someone our father knew invited us to a costume birthday party. He got costumes for us somewhere, a princess outfit for Eve and a frog costume for me. He dropped us off in front of the house. "I have an appointment," he said. "You girls have a good time, and remember your manners. Love you!" He zoomed off, and we went to the front door of the house to ring the bell.

The father of the birthday girl answered the door. We didn't see any decorations or hear any noise coming from inside. He looked at us in our costumes. "What's this all about?" he said smiling, waiting for an explanation. "Halloween again? So soon?" When we didn't say anything, he said, "What are you girls all dressed up for?"

Eve stepped behind me, hiding. I said, "I'm Mimi Burke, and this is my sister, Eve. Our dad dropped us off for the party. The costume birthday party for your daughter."

"Uh-oh," he said. "Fran! Franny! Could you come down here a second, please?" His wife appeared, and then I knew for sure there was no party. Her hair was in rollers, and she had no makeup on. "George Burke's kids," her husband filled her in.

Fran's mouth fell open. "Oh, no! Is your dad—" She looked out at the empty driveway. "I'm sorry. I had to postpone the party. I canceled it a couple of days ago. I've got three kids upstairs with chicken pox. I didn't call your father because he said you wouldn't be here this weekend."

"Change of plans," I said. I wanted to evaporate on the spot and take my sister with me.

"I'll just call your dad in a few minutes and tell him to come back for you."

"Our dad wasn't going home," I had to tell her.

"Oh?"

"He had an appointment."

"Oh, boy," she said. "I guess you don't know where." I shook my head. "I hope you girls have had chicken pox."

"Yes," I said. "A long time ago."

"Come on in then, and get comfortable."

We sat on their couch in our costumes and worked on tattered jigsaw puzzles with pieces missing and watched reruns of television shows we had already seen. Fran tended to her sick children, and her husband mowed the lawn and weeded the flower beds. Our father didn't pick us up on time; we had grown to expect that. But when he was more than half an hour late, I couldn't stop looking at their kitchen clock, a turquoise oval that matched their wall phone. He was forty-five minutes late, then an hour.

"I don't understand this," Fran said, looking out the living-room window. And then when she saw our worried faces, she added, "Traffic can be mean around here."

An hour and forty-five minutes past the time he said he would pick us up, I asked Fran if I could use her phone to call my mother. "It's long distance," I said, near tears.

"Go ahead, sweetheart," she said, handing me the phone. "You just go ahead."

In another hour, our mother arrived to pick us up. We climbed into the car, and she drove us back to our father's apartment. The building manager had a key. I hung the two costumes in the closet, and we got the rest of our stuff packed up.

We never saw our father again. Several times, detectives came to see us, to ask us if our father had mentioned going on a trip, if he had said where he might be going. Had we seen a plane ticket, perhaps, heard him talking on the phone to a friend about his plans? Just any little detail might help a lot. We didn't have any information to give the detectives, and I was sorry. I loved my father and wanted him back. I don't know when I stopped thinking he was going to show up again someday, sorry for all the worry and trouble he had caused. When we found out that he took all the money that he was supposed to be raising for a new coronary care wing of a hospital, it was a shock. But this news didn't hurt us nearly as much as the fact that he didn't come back to pick us up from the house where the birthday party was supposed to be. I never stopped trying to imagine where he went with the money. Sometimes I saw him living happily in a tropical paradise; other times I pictured him in a cold place where people spoke another language. Sometimes I thought he might be just around the corner with a new face and name, and some more kids we had a lot in common with.

The last day I saw my dad was the day I decided never, ever to be late, no matter what. Naturally I didn't know then that I would drive my own children crazy trying to be punctual. And I had no way of knowing how many times I was going to feel abandoned and betrayed all over again with a magnitude of emotion that was out of proportion to the situation, how many times I would be let down by other people who didn't share my need to be on time. I hadn't told my children about my father not picking us up that day, or explained to them that this was the reason that I was always at least ten minutes early to pick them up from anything. They knew that their grandmother was divorced when Eve and I were small, and they knew that we didn't know where our father was. That was all; that was enough.

Henry arrived at our house before I was ready. I stayed in the bathroom with the door shut. Melanie let him in. "Sorry," I heard Henry say. "I always do this. Things never take as long as I think they're going to."

Daniel said, "Hi, Henry. Cool shirt. Want to see a shadow box I made for school? It's really great." He hurried to his room.

Melanie called after him, "He doesn't want to see your dumb homework, Daniel."

"I do, though," Henry said. "I love homework." I heard Daniel come back with the shoebox in which he had made a scene from the California gold rush, a little aluminum-foil river and modeling-clay people holding bottle caps for mining pans.

Melanie said, "Mom is still getting ready. She has a long way to go." Henry laughed, and I turned on the blow dryer.

When I turned it off, my mother was there. They were all in the kitchen. Henry was talking. "I have three sisters," he was saying. "I'm the youngest. They all live in other places. I'm closest to Jeannie, the oldest, who lives in New Jersey. We grew up there. She has three kids, and she works in the office of their school. We talk on the phone a lot. My middle sister, who's also in New Jersey, does bookkeeping for a dental practice. She's married, no kids. My youngest sister lives in Colorado with her husband and two daughters. She hasn't worked since she had the kids. My dad's a retired plumber. My mom is a housewife."

"How did you end up here, after growing up back east?" My mother was talking with her mouth full. I hoped she had gotten out the vegetables and dip I had rushed to get ready.

"I went to UCLA. I met someone. We lived together

through graduate school and just split up six months ago."

"Oh, dear," said my mother.

"Had to happen," Henry said. I couldn't see him, but I pictured a shrug. "I moved here when I got a job offer in the area. It was a good chance to make a clean break."

"I see," my mother said. "And how are things working out?"

"Not perfect. I think the company I'm working for is about to go belly-up."

"Goodness me," said my mother.

"Yeah."

"I hear you were at my daughter's wedding."

"Yes. I went with my friend from work, John's cousin. I didn't know anybody else there. I'm glad I went, though."

My mother said, "So am I." I could tell from their voices that they were both smiling. In two minutes, she had gotten him to say about ten times more than I had in two dates.

"Well, don't you look nice," my mother said as I walked into the kitchen. "Now you see how pretty your hair can be if you take some trouble with it. You should do that every day. It almost makes it worth it to have a birthday."

Daniel came over to touch my hair, as if checking to see that it was real. I took his hand and gently pushed it down.

"Earrings!" Melanie said. "I don't believe it! Where did you get those? Wait a minute! Are those mine?"

"Of course they're not yours," I said, frowning at her to get her to be quiet.

"Hi, Mimi," Henry said, suddenly soft-spoken. "I like your sweater."

"Thank you," I said. I felt like walking out the door and leaving them all there. I smelled something. "The cake!" I said. "It was supposed to be out of there ten minutes ago." I pulled open the oven door. The cake looked shrunken and too brown on top.

Melanie said, "The timer didn't go off, Mom. I swear. I didn't forget. The timer didn't go off!"

"It's not your fault, honey," I said, "It's mine. Look, I set it, but I forgot to push start. Shoot! What a dope."

My mother said, "Maybe it will taste all right once you get the frosting on it. The frosting is the best part anyway."

I put the cake pan on the counter to cool. I checked the oven for the rice casserole Eve was bringing. Not there. "Where's Eve?" I said to my mother.

"She'll be here in a minute," she said.

The doorbell rang. "Here she is," I said on my way to answer it. "About time." I opened the door. It wasn't Eve. It was my mother's friends, Dot and Helen. They were standing there smiling, holding their presents.

"Come in," I said. "Here, let me put your presents with the others."

"Where's the birthday girl?" Dot said. "You look nice, Mimi. I hardly recognized you." I glared at her, but she was already on her way to the kitchen to find my mother. "Happy birthday, Joyce!" she said.

"Thank you," said my mother. "This is Mimi's friend Henry. This is Dot. And this is Helen."

"How do you do?" Henry said.

"Nice to meet you," said Helen.

"Hi, Henry," said Dot.

I joined them all in the kitchen. "I better put the burritos in," I said. My mother, Henry, and the kids were eating crackers out of a box. "You guys," I said. "I cut up about a million carrots and celery stalks so you wouldn't fill up before the burritos. And Eve's bringing that rice casserole she does and a salad." Henry folded in the box top and put the crackers away in the cupboard. I pulled a plate of cut-up vegetables and dip out of the fridge.

Dot said, "Excuse me, but is that something Mexican I saw you put in there?"

"Burritos," Daniel said. "Yum! Yum!"

Dot was shaking her head. "I can't eat any of that. I'm going to have to have something else. I've got a very finicky stomach."

"Oh," I said. "Hm." I handed the plate of vegetables to my mother. "Would you take this out to the living room, Mom? I'll find you something else, Dot."

Dot said, "Thank you, dear."

"What does everyone want to drink?" I took orders.

"I'll bring out the drinks," Henry said. Everyone else followed my mother out to the living room.

I started pouring things into glasses. "What am I going to give her? Maybe she could just eat Eve's rice—it's pretty mild—and some salad."

"Mimi," Henry whispered. "I brought you something." He pulled a small gift-wrapped rectangle out of his pocket. "Finally I remembered you from the wedding. You sang. It was the best thing that happened."

"Thank you," I said. I opened it. It was a tape, James. "Oh! James," I said. He nodded. "I love these guys. That was very sweet of you." My face burned and my eyes filled with tears. It had been a long time since I got a present for no reason. I said, "Geez, look at me. I don't know why I'm so emotional."

Melanie walked in and picked up two glasses. "Maybe you're getting your period." She walked out.

Dot came in. "Oh, is that my Diet Coke? Thanks so much."

We brought out the rest of the drinks. Melanie took the tape out of my hand. "Cool! Where did you get this?"

"A present from Henry." Melanie put the tape on. Everybody stopped for a minute and listened, then went on talking. Helen, who taught fifth grade, was listening to Daniel hold forth on the gold rush. He wanted to visit a ghost town. Melanie, Dot, and my mother were talking about shoes. Dot had some ideas about where Melanie could get high heels that weren't too expensive and wouldn't hurt her feet.

"Heels?" I said. "Melanie, your feet are still growing. You're too young for heels."

She said, "Still growing? I hope not! They're size ten and a half already!"

"Just wait," my mother said. "Mine are ten, your mother's and Aunt Eve's are eleven. Who knows—yours could be twelve."

"Is it time to eat?" Daniel wanted to know.

"We're just waiting for Aunt Eve and Uncle John," I said.

Daniel said, "How come they're always so late?"

"Why don't you put the frosting on the cake?" I said. Daniel went to the kitchen. I called Eve and John's house. "No answer," I told everybody, listening to it ring. "They must be on their way."

"The cake is still kind of hot," Daniel said. "Is that OK?"

"No," I said, "but put the frosting on it anyway."

We waited some more. By the time the tape turned itself over, the burritos were ready. I let them overcook a few more minutes while I pushed redial on the phone and waited until I heard Eve's answering machine start and hung up. Then I heated some leftover macaroni and cheese in the microwave for Dot and served burritos to everyone else. Without the rice and salad, they looked pretty pathetic alone on the plates.

Henry and Daniel were having seconds when John and Eve arrived. Their hair was wet. "Hi, Mom. Happy birthday," Eve said and kissed our mother on the cheek.

John said, "Happy birthday, Joyce," and gave her a long hug.

Next was going to be my turn. I braced myself. John hugged me. Over his shoulder, I kept an eye on the plate I was holding, making sure not to dump my burrito on the floor. He squeezed me. He rubbed my back. He whispered, "How *are* you?"

"Fine, thank you," I said. He allowed me to pull back a little, and looked into my eyes, as if to read the true answer there. I looked away. He let go of me, then took my free hand and kissed it.

"John, Eve," I said, "this is Henry."

Henry rose to shake their hands.

"Hi, Henry," Eve said. You're brave to come to a family dinner."

My mother said, "Now Eve, don't scare him. We're not so bad. Are we?" She looked around, but no one answered.

"How come your hair's wet?" Daniel wanted to know.

Eve said, "A friend of John's, a therapist, went to India for a few weeks. He's letting us use his exercise room, sauna, and Jacuzzi while he's gone. Can you imagine having all that in your own house? His specialty is fear of success. He's made all these videos and—"

I said, "Eve, did you bring the rice and the salad?"

Eve closed her eyes and put a hand over her mouth.

"Let me get you both some food," I said, pulling my hand away from John. "What do you want to drink?"

Eve followed me into the kitchen. "God, I'm sorry. Did I say I was going to bring rice casserole and salad? I did, didn't I?"

"Oopsie," Daniel said.

"You forgot, Aunt Eve?" said Melanie. "You're kidding. You forgot?"

"Nothing for me, Meemers," John said.

"What?" I said. "You're not going to eat? How come? What do you want to drink?"

"Oh, I'm fine. Nothing."

"No burrito for me, either, thanks, Mimi," said my sister.

"Wow, quite a haul here, Joyce," John said about the presents on the table. "Look at all this." John put a small box in silver paper with the other presents.

"Wait a second," I said. "Am I understanding this correctly? You guys aren't having dinner with us?"

At the kitchen door, John said, "No thanks, Meemers. We just ate dinner with friends."

"Mimi," I said. "It's Mimi. But I made all these burritos. I started yesterday." Truthfully, there weren't many burritos left. Without the side dishes, people were eating more of them than I'd expected. Henry took a third one now and gave my mother a second. "And you were supposed to provide half the food. You offered. You're half an hour late. What is this?"

"See?" Eve said to John. "I told you she'd be mad."

"She's not mad," John said.

"Mimi, these are delicious," my mother called from the living room.

I said, "They're way overcooked."

"I like them a little crunchy," she said. "Shall I help you with these plates? Oh, listen to me. It's my birthday, what am I talking about? I'm not lifting a finger. Melanie, I think Dot and Helen are finished. Why don't you pick up their plates for your mother." Melanie rose to get the plates from the two women. Daniel brought Henry's plate and his own to the kitchen. He rolled his eyes at Henry, who gave him a sympathetic smile.

"You should have told me," I said to Eve. "You should have called."

John said, "Looks like everyone got enough to eat, though, and there are a couple of burritos left over here. You'll have those for tomorrow night." He started wrapping the leftovers in foil to put them in the fridge.

"It's not that," I said, piling plates in the sink. "It's just that the invitation was for dinner, and you accepted. We were all expecting you, not to mention the fact that you said you were going to bring some of the food. It was Eve's idea."

John said, "Mimi, I'm sorry."

Eve said, "We're both sorry. We screwed up. We admit it, and we apologize. That's the best we can do. Now please don't make this into a bigger deal than it is."

"What's that supposed to mean?"

"You know. Just that you have a tendency to hang on to these little things for a long time. I don't want to keep hearing about this for years to come."

I said, "*I* hang on to things? *I* keep bringing them up?"

"Yes," Eve said. "You do. Maybe I do too. If I do, I'll try not to. From now on."

John put the burritos in the fridge. I didn't say any more. Melanie joined us, waiting for me to tell her what to do next. "Let's get started with the cake." Melanie took yellow birthday candles out of a drawer and started looking for matches. She got down some plates. I looked at the cake. There were bare patches on it where the icing had melted because Daniel had frosted it while it was still warm. "I'll be right back," I said. I picked up a pair of scissors and a flashlight and went out into the backyard.

It had grown cold outside and everything was damp. I shivered and pointed my flashlight to examine shrubbery. Checking first for snails, slugs, and spiders, I chopped off a piece of a bush. I moved on to the next one.

Henry was right behind me. He said, "Mimi? Are you OK?"

"Yeah, I'm fine," I said. Then I whispered, "I don't like the way my sister behaves now that she's with John. That was rude of them. My sister knows better than that. What's happened to her anyway? I mean, is this the way it's going to be for the rest of our lives, or is she going to snap out of it at some point? I would just like to know." Henry was quiet. I yanked a stalk, chopped it, then another.

"What are you doing?" Henry said after a minute. "Why are you hacking at those bushes?"

"I'm getting flowers for the cake. The icing looks lousy and I thought flowers would help."

"Oh," he said. "Mimi?"

"Yes." I snapped off a bloom. I got goose bumps from the cold and began to hurry. "Freezing out here," I said.

"Can I help you with that?" He moved closer, pulled back branches to look for blooms. "Here's—no, that looks kind of chewed." He let the branch go, grabbed another. "You have a nice family." I looked at him. "I know they're driving you crazy right now, but I mean, in general, they seem nice."

"I guess," I said.

"I like your mom. I'm glad she asked me."

I grabbed something with thorns, gasped, and let go. "Ow! Yikes!"

"What? Are you OK?"

I licked a little blood off my hand. "It's fine. Let's go back in. I think I have enough. I'm cold, aren't you?"

Inside, John was making coffee; everyone else was in the living room, talking quietly. Henry cut the flowers away from the stems and leaves and handed me the blooms to put on the cake. "Like this?" he said. "This OK?"

"Perfect," I said. I put a candle in the middle and surrounded it with three camellias.

John looked over at the cake. "Oh, Meemers, that's exquisite!" he said. "You really have a touch."

"Mimi," Henry said.

I turned around, but he was talking to John.

"It's Mimi," Henry said, "not Meemers. She told you that."

John laughed. "Excuse *me.*"

I said, "Isn't it kind of late for coffee? Is anyone going to drink that?"

John took a step backward. "I asked," he said. "They told me they wanted it."

"Well, I guess," I said. I took the cake out to the living room. I began singing, "Happy birthday to you," and everyone joined in. I cut the cake.

John came in with a tray of cups. At the sight of the coffee, everyone seemed to sit up a little straighter. Dot reached eagerly for her cup. John made his way around the room.

"Good coffee, John," Dot said.

"This is good," said my mother. "Mmm."

"I want some," said Melanie. But then she looked at me and didn't ask again. No one commented on the cake, which was dry and hard with places that tasted charred. I collected a lot of unfinished pieces.

"OK," I said. "Presents."

My mother took the presents on her lap. She opened Henry's first. It was a picture frame with spaces for two photographs. "Thank you, Henry," she said. "How pretty. I'll put pictures of my two grandchildren in this." There was a T-shirt from Helen that she had painted herself—a picture of a mouse jogging. Dot gave her a pasta cookbook. I gave her the new pajamas she had asked for. Melanie gave her earrings that she had made in art class. Daniel gave her slippers that I had helped him pay for. "Wonderful!" she said. "I'm so lucky. Look at all my beautiful things!"

Henry said, "Wait. Here's something else." John and Eve's present was still on the table. He handed it to her.

"More?" my mother said. "Goodness me, I don't know if I can take any more!" She opened the little package. It was a bracelet, gold, a bangle etched with tiny flowers. She didn't say anything for a minute, then she said, "How lovely. How perfectly lovely." She put it on. Everyone gathered around to look.

"Wow," said Henry. "Nice." He bent to admire the bracelet, then looked at me over the heads of the others and tried to read my reaction.

Eve said, "It just reminded us of you, and we couldn't resist."

Melanie said, "May I try it on, Grandma?" My mother slipped the bracelet over Melanie's hand. It made her wrist look small and fragile.

"Pretty," I said without wanting to. Melanie took it off and handed it back to her grandmother.

"You may borrow it sometime," my mother said to Melanie. "And now, I'm going to gather all my lovely gifts and go home. Thank you, everyone."

I got her a shopping bag to put her new stuff in. She wore the bracelet. We all went out to the driveway. I rubbed my hands up and down my arms, trying to get warm. Dot and Helen thanked me and left.

Eve said, "Good party, Mimi."

John said, "I'm sorry we were late—it was all my fault. Will you forgive me?" He kissed my cheek and the two of them left.

My mother hugged the kids, then me. She said, "It was a wonderful party, honey. Thank you. And Henry, thank you so much for my nice picture frame."

"You're welcome," he said.

After she drove off, Melanie, Daniel, Henry, and I went back inside. I said, "It's a school night, and I want you guys to get ready for bed right now."

Melanie said, "Does that mean we don't have to help clean up?"

"It's your lucky night," I said. "I'll take care of it."

"Night, Mom," Daniel said. "Night, Henry."

Melanie said, "Night, you guys."

Henry was trying to help with the cleanup, but he kept

getting into my way. When I went to dump some leftovers in the trash can, he had taken the bag out and was trying to find a new one. "Under the sink," I said.

"Got it."

Then he started to put the cake in the fridge. "You can throw that out," I said. "No one's going to eat that."

"Sure? OK." He went to the garbage can and turned over the pan, but the cake didn't come out. He found a spatula and scraped at it for a minute until it came loose. Then as he turned it over, he missed the trash, and most of it fell on the floor.

"Oopsie." Daniel was standing in the kitchen door in his pajamas. He got Henry the broom and dustpan. "Mom, I forgot, I'm supposed to have my book list ready for tomorrow. It's the last day."

I said, "It's on the fridge. Put it in your backpack now, so you won't forget it."

He took the paper to his room, while Henry finished sweeping. I was trying not to look at my watch. I wanted to get up at five the next morning to work on my mother's desk before I had to take the kids to school. If I didn't get to bed soon, I wasn't going to be able to get up early. Henry put the broom away and walked over to where I was standing by the dishwasher, putting in the last coffee cup. He stood behind me and we looked at our reflections in the window behind the kitchen sink. Suddenly, I thought of Bill for the first time all evening. What made me think of him just then was our reflections in the dark window and seeing the barbecue and the deck railing through them. Henry and I looked like two ghosts. I thought of the fact that since Bill died, I had never heard from him. And I had truly believed I would. He promised me.

Early on in Bill's illness, we both knew that he was going to die. The closer the moment came, the more frightened I was of being without him. I was terrified by the thought of the emptiness that I imagined opening up where he used to be. It took me weeks to bring myself to talk to him about it. Then one night when he was starting to seriously decline, to slip away, I blurted out, "Bill, you can't die. I don't want to be alone. I can't do it."

At first he didn't answer, and I wasn't sure that he had heard me. By this stage, he would drift off into sleep suddenly, right in the middle of talking to me, or lose track of what we had been saying. His mouth used to get so dry. I kept a glass of 7-Up next to the bed. I picked up the glass then to see if he wanted some. He opened his lips a little bit and drank for a long time. Then he pressed his head slightly deeper into the pillows to let me know that he was finished. I withdrew the straw and put the glass on the bedside table. He took a breath and spoke with frequent pauses. A simple sentence had become a major project, involving many difficult steps: formulating the thought, holding on to it, getting air, saying words with enough volume so that they could travel the distance to my ears. He said, "I won't. Leave you. You wait. I'll be. Here."

I was so desperate at that moment that I had almost no regard for his pain or exhaustion. I said, "How will I know? How will you show me that you're still with me? Do you think I'll see you or hear you talk to me, or what?"

He laughed—just a slight stretching sideways of his lips, a couple of voiceless ha-has—and then he said, "You'll know. I'll be. Relent. Less. You won't. Be able." He paused for breath. I gave him another drink. He went on. "Able. To get. Rid of. Me. Like those. Skunks. Under. The deck." His lips stretched again, then slackened, and he fell asleep.

Skunks had been a problem since we had lived in the house. For a few days or weeks, we might think they were gone. Then we would smell them again or see them, checking out our garbage cans when we threw away leftover pizza or peering in the sliding-glass doors to the kitchen when we were just about to turn out the lights for the night. When he said that about the skunks, I felt reassured. I believed that he wouldn't leave me alone and because of this, I felt I might be able to handle his death.

I wanted to be with him when he died, but it didn't work out that way. For what turned out to be his last week, his mother came from Virginia to help me. The kids were at Richard's a lot during this part of the illness. Bill didn't want them to see him deteriorate any further. One afternoon, his mother offered to sit with him while I went for a walk with Patty. "You need some fresh air, a little break," my mother-in-law said. Bill was asleep when I left; when I came back, he had died. I remember my first reaction was to be mad that he hadn't at least waited until I got home. It seemed to me, at the time, that he had sneaked off without me.

Once he was gone, after the funeral and all the sympathy I got and all the crying I did, I found that he really was gone. Completely. He didn't leave anything behind. There was no lingering presence of Bill, no hovering translucent vapor or scent of him to startle me when I came into a room, no voice inside my head. I was alone, and it was as bad as I had feared it would be.

Henry's hand felt especially warm around mine now, like a baby's skin after a nap under a blanket. I turned to face him, wanting to press my body against his, to absorb some of his heat.

He said, "I know you want to get up early, so I'm going to take off." Squeezing my hand again, he said, "OK?"

"OK," I said. His hand slipped out of mine, and he went.

CHAPTER 7

Brake Lights

Sunday evening, Eve and I were in Pic 'n' Save, my sister's favorite store. Brightly colored plastic things and products that had never been good ideas in the first place—knockoffs of cheap clothes, refills for gadgets nowhere to be found—were all sold here at drastically reduced prices. My sister had just discovered a rack of overalls, giant bibbed flowered cotton shorts. Her eyes were glittering: she had found something good, something she wanted.

Melanie and Daniel were at home, staying alone. They didn't want my mother or Richard to stay with them every time I went out. "I'm twelve years old," Melanie said. "I've taken the baby-sitting course at the Y. I can baby-sit for other people's kids. Why can't I be our baby-sitter?" Of course, I had left Melanie alone in the daytime while I took Daniel to soccer practice—but then I worried about her the whole time. And now the two of them wanted to stay alone in the evening.

"Other kids do it all the time," Daniel said.

I said, "What if you need to get in touch with me?"

Melanie said, "Get a cellular phone. A lot of moms have them."

"Are you serious?" I said. "A cellular phone? Me?"

"OK, a pager, then," she said. "It's cheaper."

I thought it over and decided it was not a bad idea. I got one. Tonight before I left, I clipped the little black plastic thing to the waist of my jeans. "Maybe people will think I'm a doctor," I said.

"Yeah, Mom," Melanie said, checking me out before I left with Eve tonight. "You look just like a neurosurgeon. Totally. You're getting the hang of this now. Go out. Have fun. Relax. You'll know right away if we need you. I promise."

Now, while my sister shopped, I glanced down at the pager, touching it, making sure that it was still there and working.

There were certain things Eve didn't like to do alone. When we were growing up, she preferred to have me sit and talk to her while she took a bath. I would sit on the lid of the toilet in my clothes while she lay naked in the steaming water, and we would talk. Even as an adult, the times when she was back from her doll-selling trips, staying at our house, I would sit with her in the bathroom while she told me things. Every once in a while she'd say, "Hold on a second," as if we were on the phone together and she had to answer the door. Then she would slide down under the water to rinse her hair before resurfacing to finish her story.

She didn't like to shop alone either. I was her favorite shopping companion. I don't know why. Shopping was one of my least favorite things to do, and I only did it when I felt I had no choice. As my sister knew, I wore only plain clothes, sticking mainly to neutral colors, favoring striped T-shirts, solid pants and shorts, the occasional skirt. Since high school, I had stuck with this uniform, buying new things not for fun, but when the old ones wore out. Many times, she had tried to take me in hand, broaden my range, loosen me up, even buying the clothes for me: floppy hats with flowers sewn to them, backless nightgowns that she insisted I could wear as dresses, glittery shoes with tall sharp heels, silk neckties she said would look great with this or that shirt. Despite her efforts, I still had a drawer full of T-shirts, most of them striped, a drawer full of pants and shorts in black, white, tan, and denim.

I suggested that Eve and I go shopping together because I wanted to erase the fight we had had at my mother's birthday party. At work all day Saturday, in the many unfilled spaces between customers, we hadn't said much beyond what we had to: "We need to order paper." "What do you want for lunch?" "Was that your last page, or is there more?" Going shopping was a chance to get past the fight.

I always felt that I was the one who raised my sister, though this couldn't really be true, as I was only two years older. Our mother went back to school to get her teaching credential after she and our father split up, then got a full-time teaching job. It seemed then that she had to spend a lot of time away from us. When she was with us, our mother seemed distracted and tired, and I got the idea that Eve was my responsibility, that we should not trouble our mother with problems. I remembered snapping her pajama top to the bottom, working bubble gum out of her hair, rubbing her back in the middle of the night when she had a bad dream. It seemed to me that in the gaps between visits to our father's, he got out of step with us. I was the one who told him when Eve needed to go to the doctor with a sore throat that might be strep. Away from our parents too, I felt it was my job, as the oldest, to watch over Eve. At school when we were little, I made the other first-grade girls move over at the lunch table so that Eve wouldn't have to sit with boys. In high school, I told her which teachers to choose and brought her with me to parties. I was the one who was with her in all of her worlds—at our father's, at our mother's, and at school.

When I was in twelfth grade and Eve was in tenth, she had a boyfriend, Scott Baker. Not only was he her first boyfriend, but he also had long hair and knew how to play an electric guitar. Eve was happy, smiling all the time, actually helping our mother with the laundry and dishes. One day I saw Scott Baker kissing another girl in the parking lot of the Dairy Queen near school. I said nothing to my sister, telling myself it was a one-time lapse, that there was no need to upset her. A week or so later, I went to the movies with Patty and saw Scott Baker with his hand deep inside another girl's scoop-neck tank top. Again, I didn't tell my sister, but a lump of deceit settled itself within me, expanding a little bit each day until I started to feel clogged, the way I imagined a fur ball would feel, growing in the stomach of a cat. Then one day, Scott Baker stood behind me in the cafeteria line at school. Ever so lightly, he rubbed his hand across my behind. "Hey, Mimi," he whispered into my hair. "Want to go out with me tonight?"

That afternoon, when I told my sister about the two other girls, leaving out what had happened at lunch, Eve cried and threw things. I couldn't blame her for being mad. But she was mad at me. She said I didn't like Scott because he liked her and not me, that I was jealous. She threw a math book across the room, and the corner of it hit my cheekbone. Then she ran out of the room, out of the house, and didn't come back until bedtime. When she returned, she was no longer speaking to me.

For a while, there was a triangular bruise on my face where the book had hit me. Even after the bruise was gone, my sister still didn't speak to me. I was lonely. I spent a lot of time with Patty, but she was no replacement for Eve. Patty didn't like music. She didn't listen to the Beatles, the Kinks, Rod Stewart, and the Rolling Stones, not the way we did. After doing homework, she didn't turn on the stereo loud and dance with her reflection in the sliding-glass doors of the family room, the way Eve and I used to every night at home. She didn't speak ob (*Dob-o yob-ou lob-ike mob-y nob-ew shob-oes?*: Do you like my new shoes?), so I could never tell her a secret in the middle of a crowd, the way I could with Eve. She couldn't lip-read, either. Every time I tried to tell her something in geometry—even easy stuff like "Let's ditch after lunch"—she would whisper hoarsely across the room, "What? Mimi! What did you say?" until we both got demerits for talking.

Patty didn't smoke. My sister had started smoking about six months earlier. At night before we got ready for bed, Eve would say, "Mimi," and jerk her head in the direction of the door. I would follow her outside, where we would sit on the curb, talking, while she smoked. My sister always looked great, sitting there with her cigarette, the smoke rising up and disappearing into infinity, her eyebrows tweezed into perfect arcs, her full lips dark with lipstick, the layers of her shag haircut looking tousled but never messy, her giant gold hoop earrings jiggling back and forth as she moved, her bell bottoms falling just over the tops of her platform sandals—never too long and never, ever too short. There was no one else like my sister.

Then one day, weeks after she stopped speaking to me, the nurse's office sent a note to my English teacher, saying that I was to drive Eve home. She had a stomach virus. Since learning to drive, I was the backup emergency person on my sister's file card at school. Our mother was on a field trip with her fourth graders. I found Eve lying motionless on a cot in the nurse's office, her face pale green. I took her home and sat with her all day, though she didn't throw up anymore. That night, she said, "Thanks for taking me home. Thanks for taking care of me." She choked on the last word and had to wipe away a couple of tears.

I said, "Hey, don't cry. It's OK. You're welcome. We're friends again, OK? Like always." She nodded and sobbed into her pillow for a while. That was the end of her being mad at me.

During the next several weeks, I did notice the swelling of her breasts, the vomiting she did in the bathroom in the mornings before school, her brooding silence, and the weight she gained. But I dismissed the changes in her body as simply a continuation of puberty. And I told myself she threw up because of that virus she had been sent home with a month before. The fact that she was in a quiet, bad mood all the time and prone to crying over nothing, I decided, was the aftermath of breaking up with Scott.

One night she came into the room we shared and said, "Mimi, you're going to have to quit pretending you don't know I'm pregnant because I need another hundred dollars." Since our mother didn't like to know or think about bad things, I was the one in charge of finding a way out of trouble. I gave Eve the money and went with her to get the abortion.

Aferward she used all that was left of our money to buy us both milk shakes. Giddy with relief, she turned to me with a little stripe of chocolate on her upper lip and said, "Mimi, you can be a real jerk and a pain, but I'm glad you're my sister." We both regretted the many times we had wanted to disown or murder each other.

After that, I never interfered when I thought she was with the wrong person. I didn't tell her that I thought the guy she was living with in college was shallow and didn't appreciate her. I didn't tell her that I thought a later boyfriend was an alcoholic. I let her figure these things out herself. Sometimes it took a long time. Then I helped her move or stayed up with her all night while she cried, whatever it took. My mother didn't say anything about her choices either, of course. "People have to make their own mistakes," she would tell me. "You'll never change her mind by interfering; you'll just make her mad at you." Though I knew this was another justification for my mother's system of denial, in a way she was right. When Eve got involved with John, anything I said or asked about him had caused her to bristle. "He's never been married?" I said. "Really?"

She said, "Is that something that needs to be explained, accounted for? Never having been married? *I've* never been married. Does that mean there's something wrong with me?"

"Of course not," I said. "I was just curious about his life, that's all."

Another time, I said, "What does he do all day, if he doesn't work?"

"Is that a crime or something, not having a job? I happen to find it refreshing to meet someone who isn't a slave to some miserable occupation he can't stand." After a few conversations like this, I found it best to stick to other subjects, to talk about anything else but John.

At first, I thought it would be easy, not talking about him. But avoiding this one topic made a big poisonous pit open up between us, a gaping dark hole that was always there, ready and waiting for us to fall into it, as we tread with utmost caution around its crusted edges. Not discussing John seemed to change everything we did talk about.

For the first several minutes we were inside Pic 'n' Save, we spoke about only what was immediately facing us. "Look at this!" I said. "A skateboard for only fifteen ninety-nine! Of course, it's probably a lousy one, and how would we know?"

Eve said, "We wouldn't. Don't even try to figure that out. Look! Over there! Those are the ugliest place mats I ever saw! Maybe I should get some."

Later as she was going through a mound of T-shirts on a table, she said, "Did the kids help you clean up the other night?" She was edging closer, showing me that she was ready to make up.

"I sent them to bed. There wasn't that much to do. Henry helped me." Bringing in Henry's name was a peace offering. I was saying I was willing to move past the fight too, by allowing her to give her approval of a new boyfriend.

"He seemed nice enough," Eve said.

"Henry's very nice," I said. For some reason, I thought of all the things we didn't do the other night, picturing in my mind the things that might have happened between us—whispering, kissing, touching—and hadn't. A hot feeling came over me. I looked quickly at a row of $1.99 vases shaped like donkeys pulling carts; the cart was where you put the flowers. I wanted to talk to her about the fact that Henry and I had not even kissed. Did she think I would have to call him if I wanted to see him again? And did I want to see him again? Once we got back on the right track, Eve would discuss all this with me, I was certain, and then I would be able to sort it all out.

"You're blushing," she said.

"I am not." I felt my face heat up more.

"You had sex with him and it was great. Hey, you're only human." She scanned the store for the fitting room, found it. "Come on." I followed her. With these offhand comments, Eve had just negated the headway we had made.

I watched Eve try on a pair of the overall shorts. They were even bigger than they had looked, apparently oversized for overweight women. She picked up a belt that someone else had dropped on the floor and buckled it tight around her small waist, and suddenly the shorts looked great. How did she do that? "Good," she said, checking herself out in the mirror. "I'll get a couple of these. You want one? Nobody else will have them; no one shops here but me." This was a big consideration with my sister. She didn't mind being out-of-date or looking silly, as long as no one else would be seen wearing the same outfit she had.

"No, thanks," I said. "That would look ridiculous on me."

"I'll get one for Melanie," she said. "I'll show her how to belt it." Sorting the clothes into piles of what she was going to get and not get, she said, "To me, Henry didn't seem like your type. But what do I know?"

"My type?" I said. "Do I have a type?" Instead of warming up to my sister, as I had hoped, defensive anger began to prickle inside me. I set my jaw as though trying not to bite.

"I'm just saying he's very young for you. He seems so, I don't know, just *young*. And *small*." She flicked her hair back as she left the dressing room with her piles. I followed her.

"But Eve," I said, "he's so nice and smart, and he likes me. I like him." The way I had thought it was going to be was that I would tell Eve all my reservations about Henry and allow her to talk me out of them. I had imagined her pushing me into seeing more of him, telling me that I owed it to myself. She was going to reassure me that I hadn't blown it, that there was no such thing as blowing it when you were meant to be with someone. I was going to say, "Do you think he's too young for me?" And I imagined her saying, "No, of course not. What difference do a few years make? Don't be so hung up on meaningless details. Mimi," she would urge, "you've been alone long enough. It's time."

Out of the dressing room, she started looking through more stuff. "I'm sure he has many attractive qualities," she said. "I just don't want to see you hurt."

I searched for another topic, one we could agree on, that would get this outing going in the direction it was supposed to. "Wow, pretty nice photo albums for only three dollars. Why don't you get one of those? You could start it with your wedding and honeymoon pictures. Wouldn't that be neat?"

She curled her lip. "When I buy a photo album," she said, "it's going to be a nice one, a good one, not some piece of crap from a discount store."

"Oh," I said. "Sorry. Excuse me." To hell with it; now it was her turn to make an effort.

"Look at these great hair things," Eve said, heading for a rack. "I'm going to get Melanie some."

"Please don't get her more hair stuff," I said. "We're up to our knees in barrettes as it is."

"All right," she said crisply, moving on.

For a while, we went our separate ways. I picked up a sports bottle decorated with characters from a cartoon show that wasn't on television anymore. I put it down. I couldn't figure out how Eve could find anything she wanted in this place, why it cheered her so to be here. A whole aisle of artificial flowers was finally too much for me. Near the front door, I stood waiting for Eve to finish. I looked out at the cars in the parking lot to rest my eyes.

"Mimi! Come here!" my sister called to me from beside a rack of cassettes. I hurried to see.

"Lisa Bates! There are a whole bunch of Lisa Bates CDs here. Look at this. Every Emotional Blackmail CD and cassette ever made. One ninety-nine for a tape and two ninety-nine for a CD." She looked at me, smiling.

Lisa Bates was someone we liked on the radio, but we had never found any of her CDs or tapes in a music store. For a moment, we didn't make a move but just looked at the stuff in the racks where it seemed to be begging us to grab it. We smiled at each other before we each stretched an arm out for the little plastic boxes with pictures of Lisa and her band at various stages of their career.

There were a few other things Eve picked up on her way to the cashier: a pair of sunglasses with turquoise frames, a baseball cap, a teapot in the shape of a pumpkin, a pair of men's shorts. Everything she got came to under twenty-five dollars, and each item would work out; my sister almost never bought anything that had to be returned or that ended up brand-new in the Salvation Army bag.

When we got out of Pic 'n' Save, we went to the pizza place next door and ordered a large with extra cheese to bring home to eat with Melanie and Daniel. Waiting for the pizza, Eve said, "I'm putting on these shorts as soon as I get to your house. I love them." She peeked into the bag, gave a little shiver of pleasure.

I said, "I'm going to play this tape in the car." I scratched a tear in the cellophane, peeled it away from the plastic box. Taking the hot pizza to the car, I was thinking, Everything will be fine; we can smooth over the stuff about Henry later. As long as we stay off the trouble John is in, as long as Eve doesn't tell me anything I don't want to know, this will be fine.

In the car, I slid the new tape in before I turned the key in the ignition. When I started the engine, the car filled with the smell of hot pizza and the introduction to a song I knew I would love called "One More Fucking Heartbreak." There were green lights all the way from the pizza place to the freeway. Though it was Sunday evening and there could have been heavy traffic going north, I glided on easily between a white pickup truck and a station wagon. Traffic was moving steadily forward. We would go to my house, eat with the kids, and it would be the way it had been before, like a year ago, just the four of us together.

Then I saw a lot of brake lights ahead of us and we weren't even close to the usual bottleneck of the 5-805 merge. I had to slow down, coming to a full stop. We didn't move at all for several minutes. I worried about the children at home alone. I looked at my pager, in case I hadn't heard it go off while I was driving with the music on. It wasn't lit up. Maybe

I should have gotten that cellular phone, instead. Then I could have called Melanie and Daniel myself, told them where I was, that I didn't know how long I would be. It made me nervous, not knowing what they were doing. At least I had my sister with me, I thought; we weren't arguing, and nothing unpleasant had been said since we were in the store.

Eve sighed and said, "If John has to go to jail, I'm going to kill myself."

"What?" I said. "No, you're not! Jail? What do you mean, jail?"

"I just mean it would be the worst thing that could possibly happen. Jail would."

"Well, yes. It would be pretty bad," I said. "*Jail*. I mean—" I was trying not to let the panic in my stomach creep up into my voice.

She lifted the pizza box off her lap. "This thing is cooking my thighs. I know you want to know what this whole thing is all about, so I'll tell you."

I shook my head. "That's all right," I said. "You don't have to get into the details." I held up my hands. "Not necessary."

"Let's see," she said. "Where shall I start?" Staring straight ahead at the truck in front of us, she twiddled her earrings.

I leaned to the left to try to see how far ahead the cars were stopped, how long we were going to be sitting here. I couldn't see anything but the truck in front of me, a Toyota. Across the back, most of the letters had been removed so that it said simply "YO."

"Okay, first of all, when John was in Los Angeles and living with this evil witch of a person, he was a restaurant manager." She looked at me. "You knew that much, right? That he was in the restaurant business?"

I nodded and stared at the back of the truck. Silently I told it, *Move!*

"He was working for these guys who had a successful place

in Hollywood. They wanted to open another one in Santa
Monica, and they needed someone they trusted to run it. John
had worked with them for three years. They liked him, and
they wanted to stay at the original place themselves, so they
put him in charge of the new one. He hired the chef, the wait-
people, everybody. He made all the decisions about food and
wine, even the design of the menu. In the first few months it
was open, this new place got to be very successful, and John
was responsible. He showed me pictures. The place was gor-
geous. He was proud of it. Because of the Witch, his home
life was lousy, but that just made him work harder. He spent
all his time at the restaurant.

"Then one day, he came to work and found the place shut
down. He was fired. The place was bankrupt, a total loss. All
that money was gone. Disappeared." Eve brought her hands
together, then opened them, as if releasing a puff of smoke
into the atmosphre. "Pffft. The people who owned the place
think he took the money. They really believe that he could
have stolen huge sums of their money, and they refuse to
speak to him, to have anything to do with him." Eve paused
for a moment to touch her earrings: on one side, a cow jumping over a moon; on the other, a dish and spoon, smiling,
holding hands. "Now, it's true John *could* have stolen the
money," she said. "He was in the restaurant business so long
that he knows every scam there is. That's partly why these
guys hired him, right? Because he's been around. I mean, he
knows how to work the system. When he was younger, he
used to skim money from this place he worked in Malibu.
But"—Eve waved her hand around to wipe away this irrele-
vant aside—"he was, like, only twenty or something. Another
lifetime. Uh, where was I?" She looked at the truck bumper,
then resumed her story. "So after the place got shut down, he
had to completely regroup, it shook him up so much. He
put his house on the market, and it sold immediately. The

Witch didn't like that at all. They split up, and he came down here. He found a place to live and started trying to get straightened out emotionally. It turned out that the whole greed scene was totally wrong for him, although he had been really successful in it for years."

"Greed scene?" I said. I inched the car forward almost to the truck's bumper: "YO."

"You know, the insatiable appetite for profit, getting more faster, that kind of garbage. I mean, granted, some people are most themselves in that framework. John did make a lot of money. He had several nice cars, a good house. He was *talented* at making money, but he wasn't *satisfied* doing it. The money never did it for him." She put out her hands, palms up. "I mean, how much do you have to pile up before you realize that the pile could always be bigger? He needed to spend some time with himself, to cook and think. That was when he started enrolling in every self-help workshop he could find, trying to work through what had just happened to him. And you know, once he was on the self-help circuit, he was bound to run into me eventually." She laughed. "When we met at the Valentine's Day thing, that was *it* for both of us. You know how it is, once you get centered inside yourself, everything around you kind of falls into place."

"Mm-hm, yeah," I said. I rolled down my window and leaned out: brake lights as far as the eye could see. "Come on," I said, banging my hand against the steering wheel. I rolled up the window.

Eve looked inside the pizza box. "This isn't very hot anymore. By the time we get there, it's going to be cold. I'm starving." She took out a slice and bit into it. "Want a piece?" I shook my head. "So everything would be perfect," she went on, "if it weren't for this ridiculous investigation. They're going through every single financial transaction John has made for the past five years, buying and selling his house, his cars.

Checking out his bank accounts. The thing is, John didn't keep very good records of anything. He was going through this antimaterialism thing, and he threw away a lot of papers." Eve ate her pizza, finishing the whole slice.

The truck moved forward, stopped. I moved up too, pulling as far as I could to the left, trying to see ahead. "Way, way up there," I said, "I think I see something moving." I squinted. "Or maybe not."

"We'll get there," she said. "One of these days." She took another piece of pizza out of the box. "The minute I saw John, I knew I would love him. I mean, I got this feeling, as if I had just arrived home after a long trip. It's hard to explain. It was a physical sensation, like suddenly gravity had this extra hold on me, pulling me down into the place I was standing, looking at him. And that feeling of being rooted has never left me for an instant since we met." Holding her pizza, she looked thoughtfully out the front window at the back of the pickup. "And OK, so he may not be perfect. He may have done some things in his life—some lying, maybe, or tax evasion, using what didn't exactly belong to him, whatever—some things he's not proud of. But—" She stopped, took a bite of pizza, and chewed. "I love him anyway."

I wanted to get out of the car. It was too small in there. Reaching down near the floor, I pulled up the lever to push my seat back, to give myself more space. I couldn't just sit here anymore. I looked into the other cars. How could people tolerate going nowhere like this? I opened the window and stretched my hand into the air outside. "I can't stand this!" I said.

Eve turned to face me, alarmed at the strength of my frustration. "It's a traffic jam," she said. "A few more minutes. Take it easy."

Just then the pickup moved forward a little, then a little bit more. We started to move. In a couple of minutes, we were going forty miles an hour. We passed a van with its hood up, the cause of the delay. When we hit sixty, I took a deep breath and let it out.

Eve said, "You know, maybe you should start meditating. You're so tense." She chewed her pizza. "The next time it's offered, I want to take the workshop on abundance. It's supposed to be really good."

We had reached our exit. I had told Melanie and Daniel we were going to get back around seven, and it was almost seven-thirty. I had a hurry-up feeling in my chest, hot and squeezing, as I willed the traffic lights to be green. I tried to reassure myself: I had my pager, and if they needed me, the kids would let me know.

As I pulled into our street, I saw there were several cars parked in front of our house. What had happened? I zoomed into the driveway, parked crazily behind Richard's car, jumped out, and ran to the front door. My brain was moving slower than my legs, but I finally recognized one of the other cars as John's. I identified the third car last: Henry's. A girl's bike, Melanie's friend Janine's, was parked on the front step. The front door was unlocked. I threw it open. Six startled faces turned to me. "What happened?" I said.

Melanie took the pizza box from Eve, who was now behind me. "Nothing, Mom." She patted my shoulder. "Is this plain cheese? I hope it's plain."

"Of course it's plain," Eve said. "We know you guys don't like anything." She sat down next to John on the couch. "Hi, baby," she said, kissing his mouth.

"Melanie," I snapped, still flustered from seeing all these people here, "you are not supposed to have friends over when I'm not here. You know that."

Melanie looked at me. "But I didn't know Janine was going to stop by, and Dad was here," she said.

"Oh. Well. The whole time? I see, OK, that's all right, I guess."

"Where were you?" John said, pulling Eve close. "I had to wait so long."

"The pizza place was crowded," she said. "We got into a little traffic jam on the way back. I thought you weren't going to be home yet."

"Change of plans," John said. He kissed Eve again.

I needed somewhere else to look. I turned my head and there was Richard, looking at me. I turned the other way, and there was Henry. This was really too much, his being here again so soon. People ought to give you a chance to breathe.

"Hi," said Henry.

"Hi," I said. "I— What a surprise. I wasn't expecting you."

"I just thought I'd stop by. The kids told me you'd be right back, so I thought I'd wait. Daniel showed me his book report."

Turning back to Richard, I said, "What are you doing here?"

"I thought we could share a pizza," Richard said, as if this were something we did. I didn't say, "Since when did you start dropping by without an invitation?" because Eve and John, the children, and Henry were all there. I would save it for tomorrow, by phone, when no one else was listening.

I turned back to Henry. I said, "I guess I should have gotten two pizzas." I went into the kitchen, and he followed me. Daniel and Richard stood up and came too.

Richard said, "You left the kids by themselves? What's going on here?"

"I have a pager," I said. "Look." I held it up to show him. "They can reach me anytime." Then I borrowed Melanie's defense. "Besides, you were here."

"Only for a little over an hour," Richard said.

I looked at my watch. "We were gone an hour and a half," I said.

"You could have dropped them off with me. Why didn't you just call me?" Richard said, stepping in next to me at the counter, a little too close.

"They had homework to do, and they like to stay by themselves." I turned to him and spoke quietly right into his face, which was only inches from mine, "Could we talk about this another time?"

Richard turned to look at Henry. "Sure," he said. "We could do that. Want me to hand out those plates for you?" He said this to show Henry how helpful he could be, how supportive.

I had cut some of the pieces in half so there would be one for everyone. Once we passed them out, the pizza was gone. But John had ordered two more pizzas while I was in the kitchen. Pretty soon the new pizzas arrived. John jumped up at the sound of the doorbell and paid before I had a chance to reach the door. These were the fancy kind with leaves of fresh basil attractively withered on top. "The guy who owns this place is a friend of mine," John said, going around the room with the pizza box and a spatula like a solicitous host. It was just like him, I thought, to know somebody who owned a gourmet pizza place I'd never heard of after living here all my life.

Daniel looked at the pizza on his plate. "Mom," he said. "What's that green stuff?"

"Basil," Richard said. He reached over, plucked it off Daniel's pizza, and ate it. "Mm," he said.

The children kept eating and eating, as if it had been a very long time since their last meal. Henry was trying to catch my eye, to say something to me without speaking any words. What was it? *I'm glad to see you.* Or, *This time, I promise I'll kiss you.* Or, *Good pizza.* I couldn't make it out. Impatiently, I shook my head at him, meaning, *Tell me later; I don't get it.* Richard was asking a lot of questions to show off that he knew a lot more about us than Henry did. "Melanie, how was the test the other day?"

Melanie said, "What test?"

"Math," he said.

"Good," Melanie said, not looking up.

"Janine, how's your mom's new job?" Richard said.

Janine said, "Good," and reached for more pizza.

After the pizza, Richard stood up. "I have to go," he said, as if we would beg him to stay. He kissed Daniel, then Melanie, and for one awful moment, I thought he was going to kiss me too. But he just patted my shoulder and said, "See you."

When the door shut behind him, I sighed loudly without meaning to, relieved that he was gone. Eve and Henry laughed. I smiled at them, embarrassed by my transparency. Then John laughed. I picked up an empty pizza box.

Daniel said, "What's so funny?"

"More pizza?" I said. "Or have you had enough?"

"Enough," he said and took his plate to the kitchen.

I wanted Janine, John, and Eve to go home and my kids to go to bed. I wanted five minutes alone with Henry. I suddenly felt resolved about him. Having him appear like this without warning had somehow cleared up my feelings. "This just isn't right for me," I could say. Was that enough? Or would I have to give more of a reason? But the kids were there, and as soon as the pizza things were cleared, they turned on the television. Janine had brought a video with her.

"We're going to go," Eve announced.

"OK," I said. "See you tomorrow."

"Good night," John said.

"Thanks for the pizza," I said.

When they were gone, Henry followed me into the kitchen. "I just stopped by to tell you some ideas I had for your store," he said.

I turned to him.

"What about big signs, visible from far away?"

I nodded.

"You could offer super cheap copies," he said, "just to get people in the place. Once they were there, they would spend money in other ways."

I said, "You mean like a big banner, reading 'Three-cent copies!'"

"Yes," he said. "Exactly."

"I've already ordered one for the front window. It will be visible from the street."

"Oh," he said, a little let down that I had already thought of his idea. "Great minds think alike." He smiled at me. Then he said, "Mimi, I've been thinking about you a lot and—"

Melanie was standing in the doorway. "We want popcorn," she said.

I said, "OK. You make it. I'm going to show Henry Grandma's desk." He followed me to the garage.

It smelled like sawdust, making me want to plug in my sander and make more. "Wow," Henry said, leaning down to get a closer look at the desk. "This is impressive. You *made* this? How did you learn to do all this?"

"Bill, my late husband, showed me some things. After he died, I took a couple of adult ed courses, looked at some books. Then, I don't know, I just figured stuff out. I asked people when I got stuck, that kind of thing."

"I can't do anything with my hands," Henry said, struggling with a drawer; there were no knobs on it yet. He wiggled it open and looked inside: sawdust.

"The trouble is, I think about it all the time when I'm not working on it," I said. "I keep wanting to get back to it." I felt the wood, examined my work on the corners.

"Hm," he said. "Like being in love." He blushed. "I mean, you know, like thinking about someone all the time when you're apart."

I said, "I guess so."

Melanie came out. "Popcorn's ready."

"OK," I said. "You guys go ahead and eat it." She backed inside and closed the door. When I looked at Henry's face, so sweet and serious, I knew exactly where this was going to go if I didn't do something right now. There would be shared jokes and secrets, sex, a private little world forming, appearing miraculous at first, then comfortable, then too confining and predictable, and finally suffocating. At that point, one of us would have to get out, escape, tearing the little world to shreds, fighting to break free.

I bit my lip and looked at the desk. I ran my hand over the top. "Maybe I should sand this one more time. What do you think?" I glanced at the shelf to check my supply of sandpaper. "There's going to be another piece attached across here with pigeonholes for letters and papers and a phone." I couldn't bring myself to say what I wanted to.

"I want to see you tomorrow," Henry said. "Alone." He folded his arms: He had decided; he wasn't asking me—he was telling me.

"No," I said, shaking my head. "This isn't right for me. I mean, I like you. You're very nice. But it's not enough."

"You don't know yet. This is only the beginning. How could you know?" He had a trusting smile, the sides of his mouth curling optimistically upward.

I said, "Oh, yes. I know right now, and I can't do this. Sorry." I felt mean and guilty for turning him down, the way

I used to when I wouldn't buy my kids a cheap toy they wanted that I knew would fall apart right away.

Henry's smile went away, and he didn't speak. He glanced up at the garage rafters for a second, then looked straight at me.

"I'm sorry," I said again. "I just don't think it would work."

"Nothing to be sorry about," he said. "It's either going to happen or it isn't. And it isn't. I understand." He left quickly.

I plugged in the sander and went over the desktop one more time.

CHAPTER 8

The Meaning of Skunks

Saturday afternoon near the end of Daniel's soccer game, Melanie, Patty, and I watched a moving, changing clump of boys follow the ball around the field. Daniel was always on the periphery, staying just outside the little group of boys, near them but slightly separate, like a sheepdog and its herd, or a moon and its planet. The score was tied. It started to drizzle.

Patty held a newspaper above her head. "Snakes and spiders!" she said. "I have an open house this afternoon, and my hair's going to be all flat."

It started to rain a little harder. Melanie put her hands on her head and said, "Mom, do you have an umbrella in the car?"

"No," I said.

"How come?" Melanie wrinkled her face. One of the boys slipped and fell on the wet grass, but he was up and running again in a few seconds. "I'm going to sit in the car then," Melanie said. "I'm not getting soaked."

"Stay here," I said. "You don't want to hurt Daniel's feelings."

"He doesn't care whether I'm here or not. He's barely here himself. I'm going to the car."

"Wait." I hooked my arm through hers. "This is almost over anyway. Two minutes and the score is tied; how can you even tear yourself away?"

Melanie whined, "I'm getting all wet."

"It's a drizzle, honey, a heavy fog. We have to be here."

"Mom, look at him. He's just trying to stay out of the way. It's sad. You should get him out of this. There are other boys who want to play, who actually enjoy this game."

"I was hoping they would get one more goal and win. Maybe that would cheer him up."

The coach, normally a patient man, had yelled at Daniel during the warm-ups for his lack of effort, poor concentration, and aimless, half-hearted kicking. "Daniel Hawkins!" he shouted. "Hey, you! Wake up! No sleeping on the playing field!" Probably because of the yelling, Daniel had closed up, withdrawn to a place no one could reach him for this game.

Melanie pulled free of me and started walking back to the car. This time I didn't try to stop her. Suddenly, the ball shot wildly out of the knot of boys and rolled straight toward Daniel. He looked left and right before extending his foot to meet the ball, which went from his foot straight through the legs of the other team's goalie, scoring the winning goal for Daniel's team. Parents screamed and yelled, and the boys crowded around Daniel so that for several seconds I couldn't see him. "What happened?" Melanie said, running back.

"Daniel scored the winning goal!" I said.

"No way," she said.

"Way!" I was more surprised than proud. My son scored the winning goal. The crowd cleared and Daniel made his way toward me. He was smiling, for a change.

"Congratulations!" I said, and I hugged him. "Wow! The winning goal! You did it!"

"Yeah," he said. "That was weird, wasn't it?" He laughed. "Let's go. I hate soccer."

In the car, I said, "Wow, Daniel, how do you feel?"

"Regular, Mom," he said.

I looked at him in the rearview mirror. "Regular? You just scored the winning goal!"

"Mom, please. The ball came to me because it didn't know any better. By accident, it hit my foot and went where it was supposed to go. You saw what happened. Drive, Mom. I want to get out of here." I backed out of the parking space. "I'm quitting," he said. "I'm not doing this anymore. This was my last game."

I said, "Luckily, there are only a few more games. If you never want to play soccer again after that, it's fine with me. Next year, you won't have to do this."

"I'm quitting now," he said.

I said, "No, you're not."

No one said anything the rest of the way to Richard's.

I parked in front of Richard's apartment and followed Melanie and Daniel to Richard's front door, helping them with their stuff. As soon as their father opened the door, Daniel said, "Dad, I'm ready to quit soccer." He went inside.

Melanie followed him in, saying, "He just scored the winning goal of the game. He's depressed. You understand."

Richard looked at me. "Am I getting this right? Daniel scored the winning goal? Wow! And you want to quit now? Well, if you're sure about your decision, I'll talk to the coach."

"Wait a minute." I shook my head. "I didn't say—," I began, but Richard cut me off.

"What?" Richard said. "I thought it was all decided."

"For next season," I said. "I still want him to finish the last few games. I think it's important to do what you say you're going to do," I said to Daniel. "And look how good you've gotten, honey!"

Richard looked at me. "Why does everything have to be so absolute with you, Mimi? He should be allowed to change his mind. He's given it more than a chance, he doesn't like it, he wants to quit. I don't see anything wrong with that. Why keep doing something he doesn't enjoy?"

He kept looking at me, so I said, "Daniel, you did a great job out there today, and I'm going to be very proud of you for doing your best in the remaining games."

Daniel flopped down onto the sofa. "Mom, you're dreaming," he said. "I didn't *make* that goal. It *happened* to me."

Richard turned to me. I was backing out the door. "Mimi, where are you going? Aren't we going to talk about this?"

"Listen," I said. "As far as I'm concerned, there's nothing to talk about. We've discussed all this before and made our decision. And besides, this is not a good time for me to talk. I have to get to work. Eve's there all by herself. Bye, guys," I said. "I'll see you tomorrow. OK? Have fun." I threw kisses to the kids.

"Why are you always rushing off?" Richard said. "Why don't you stick around? Eve can cover you through lunch, can't she? I made chili. You can have some with us."

"Yuck, Dad," Melanie said. "We hate chili. What's in the freezer? Am I going to have to make pancakes again?"

"*Stay,*" Richard said to me.

I shook my head. "I have to work. Have fun." I started walking to my car.

"All right, go then." Richard pressed his lips together in frustration. He had come over to my house twice lately for no apparent reason and kept asking me to stay when I dropped off Melanie and Daniel. "What do you expect?" he had said when I spoke to him about it. "I've known you longer than anyone. You're my best friend." I'd said, "Richard, this isn't the way things are supposed to be." And he'd said, "Oh, really? And how *are* they supposed to be? You mean, I'm not supposed to want to talk to you anymore because we're divorced? Forget it. Like it or not, you're my best friend."

"I'll see you tomorrow," I called to him as I got into my car.

When Richard and I split up, I thought it meant that he would leave our family, but that wasn't what happened. The reason I made him move out was that he had an affair. Immediately, he broke it off with the woman he was seeing and wanted to come back. I said no. To convince me that he had reformed, he didn't date anyone else and made a big effort to do better with the children. He took a cooking course so that he could make nutritious dinners for Melanie and Daniel when they came to visit. He taught them both to swim in the pool at his apartment complex. He had a neighbor show him how to put ponytail holders in Melanie's hair. He sent their clothes home clean and folded. He learned to listen to them when they told him things. When it was time to buy them Christmas presents, he talked over the choices with me. Through the separation, he became a better father. He kept trying to talk me out of going through with the divorce. He wanted us to get back together, but I couldn't do it. I couldn't make myself forget that he had had an affair, that he had lied to me. Once I found out that he was capable of that kind of betrayal, I never felt as close to him as I used to. Around the time I married Bill, Richard finally met someone else too and lived with her for two years until she moved to Chicago for a promotion. Soon he would have another girlfriend, I felt sure, and the shape of our family would change again to accommodate someone new.

"How's it going here?" I said to Eve when I came into the store.

"Not our best day," she said. "I did twenty bound copies of this report for that software guy." She held one up for me to see. "When he came in to pick them up, he freaked out because the pages were two-sided, instead of one-sided. He said he told me they were supposed to be one-sided, but I know he didn't. There was a minor confrontation, but I backed down and did them all over again. I figured we can't afford to lose anybody right now. He'll be back for them in a few minutes." She picked up her jacket. "I'm going to get something to eat. I don't want to be here when he gets back. Want anything?"

"Not yet, thanks." I said.

"There are a couple of other people coming back for stuff. It's all on the shelf. And those flyers from the car wash need to be done."

"OK," I said. "I'll do those first."

She went out and came right back in. "I keep forgetting to ask you—are you doing anything tonight?"

"No," I said.

"Our garage-door opener is broken. The door opens half-way, then stops and goes down again. Sometimes I can get it open by pushing the button again, and sometimes I have to force it up by hand. I was wondering if you could take a look at it."

"OK," I said. "I thought you were going to invite me to a party or something."

"No, sorry," she said.

"Sure. I can come by after we close. I'll just stop by my place to get my toolbox."

"I hope you can fix it," Eve said. "Do you know how much those things cost? I'll be right back."

At my house after work, I put my toolbox in the car. Then I went inside, brushed my hair, and put on lipstick. I thought maybe Eve and John would invite me for dinner in return for working on their garage-door opener. But when I arrived, they were getting ready to go out to dinner with people I didn't know.

I took my toolbox to the garage. I would work on the door while they were gone. I could spend the evening here, taking the thing apart and putting it back together. I would bring Eve's boom box out to the garage and play some of her tapes. If I needed more tools I could always drive home and get them.

I was just opening my toolbox when Eve and John were ready to leave. Eve said, "Good luck. I hope we're not going to come back at midnight and find you still working on it."

"I won't leave until it's fixed," I said.

"That's what I mean," Eve said.

"I think we're going to need a new one," said John, picking up his keys. "These things don't last forever."

I said, "If I can't get the door working again, if it turns out it's a lost cause, I can install a new one for you. I watched a whole Bob Vila program on it, how to brace it from the ceiling, how to install the chain. I could do it; it would be fun. It would save you some money."

Eve said, "I hope you don't have to."

They stood there while I pushed the button for the door. Sure enough, it started to open, got about a third of the way up, then stopped and went down. I pushed it again, and the same thing happened. I opened the door of Eve's car and stood on the seat. I sprayed WD-40 on the track of the door opener. I went over to the button and pushed it again. We all watched while the door opened smoothly. I pushed it again. It closed.

Eve said, "You fixed it?" She pushed the button. The door went up once more. She pushed it again, and it went down. "She fixed it," Eve said to John. "My sister fixed the door!"

"No," I said, holding up the can. "I just—"

"It's really amazing," Eve said to John, "the way some

people are mechanical and some are not. I'm not. That's for sure."

"I'm not either," John said. He stared at the door in amazement. "It's good to know someone who is, though."

"You guys," I said, "this has nothing to do with being mechanical. I just sprayed this stuff on it. Anybody could have done it."

"I couldn't," John said, shaking his head. "I wouldn't have thought of it. Not in a million years."

"Me neither," Eve said. "Let's go, honey. Now that the door works, we can take my car." She pushed the button again. She laughed happily when the door opened. "You're a genius, Mimi."

She got in the driver's seat of her car, and John got in on the passenger side. As she backed out the driveway, he rolled down his window. "Why don't you stay? There's a good movie in the VCR. *Philadelphia Story*. Ever see that? It's not due until tomorrow."

"Have fun," I said. I waved and put the garage door down again.

I picked up my toolbox. I wasn't going to stay. I had my own empty house to be alone in. The phone rang. I walked to the kitchen to answer it.

"Hello," I said.

A man's voice said, "Hi. Two witnesses came through for the other side. They've got some pretty convincing testimony, apparently. I want to go over names and dates again with John. We're going to have to do everything we can to come up with some more people."

I said, "Who is this?"

There was a slight pause. "Eve?" said the voice. On the phone, my sister and I sounded alike. The only person who never mixed us up was our mother.

"No," I said. "This is Mimi, her sister."

"I'm sorry. You sounded exactly like Eve. Excuse me. Is John there? Or Eve?"

"No, they went out," I said.

"This is John's lawyer. Do you have a number where they can be reached?"

"No," I said. "They went out to dinner. I don't know where."

He said, "If you hear from them, please tell John to call me right away. It's urgent." He hung up.

"Thanks for calling," I said to the dial tone. My heart was pounding, and my palms were wet. I wanted to get out of there quick. I could leave John and Eve a note about the witnesses, but the lawyer said it was urgent.

Eve's calendar lay open beside the phone. For that night it said "Bonsalls 7:00—Casa Maria." I hurried across the room to get my toolbox, went out the front door, locking it. I had my own key. I walked quickly down the front path to my car. I felt as though I had just done something wrong and was about to be caught.

On the way to the restaurant, I couldn't help thinking about our father and the investigation after his disappearance, the way my heart raced as the detectives asked me questions. I was always afraid I would say the wrong thing and get him into more trouble. Our father used his charm and appealing personality at his job as fund-raiser for big medical charities and hospitals. After our parents' divorce, he began working in Orange County, about an hour away from where we lived, raising money for a new coronary care wing of a hospital that would be built in Newport Beach. He gave speeches about the new wing, showing slides of the most advanced medical equipment of that time and a model of what the wing would look like when it was completed.

Sometimes our father had to work on weekends when we

were visiting. He met with wealthy potential donors in their own homes. Many were heart patients themselves. He told them how much their money could do to help others. When he had nowhere for us to go, no birthday party or neighbors' house where he could drop us off, we would go with him, all dressed up in the party dresses and patent leather shoes that he insisted we keep at his house. He would talk about the hospital, the words *facility, technology, generous donors, gratitude, healing* occurring over and over. Occasionally he would talk about us, his girls, saying that our mother was a teacher and that the two of them were very proud of us. He would say that we had big dreams, that I wanted to be an astronaut. I didn't mind him telling this to strangers, because I liked the way he whispered the word with such deep awe and then looked at me, glowing from inside. And Eve, he would say, wants to be a teacher like her mother. Everyone would smile at her, while Eve turned as pink as the inside of a seashell, twisting her hands in her lap. "It's very important for children to have dreams," our father would say, and the people we were visiting would have to agree with him.

Then our father would talk about Eve and her defective heart. "My little girl here would not be with us today if it were not for generous people such as yourselves." As he said this, I would watch the woman's eyes opening wide, the man leaning forward in his chair. My dad put his arm around Eve's shoulders. "It took those doctors nine hours to repair our baby's tiny heart. And that surgery was only possible because she happened to be born in a hospital outfitted with the latest coronary care equipment. She stayed six weeks. She weighed only three pounds at the time of the surgery, and it was touch and go for quite a while. Every day I thank god that our baby made it. I guess you could say that my work for the hospital is my own personal way of expressing my gratitude." He took out a handkerchief, apologized for becoming so emotional, saying he didn't mean to talk about Eve; he shouldn't let himself get so personal, so carried away.

I got choked up too, thinking about how Eve might have died, picturing those doctors with their big hands in her tiny baby chest as they worked to save her. It made me love her more, knowing that I might have lost her. As I sat there listening, I resolved to be more protective of her. I would never kick her again or pound her with my fists or steal her candy out of her secret hiding place. From now on, when she climbed up to the top of the jungle gym, I decided, I would stand on the ground beneath her, my arms stretched up and ready.

We usually got a snack at these houses, soda or a piece of chocolate, things we weren't normally allowed in the middle of an afternoon. Then one of the people we were visiting, the man usually, would write out a check and hand it to our dad, who would hold it reverently and say, "Thank you, sir, thank you very much indeed."

"No," the people would say, shaking their heads. "Thank *you*." And they would smile at our dad, at us, for letting them help.

For not talking or fidgeting during our father's speeches about the hospital, he took us to play a game of miniature golf, then dinner at McDonald's. While we ate, our father, his collar unbuttoned now and his tie in his pocket, made calculations on a napkin with a silver pen.

I think I was in junior high, maybe even high school, before I figured out that Eve never had anything wrong with her heart. I thought about it a lot and realized that I had never heard anyone mention it, except our father on those few calls he made. True, our mother didn't like to talk about ill health or problems of any sort. But wouldn't there be some stories about Eve's long hospital stay when she was a baby? Wouldn't she have a scar? I asked my mother, "How long did we stay in the hospital when we were born?"

· My mother said, "In those days, it was a long time, five days."

"Did either of us have any problems that would make us stay longer?"

"Problems?" she said, looking up. "You both had a little jaundice for a day or two, but that's not unusual."

"How much did we weigh?"

"You were seven pounds six ounces and Eve was seventen. Why all the questions?"

I even asked our pediatrician if I could see our records. There was nothing in either of our files about heart problems or surgery. Our father made up the story about Eve's heart, the same way he made up the coronary care unit of an imaginary hospital. By the time I put all this together, he had already been gone a long time, and I had been trying to shield my sister from harm for years.

I was dressed all wrong for the restaurant. I was wearing shorts and a sweatshirt with dirty high-top tennis shoes. At the door, the maître d' stepped in front of me, as if to prevent me from making a loud, crazy scene. I said, "I need to speak to John Gates. He's with the Bonsall party." I could have phoned this place, had him paged, but it was too late now. A busboy was summoned to fetch John, who appeared chewing, a white cloth napkin in his hand. "Meemers!" he said, beaming a smile at me, as if it had been ages. He hugged me, holding me close and too long. "Glad to see you. Change your mind about tonight?"

I pulled away. "Your lawyer called," I whispered so that the restaurant employees wouldn't hear me. John stopped chewing, leaned forward, swallowed. "The prosecution has testimony from two witnesses."

"When? He called just now?" he said, looking at his watch. He shook his head, smiling. "That guy doesn't let up."

"It sounded important. I thought you should know. He said to call him right away."

"That was nice of you to come all the way down here. Want to join us for dinner?" He put his hand lightly on my back to walk me into the dining room. "Do you know Pam and David? You'll like them."

I stopped, and his hand kept pressing. "No," I said. "No, thank you. I just wanted to tell you about the phone call."

"Good, then. Thanks a lot for your trouble." He smiled at me, as if I had just come to tell him he had forgotten to turn off his headlights. He took one of my hands in both of his and kissed it. "You are a treasure."

"See you," I said. I went outside to my car.

I pulled up in front of my house and parked in the driveway. There was no longer any room for a car in the garage, now that I used it as a workshop. I popped open the trunk with the lever next to my seat, got out, locked my door, and went around to get my toolbox from the trunk. There were a whole bunch of Daniel's school papers and art projects in there that I had to push out of the way. I was going to have to find a place for those, a box or something. I slammed the trunk closed just a fraction of a second before I realized I had put my keys down in it. I checked all the car doors to see if they were really locked. They were. I went all around the house and checked all the doors to see if they were locked too. They were. I was careful about things like that. I put my toolbox on the front step and sat down beside it.

For several minutes, I just sat there. And I thought, This is my life: I run a small, failing business with my sister, who is married to a criminal. I have two children, an ex-husband, and a mother. I've been on two dates in three years. I am forty years old, and I'm locked out of my house. Maybe because I had listened so hard to all those song lyrics for so many years, I thought that the things that happened were supposed to have a larger significance than they seemed to now. Something that was supposed to happen to me hadn't. It wasn't that I thought I was going to be rich by now and wasn't. It wasn't that I thought I would be famous or beautiful, either. What was missing was nothing so simple or easily achieved. *Meaning*— that was it. I had expected that the things that happened would mean something, and they didn't.

I decided I would keep sitting there until something happened that meant something. I waited a long time. A bathroom light went on next door and off again a short time later. Down the street, a party took a long time breaking up.

I thought back. It had started with the Beatles. I remembered the way I used to stay up late with my transistor under the covers, waiting for a brand-new song to be played on the radio. The first time I heard the Beatles—on that famous *Ed Sullivan Show* so long ago—it was like waking up, as if my first ten years had only happened to get me to this moment, and now my real life had started. My sister and I joined the Beatles Fan Club. This was around the time of our father's disappearance, and Beatlemania may have been something we particularly needed. We even took guitar lessons until we found that we had no musical ability. We listened hard to every song and learned each one by heart as if it were in a secret language that only we could understand, as if each song contained a message just for us.

Eve loved Paul, and I loved John. When John said that some teenagers cared more about the Beatles than they did about Jesus, I agreed with him. I knew I certainly did. In eighth grade, I became a vegetarian because George Harrison was, even though he was not my own personal favorite. Every day I tried to meditate by staring for a long time at a string of red beads. We talked local record-store owners into giving us Beatles posters when they were finished with them and taped them up in our room to gaze at every chance we got. When John married Yoko, I was puzzled, but I bought her book *Grapefruit* and read the whole thing. I liked it, and I grew to love Yoko too. When the Beatles broke up, Eve and I tried to take it in stride. I was in high school by then, and I remember thinking immediately, Maybe they'll get back together. I bought all the early solo albums. But the ones I loved the most, the ones I committed to memory forever, the ones that played over and over like a continuous soundtrack inside my head, were John's.

The night John Lennon was killed, I was driving home from my job making sandwiches in a deli. I heard the news on the radio and had to stop the car and pull over to the side of the road. For several moments, I stopped breathing. I sat there over an hour, frozen, a zombie with the radio on, until Richard came looking for me. Like me, Richard was a longtime Beatles fan. After John was killed, Richard wanted to take all the money we had, go to New York, and join the mourners who were to gather in Central Park and remember John. I talked him out of it. I couldn't stand to see myself as one of a whole throng of people. I believed that what John Lennon meant to me was special, unique. Instead of a trip to New York, we had several weeks of grief, during which I had to force myself to reorganize everything I thought, everything I knew, in order to continue.

I had never spoken to my children about the Beatles. They were born after John Lennon died, of course. I hadn't told them that if it weren't for the Beatles, who were the reason I started listening to music in the first place, I wouldn't be alive, not really. I'd be a kind of sleepwalker, living in a flat, colorless world. I never showed them my Beatles scrapbook or played them even one of my old vinyl Beatles albums. All that stuff was in my mother's garage somewhere. They never heard the children's tapes of Beatles songs recorded by other singers as lullabies. I didn't know how to explain to my children the deep joy I used to feel each time I heard a Beatles song, even a sad one. And I didn't know how to describe the ugly pain that came with the music now, knowing, as I do, all that had happened since it was recorded.

Whenever a Beatles song came on the radio, I switched the station, preferring new songs. This was the way I had found to keep moving forward, choosing not to pause over that complicated cluster of intense mixed feelings that always left me breathless and upset. In the early eighties I latched on to new wave music as my salvation, my escape from the sorrow and disappointment and betrayal I felt about everything that had gone wrong.

Fog had rolled in while I was sitting there on my front step in the dark, and when I put my hand up to my hair, it was wet, the curls tight and grasping. I kept sitting there, feeling chilled and damp, waiting.

Then I heard a rustling sound coming from the bushes beside the fence. My heart began to pound as I waited to see who had been hiding in the bushes all this time. A skunk walked out of the ground cover beside the house, making its way across the grass.

Shape-shifting, I thought. Someone who appears to have vanished may have simply taken on an animal form, that of a lion, say, a snake, a wolf, or even a skunk. That seemingly absent person might have simply adopted a new appearance.

I drew a breath. "Bill?" I said.

The skunk paused for a second, glancing over its shoulder at me, and continued on.

More time passed, and I heard footsteps, a man from a few doors down with a dog. Because of the fog, I couldn't see them until the last minute. The dog stopped and pulled at the leash, straining to come to me, to sniff and investigate. The man didn't see me sitting there in the dark and gave the leash a tug. "Come on, Lulu, there's nothing there. Let's go." Lulu gave up and continued on. There was another quiet period. By now I had no idea how long I had been sitting here, what time it might be.

Then Henry came up the walk, looking at the house, then at his watch. He was trying to decide if anyone was home, whether he should ring the bell. He didn't see me either. "Hi," I said.

He jumped, putting his hand to his chest. "Mimi!" he said. "You scared me! What are you doing sitting there in the dark?"

"Where did you come from?" I said. "I didn't hear a car."

"I got a flat tire," he said.

"Oh." Did he want me to change it? I wondered, because I really wasn't in the mood.

"After I got finished changing it, I realized how close I was to your house, so I just walked over. Just thought I'd see what you were doing."

"Nothing," I said. "Just sitting here."

"Could I sit with you?"

"Sure," I said, trying to sound as unwelcoming as I could. I needed to focus, concentrate. Besides, once you told someone you didn't want to see him anymore, he wasn't supposed to come back. That was the way I always thought it worked.

"Where are Melanie and Daniel?"

"At their father's."

"Oh. You know, it's kind of dark and wet out here. Don't you want to go inside or something or turn on a light at least?"

"No," I said.

He looked at me.

"Actually, I couldn't get to the light switch very easily right now," I said. "I locked my keys in the trunk of my car."

"You did?" he said. I nodded. "So you're waiting for someone to come with your keys. I see."

"No, not really," I said. "I didn't call anyone. I was just sort of sitting here." I didn't want to tell him I was waiting for something to happen that meant something; I didn't want to make him nervous.

"But how are you going to get inside?"

I glanced over my shoulder at the house. "I don't know yet."

"I see," he said. We sat there in an awkward silence for a few minutes. Then Henry said, "I got fired. I mean, laid off. Sixty-three other people and I were cut loose. A bigger company took ours over. They got rid of my whole department. Corporate bloodletting. Whatever you want to call it, I don't have a job anymore."

"I'm sorry," I said. "When?"

"A few days ago. It's OK. I'll get another job, I guess." He looked at the halo that the fog made around the streetlight. "You know what I like about you?" he said. "You know why I'm here again after you told me to get lost? You don't laugh at dumb jokes that aren't funny or wear a lot of makeup or talk too much."

"I talk a lot," I said. "And maybe more makeup wouldn't be such a bad thing."

"Come on," he said. He bumped his shoulder against mine. "You know what I mean. You're *real*, you know, genuine, not a phony."

"Thanks," I said. He looked at me, as if I might at any moment do something odd, recite a tongue twister or perform a back flip.

"And about the business," he said. "I've been thinking about that too. I've been thinking you should be more aggressive about this. Honor everyone else's coupons, *guarantee* the lowest prices, put some advertising on the radio. Offer more services, word processing, computer counseling. You could have a whole computer side to your business, maybe even buy five or six PCs and set them up for people to use. You'd charge by the hour. And hey, wait a second! I've got it! You could offer computer courses too. A lot of people still feel intimidated by the whole idea of computers." He was talking faster, getting fired up by his ideas. "I mean, they want one, they think they could use one," he went on, "but they're afraid. They don't know where to begin! You could offer crash courses. Listen to that—Computer Crash Course—it even sounds good. Do you know anything about PCs?"

"No," I said.

"Ah," he said, waving his hand to dismiss this minor glitch. "There's nothing to it. You're so smart, you'll pick it up in no time. Then you'll have a great business. I'm sure of it. This just feels *right.*"

I said, "But why would I get into a business based on something I knew nothing about?"

"Because you want to *survive,*" he said, clenching his fists, baring his teeth. "You've got to be willing to go to extremes."

"I see," I said. "Thanks for the input. What time is it?"

"Quarter to eleven."

"I have to get up early tomorrow," I said.

I stood up and went to the side of the house. The bathroom window was open, but it was very high, way over my head. I pulled a garbage can over, a plastic one with a cracked lid. Fortunately, it was packed so full that it supported my weight. As I climbed on top of it, Henry came around to see what I was doing. I felt the screen of the window. It was a little bent on one corner. I wedged a finger under it, wiggled it back and forth for a minute, and pulled at the aluminum frame. The screen came out suddenly and easily, falling from my hands and hitting me in the forehead before dropping to the ground.

After sliding the window to one side, I was able to get both my arms up on the window ledge. I tried a couple of times to hoist myself up, but it was a little too high for me. I pressed one toe halfway up the wall, then pulled, but my foot slipped and I almost lost the garbage can below me. I tried again and didn't make it. I thought resentfully of Henry standing there watching me. But aside from placing both hands on my behind and shoving upward, there wasn't much he could have done. I tried one more time, using all the strength I had, and made it, scraping a knee on the rough stucco of the house, then falling head first into the bathroom. "Shit," I said, allowing myself this because Melanie and Daniel were away. Anyway, I was inside. "OK, I made it," I called to Henry. "Good night."

I wiped the blood off my knee and put a Band-Aid on it. I checked the answering machine: no messages. I turned on the TV and watched a few minutes of CNN before deciding I was too exhausted and discouraged to take anything in. Out of habit, I went to check that the front door was locked. There was Henry, sitting out on the step.

I opened the door. "Hey," I said. "What are you doing out here still?"

He looked up. "I was waiting for you to open the door. I thought you were coming back. You left your toolbox here."

I picked it up. "Right," I said. "I forgot about it."

"May I come in?"

I said, "Do you have more to say about what I should do with my business?"

"Yeah. Lots more." He stood up. "That's the spirit. See, the trick to keeping a business alive is to be open to new ideas from different sources, especially"—he pointed to himself— "knowledgeable experts."

I didn't think I could listen to any more ideas tonight and still be polite about them. I said, "Some other time, maybe. I usually go to bed a lot earlier than this. Good night, Henry." I closed the door and headed to the bathroom to brush my teeth. Then I put on my pajamas and got into bed.

Something was crunching in the ground cover around the house—the skunk getting comfortable, I thought.

"Mimi?" Henry again. "Mimi? *Mimi,*" he called. "Can you hear me?"

I threw back the covers and got out of bed. "Everyone can hear you," I said. "Janet and Dave across the street can hear you, I bet." But I wasn't shouting, the way Henry was, so I was talking to myself. I went to the front door and opened it again. He had to come crunching all the way back around.

"Oh," he said, looking at me in my pajamas. "There you are. Are you going to bed now?"

"I thought I would," I said. "Yes."

"Can you wait a few minutes?"

"It's been a long day. It's late. I'm tired." I had to use a lot of self-control to keep from yelling at him.

"I just want to hold you," he said.

"No, Henry," I said. "I don't think so."

"What's the matter?" he said. "Don't you like me?" He looked at me, with his eyes open wide, expectantly and with such longing, as if no one had ever said anything damaging to him, like "Can't we just be friends?" or "It's not you, it's me; I just don't want to be with anybody right now."

"Of course I like you," I said. "You're very nice and—" I stopped and thought a few seconds. The way he was looking at me, I couldn't bring myself to tell him to go home, couldn't make myself say he really ought to find someone smaller and younger. And suddenly I didn't think I was up to lying alone in my bed, waiting to hear the skunk come home. "All right," I said. "Come in. For a minute."

He stepped inside, and I closed the door behind him. He put his arms around me and his head on my shoulder. Ever so gently, he kissed my cheek. Soon his hands were touching my face, my hair, unbuttoning my pajama top. My fingers were touching his mouth, opening his clothes to get to his skin. Even then, I knew that this was the start of a long and exhausing night. In the middle of it all, the thought kept coming to me, *Now everything has changed forever; now nothing can be the same again.*

CHAPTER 9

The Henry Thing

There was a cloud around me, a nice mist, an invisible haze that enveloped me. People noticed it and commented. In the store, Frances, the graphic designer, came in to get her mail and said, "Mimi, you look so pretty today. You have a glow. Is it your hair that's a little different? Or have you started wearing a new kind of makeup? Is that a new sweater?" She stared at me for a few seconds before putting the key in her box and saying, "Whatever it is, it looks good on you."

I was spacey and forgetful. I remembered about food in the most abstract and theoretical way, that people were supposed to have it to keep going, that I used to eat it too. I managed to get myself to go to the store, remembered to buy coffee for me and ice cream for the kids. When I got home, I realized I had forgotten a lot of other things. Henry would call on his way to my house: "Need anything from the store?" he would ask me.

"As a matter of fact, yes," I told him. "Milk, bread, eggs, butter, sugar, cereal, peanut butter, jelly, fruit, something to make for dinner. If you wouldn't mind, if you're sure it's no trouble."

He got everything and cooked hamburgers on our barbecue. This was a good thing, too, because I might have gotten started, then forgotten about it, neglecting to put meat on the grill or letting it burn black.

I bumped into things, walking around daydreaming, and got bruises on my shins and thighs, then couldn't remember what I had crashed into. I saw everything through my cloud, and everything looked better this way, brighter, more hopeful.

Inside my cloud, I attended Parents' Night at Daniel's school. Daniel and I got there early. Richard would arrive half an hour later, I would leave, and then he would take Daniel home. This was the way we usually did things, both parents represented without too much overlap. Daniel and I left Melanie doing her homework; I had my pager. On the way, the Cranberries came on the radio. I turned it up, and Daniel and I sang together. Now the song was about Henry. A lot of songs were about Henry, all of a sudden.

The parking space I got was a long walk from the school, but I thought, this way, we could enjoy the clear dark sky for a few minutes. As we walked, I was conscious of outer space. "Isn't it amazing," I said to Daniel, "the way that the planets surrounding us are always moving, having meteor showers, firestorms, missing and colliding with things, exactly the way they're supposed to, even when here on Earth we might not be aware of them?"

Daniel said, "What?"

"I mean things keep going along, moving ahead, whether you think they're going to or not."

"Oh," he said.

This is what I mean about my cloud; it was as though I had taken some benign mind-altering drug that helped me enormously. Through it, I saw Daniel's classroom, his language journal, his math facts notebook, the kite with his name on it that seemed to stand out unmistakably from twenty-six others, and I enjoyed it all.

Daniel's teacher, Mrs. Coles, came over to me and shook my hand. She said, "Welcome to room twenty-one! I want you to know that Daniel is a delight to have in my room, a real asset to the class."

Not all teachers were like Mrs. Coles. Some of them had missed Daniel completely, but Mrs. Coles saw the real Daniel, just not some kid at table three who wasn't too much trouble. My eyes filled with tears; Daniel shifted awkwardly, scratched his head. Mrs. Coles smiled and said, "Let me know if you have any questions. I'm always available for individual conferences. Call any time you want to make an appointment."

"Thank you," I said.

Mrs. Coles moved on to other parents.

Daniel said, "Mom, want to see my new shadow box?" He grabbed my hand—something that happened rarely now— and led me to a counter where all the shadow boxes about California history were displayed. I had already seen it, of course, as he had made it at home. But he wanted me to see it on display with a little card in front of it saying "Daniel Hawkins: Native American village before the arrival of the missionaries."

I said, "It's great; you did such a good job. You worked hard on it; I can tell." I smiled at him, and he smiled back, shutting both eyes tight for a second, then opening them wide. For a moment, he joined me in the cloud, happy and optimistic. In the back of my head, I was thinking of Henry, the details about Parents' Night that I would save up to tell him, the sound of his laugh, the shape of his mouth.

Richard arrived. I looked at the clock. He was early, but not as early as it seemed to me; the time had gone by quickly.

I smiled at him. Richard joined us near the art table and looked at me curiously without saying anything.

"Hi, Dad," Daniel said. "Dad, look at this."

"Well," Richard said to me. "Don't you look like the cat who ate the canary!"

"Pardon me?" I said.

Daniel tried to move us along, prevent something he felt coming. "The language journals are over here, Dad. Want to see?"

Richard tilted his head toward Daniel without moving his eyes. "I'd like to see that, sweetheart. One second, OK?" He lowered his voice to nearly a whisper: "What's happening? What's going on?"

"Nothing," I said. "Mrs. Coles is very pleased with Daniel's work. She said he was a delight to have in the classroom. She's right over there. You should go talk to her."

"Oh?" he said. "And what else?" He raised his eyebrows and looked down at me to make me feel that he knew everything I was trying to conceal.

But he didn't know; nobody did. Nobody knew about it but Henry and me. It was a secret, not the fact that we were seeing each other now. What was going on between us was only a secret because there were no words to tell it. To try to describe it would be like trying to demonstrate harmony with only one voice. Putting it into words would be like naming a star: you could make a series of sounds and point at an object in the sky, but nothing could summarize the power of its light.

Richard bent toward me to say something to me privately. He thought he had it. He said, "You're sleeping with him, aren't you?"

I felt myself turning a new color; my legs prickled with a desire to kick him and run. But there was Daniel, looking at us.

"Oh, no. You *are*," Richard whispered, then he spoke a

little louder. "Henry? The young kid, the little guy? I knew it. I saw the expression on your face from across the room. It's one of the more common looks we see in junior high." A bitter edge had entered his voice.

Daniel shifted his eyes from me to Richard and back again. "Dad," he whined too loudly. "Dad, stop. Cut it out. Me and Melanie like Henry. Henry's *nice.*"

"Melanie and I," Richard snapped. Heads turned toward us, then away again.

Daniel looked at me protectively. He said, "Mom, you go now, OK? You saw everything. Dad will drop me off. Go, Mom."

I walked quickly out the door. I heard Daniel say, "Dad, what is your *problem?*"

At the store the next day, Frances came in to get her mail. She looked at me and walked over to the counter. "Mimi," she said. "You look so happy. I'm just going to stand here near you and absorb some of that, whatever it is, that you're emanating." She stood in front of me with her eyes closed, holding up her hands as if to warm them by a fire. "I think it's working. I'm going to get a big design job today. I just know it."

I laughed and picked up the ringing phone. "Wrap It Up," I said. "Mimi speaking."

"Hi." It was Henry. A nice hot feeling went through me. I took the phone to the office, while Eve took care of two customers. When I came out a few minutes later, the store was full of people. Eve clicked her tongue and rolled her eyes. "Mimi," she said. "You have the stupidest look on your face."

"Hm?" I said. "What did you say?"

"Is he going to keep calling you all the time? Because I can't take care of the whole store myself."

"Eve," I said. "It was only a couple of minutes. May I help you?" I said to the first person in line.

"Just postage on this, please." I took an envelope to the scale.

Eve waited on the next customer. We worked through the line. When the store was empty again, I picked up a photocopying order due later in the afternoon.

Eve said, "I hope you know what you're doing."

"Sure," I said, looking again at the form, "one copy of each in this pile and two of each of these. Double-sided, right?" I looked at the back of the form. "Is there something else I should know?"

"Not that." She waved her hand around. "I meant with Henry."

"What about Henry?" I stopped what I was doing and faced her. "What would you like to tell me about Henry?"

"Nothing. I barely know him. I just think you should be careful."

"Careful?" I said.

"Yes," said Eve. "I mean I don't think you should just jump for the first guy who comes along."

"It's been three years since I was with anybody," I said. "I wouldn't call that jumping. Henry is a very sweet, straightforward person. You know, I really don't think we should get into this."

"Fine," Eve said crisply. "Let's talk about something else then." She stuck a label on a package. "John agrees with me, by the way. He thinks you could do better. You don't want to make a mistake you'll regret."

"Now you listen to me," I said, pointing, as if I were talking to Daniel about behavior I found inexcusable. "You listen right now. You think you're warning me about some unseen danger, don't you? Something I don't know about. But I do know.

Anytime you let somebody kiss you, you're beginning the process of risking your life. And I don't mean disease, either. I mean"—I pointed to my chest—"your heart."

Bridget, the writer, came in with her kids. "Hi, Mimi. Hi, Eve," she said, smiling at us, putting a thick pile of paper on the counter. "Phew. I didn't think I would make my deadline this time, but I did. It was a little hairy there for a while, then I—" She looked at my face and stopped talking. A young guy with a backpack and a woman with a small dog on a leash walked in and stood behind Bridget to form a line.

I held up one finger to the customers without taking my eyes off Eve. "I've done this before, as you know, and I realize what might happen." Joe, the lawyer, walked in to get his mail. I couldn't stop now; I was too mad. "He might cheat on me," I said. When he heard the tone in my voice, Joe stopped to look at us. Bridget's two children looked up from the toy cash register they were playing with and froze. "He might leave me or lie to me, disappoint me in a way I can never recover from. He might even *die!*" I turned to our customers. "You just never know, do you?" I took a deep breath and said to Eve, "Believe me, I have a full understanding of what I'm getting into here, and I'm still going to do it. A week ago, I wouldn't have said any of this, but I've changed my mind. I can't be careful anymore; I'm all finished with careful—the loneliness was killing me."

Eve sniffed. "Well," she said. I waited for more. She walked to the counter and stood in front of Bridget. "May I help you?" she said.

"One copy of each of these, please, and I'll pick it up in an hour." Bridget rounded up her children and hurried out the door.

Patty had bought a closet organizer to be installed in her daughter's bedroom. She needed some tools, she said, so

Henry and I stopped by on our way home with Melanie and Daniel. I told her I would help her put it together, but I knew from experience that I'd end up doing most of the work. After sitting with us for a few minutes, Patty had drifted off to the kitchen, and the kids had gone to the backyard, leaving Henry and me on the floor of the bedroom with the shelves, drawers, screws, and a sheet of instructions. "Are we going to have to put this whole thing together?" Henry whispered to me.

"Yes. It won't take long," I said. "I've done lots of these. Look. This drawer unit is almost together. I don't know, though. I wonder how much she paid for this. With so much plastic, I doubt it'll last Stephanie through high school. OK, now see this? Can you put these two things together? And I'll do the back piece."

"Mimi," he whispered. I looked up from the bolt I was twisting into place. "I love this." He put his hand on my knee and smiled.

I knew what he meant. We were doing something normal together; we were a couple. We weren't alone anymore. "This is nice," I said, and choked up.

Patty came in with a beer for Henry and ice water for me. "You guys want to stay for dinner?"

"Yes," I said. "You think we're doing this for nothing?"

"I better get busy then," she said. "Would your kids eat eggplant?"

"No," I said. "Not a chance."

"I didn't think so," she said. "I'll order some pizza."

When the closet was finished and the pizza was gone, I was helping Patty throw away the paper plates. Henry was outside putting the pizza boxes in the garbage can, while the four kids sat eating Popsicles in a row on the diving board, like crows on a fence. Patty whispered to me, "I like him. He's crazy about you."

"You think so?" I said, trying not to break into a big, goofy smile.

"Yeah," she said. "Head over heels. This will be just fine. This will be good. He's the first guy since Bill, isn't he?" I nodded. "Does it feel weird? Do you think about him?"

I nodded again, tears rising unaccountably to my throat, my eyes filling up. "I cry all the time these days," I said, wiping my eyes on my sleeve. "Commercials about calling home make me weep. Do you think Bill would be disappointed?"

"Disappointed?" she said. "What? To see you happy? No, he'd like Henry. Anyone would."

"Richard doesn't."

"He's having a hard time with it, isn't he?" Patty said. "The Henry thing."

"You know how Richard is," I said.

"Oh, I do," she said. "Possessive and territorial where you and the kids are concerned."

"Not all the time, is he?"

"In a nice way. He'll come around," Patty said. "And if he doesn't, to hell with him. I bet Eve is happy for you."

"Not really," I said. "She tried to warn me away from Henry. She said I should wait for someone better."

"Nice."

"It's complicated."

"Sure it is. But Mimi, you're thinking too much about how you look to other people. Very few other people care what you do. Those who do are a mess and ought to be in long-term therapy. So go ahead and be happy. You've earned it, if anyone has." I smiled at her and she hugged me. When we pulled apart, we both had tears in our eyes. She picked up a napkin and dabbed at the corners of her eyes.

Henry walked in then. "Hey," he said, "what's going on here?"

"Nothing," Patty said, and more tears filled her eyes, rolled down her cheeks. "We're just happy."

The next morning, I was surveying our breakfast options. Henry was still asleep in my bed, and I was hoping that the kids would leave for school before he got up. I didn't want them all to get talking and make everybody late. "Let's see," I was saying to Melanie and Daniel. "There aren't any muffins left, so what about Cheerios?"

"Is he going to be here all the time now?" Daniel said. "Is he going to live with us or what?"

The two of them looked up at me and waited. "No," I said. "He's just visiting. Cheerios?"

Henry came into the kitchen with his hair standing up straight, wearing the clothes he had on the night before. "Good morning," he said. There was a frog in his throat so that the first word came out a whisper and the second a croak.

Both kids studied him for a minute. Daniel said, "Henry, did you sleep with Mom last night?"

Henry swallowed and cleared his throat. Looking Daniel straight in the face, he said, "Yes, I did." Then he looked at me to see if he had given the right answer. I put the milk back in the fridge.

Melanie sighed loudly and threw herself back in her chair. "God, Daniel, what a question!"

Daniel said, "What wrong with that question? I wanted to know!"

There was a small silence. Then Melanie said, "I hope you used a condom," and left the table.

"Yes, I did," Henry said as she walked away, though in my opinion, he could have let that one go.

I went to her room. "Melanie?" I said. "Do you want to talk about this?"

"No," she said, sliding books into her backpack.

"OK, then I will. Henry—" I didn't know what I was planning to say. "Henry is very important to me." This wasn't the way to put it. I had said the same thing about having the house picked up before we left this morning. "I mean, he's— I like Henry a lot. He's a good friend."

"Give me a break, Mom," Melanie said. "So is Patty, and *she* doesn't sleep over. I don't know why you keep all the important stuff a secret. Why can't you just say what's really going on? You think we're too young, don't you? You just don't want to tell us that you're in love with him."

"Oh," I said. I had to think a minute.

"I'm not stupid," Melanie went on. "I see what's happening here. I see you walking around with stars twinkling in your eyes and your shirt on backwards. I may be young, but I know what I see."

I was wearing a T-shirt with the name of the store on the front and a picture of a present and our phone number on the back. I looked down and saw the present on my chest. I took my arms out of the sleeves and twisted the shirt around the right way. "You're right," I said, surprised. "You're so right. My shirt *is* on backward. And I guess I *am* in love with Henry. I'm in love with him," I said again, testing it out, surprised and pleased at the way it sounded. "Thank you for telling me. Thanks for letting me know."

"You're welcome," Melanie snapped, standing up with her backpack and walking to the door. "Just don't forget the rule."

"Rule?" I said.

"No sleep-overs on weeknights," she said dryly. The front door slammed and she was gone.

Henry was going to see his family in New Jersey for Christmas. The day before he left, a Sunday, he convinced me to take some time off to go somewhere outside of San Diego in the car. He was in charge of the tapes, and I was driving. As he put on *No Need to Argue,* I said again, "I really should be working on my mother's desk. I'm afraid I won't get it done in time for Christmas."

"You'll get it done, angel," he said. This was what he called me now; I liked it. "You need a break. Everybody needs a break now and then, right? It's just a day off, nothing to worry about. It's not going to hurt you. As a matter of fact"—he paused for significance—"it might help!"

"You know, we're hardly doing any Christmas cards in the store this year," I said. "I wonder what the problem is. People are sending them less or getting them done somewhere else?" Henry turned his head to glare at me. "OK, OK," I said. "A day off. I am taking a day off."

Henry began to sing along with the song that was playing. He sang badly; I joined in. "You think you're so pret-teeeeeeeeeeeeeeeee!," we sang with James with confidence and abandon, never once hitting the right note. The scenery changed from housing developments and shopping centers to small farms, horses and cows, dried grass, boulders, scrub oaks. For a while, Henry selected songs DJ style, one at a time, moving from artist to artist. While he was rewinding Mazzy Star to hear "Fade into You," he said, "By the way, where are we going?"

"Julian," I said. "They grow apples there. It's in the mountains. Hills. Higher elevation, anyway." The song started.

After a while, Henry got tired of waiting for the tape player to rewind and put on a David Byrne tape at the beginning, letting the whole thing play through. When we were almost to Julian, listening to "Strange Aliens," I saw a thin dusting of snow at the side of the road, probably from the night before when it had rained in San Diego. In the direct sunlight, the snow had already disappeared. I pulled over in a turnout. I jumped out of the car, ran to pick up a little snow in my fingertips, brought it to the side of the car for Henry to see. "Look at that! The real thing!"

"Snow," he said. But he was looking at me, smiling.

I said, "I guess it's hard to impress a boy from New Jersey with snow that only sticks in the shadows."

"No, no," he said. "I like it. I like it because you like it."

I wiped my hands on my pants and got back in the car. "Shoot," I said. "We forgot to bring jackets. I always do this. I always forget that other places have weather."

In Julian, we parked the car and got out. We held on tight to each other to keep warm. We bought a couple of apple pies, one for us and one for my mother. "We can freeze them until Christmas, then no one will have to sweat over a crust." I looked around for something else to do. Now that I had brought him all this way, I felt obliged to show Henry something more than an apple pie factory. "We could go into some of those little shops, if you want to," I said, "where they sell the quilts and scrimshaw and dried-flower wreaths. But I don't know. A whole store full of that kind of stuff makes me queasy."

"Wow," Henry said, "*another* thing I like about you!"

We bought a few bags of apples, then we started back. All the way, Henry changed tapes with his right hand, keeping his left hand on my thigh. When I didn't have to steer around curves or shift gears for a while, I let my hand join his on my jeans, where it was always waiting, warm and dependable.

We got back to San Diego just before sunset. We passed a big field where a lot of people were gathered around hot-air balloons being inflated. Henry craned to see past me, put one hand on the dash and one on the back of his headrest, and leaned down low to see the balloons rising. "Look at that!" he said. "Look!"

I glanced to my left. "You want to stop and watch?"

"No," he said. "I couldn't watch without taking a ride myself. Look at those things fill up! They're so beautiful. Wow." He stared until I turned the corner and the balloons were out of sight. "Don't tell me. You've been up in those things thousands of times and can't get excited about it anymore."

"No," I said. "Never."

"Never?" Henry said. "We have to go, then. We have to do this. The two of us. We'll float above the world, looking down. It will be great." He looked at me. "Right?"

I shook my head and laughed. "I don't want to," I said. "You know how much it costs?"

"How much it costs?" Henry said. "You can't worry about little obstacles like money or you'll never get anywhere."

"And then after you pay all that money, it's noisy and you're squashed in there with a whole lot of other people. And what about the danger? I'm a mother, remember."

"This isn't my Mimi talking. My brave, risk-taking Mimi."

"Oh, brave," I said. "I don't know. I guess I'm willing to take some risks, maybe, to save my own life, or my kids', but not to see a view."

"Don't tell me you're going to make me go up in one of those things without you."

"I guess you'll have to," I said. "I'll wave to you from below."

"Mimi, the pragmatist," Henry said, "the realist. Level-headed Mimi with both feet planted firmly on the ground."

Daniel and Melanie were staying at Richard's for the night. We were at Henry's apartment. The place had come furnished with a bed, a dresser, and a desk that looked as though they had come from some motel. When Henry and his old girl-friend broke up, he didn't take any of their things. "She cared about stuff like furniture, so it was only right," he said. "And I don't really mind this place. I don't spend much time here, and it's not forever."

At the moment, we were naked in Henry's bed, showing each other our scars and telling the stories of how we got them. "I got fifteen stitches in my head once." He pulled his hair back, trying to show me the scar. "Wait, I think it's on the other side."

"What happened?" I said.

"I was eight and I jumped off a swing, fell, and hit something hard. Now where is that?" he said, feeling his head. "They shaved off my hair in that spot. It was pretty impressive, going to school with part of my head shaved and fifteen big black stitches holding it together, let me tell you."

"Here it is," I said, pulling his hair back to look. "Nice one."

"OK," he said. "Your turn."

"This is from a chisel," I said, showing him the palm of my left hand. "From when I made that, I don't know, the wall unit maybe."

"It's still pink," Henry said.

"Yeah, maybe it's more recent." I looked for another one. "This is from my coping saw. It's actually a lot sharper than the big one. That's getting white now." I held up an index finger. "Wire cutters. Christmas Eve last year, putting in Eve's stereo."

"Nice," Henry said. "You've been busy."

"Oh, I've got some older ones too." I tipped my head back. "If you look closely at the underside of my chin," I said, "you'll see a white line about an inch long with small white dots on both sides. See that?" I said.

Henry examined me closely. "Not bad," he said, rubbing his thumb across the scar. "How'd you get that one?"

"Trying out a new bike," I said. "It's a long story."

"Tell me," Henry said. "I want to hear it, all the gory details." He leaned back against the pillows and pulled the blankets under his chin, settling in to listen.

"OK, you asked for it. The first Christmas our father didn't live with us, our mother didn't have much money. I was six and Eve was four. My mom had just started teaching when our car, a beat-up old, I don't know, something-or-other, broke down on the freeway. It never got going again. Three weeks before Christmas, she had to buy a used car so she could get to work, and the down payment nearly wiped her out. For Christmas, I wanted a two-wheeler with a kickstand. Eve wanted a doll she had seen that came with its own baby carriage covered in white eyelet. Our mother didn't have enough money to get us those things. We knew that, but somehow we expected a miracle to happen at the last minute, you know, the way it always did on TV.

"We opened our presents on Christmas Eve, because our father was supposed to have us beginning early the next morning. We each got a big ugly doll in a red dress and no underpants. I also got a new jump rope, and Eve got a Magic Slate. When she realized there was no baby doll or baby carriage, Eve cried long and loud, while I went completely silent. I remember feeling as though a small boulder of disappointment had settled in my chest."

I looked at Henry to see if he was still listening. "The scar," he said. "Keep going."

I went on. "The day didn't improve. Our mother, in her own envelope of misery, set to work making Christmas Eve dinner. When she served it to us at lunchtime, we were not hungry. Eve tipped over her glass of milk on the table and started crying again.

"Our mother cried too and yelled at us. She said we didn't know how hard it was, we had no idea. We were spoiled little girls who ought to learn to be grateful to have the presents we got. She blew her nose, cleaned the milk off the table, and we all ate without speaking. When we stopped eating, she didn't tell us to have a little more chicken or finish our peas, she just picked up the plates and dumped the leftovers in the trash. For dessert, she gave us Eskimo Pies and washed the dishes while we ate them.

"Our father called and asked our mother if he could stop by to give us presents. He wasn't supposed to do this. He was supposed to pick us up the next morning. Our mother was new at being divorced, and she said yes, it was all right with her. She almost never said no to him; maybe she still loved him, despite everything. Or maybe she was just looking for a little diversion on a long, bad day. Maybe she was lonely.

"Before the divorce, when we were all living together, our mother had bought all the presents. This year, our father had bought us presents too. 'I couldn't wait!' he said when he arrived. 'I just couldn't wait to give you your presents, girls.' He disappeared for a moment to his car. I looked at my mother's face as she held open the door for him. Despite the lipstick she had put on before he came, her mouth was a thin, tight line.

"First our father wheeled in Eve's present. She got a pair of twin dolls in a carriage with space for two babies, facing one another. Then he brought in a bike for me that was much fancier than the one I had picked out. It was pink with white tires and a little pink-and-white license plate that said 'Mary.' It had a white basket on the front with plastic flowers attached to it. He made another trip to the car to get two little cradles for Eve and a pair of roller skates for me. Our mother's face cracked and leaked two big tears before she hurried upstairs to her room.

"Our father stood helpless and confused in the middle of the living-room floor for a minute, then took us outside. I tried my new bike, conscious of Eve and our father and the smiles they wore and of my mother, hiding upstairs, waiting for him to be gone. I remember that as I rode my new bike in a wiggly line down the sidewalk, I still had the boulder in my chest, but now it had changed its shape from disappoint- ment to conflict. Sitting on the seat, I had to stretch my toe as far as I could go to reach the pavement. I found when I stopped and stood on the sidewalk that the handlebars came up to my chest; I had never owned anything this big before. My dad yelled, 'Thataway, princess!' Eve was tucking her dolls into their cradles in the shade of a palm tree, making sure they were cozy and snug. I heard Eve say, 'Daddy, this is the best Christmas I ever had!' And then I crashed my bike on purpose into a chain-link fence."

I looked at Henry. His mouth opened in amazement, then he closed it and kissed the palm of my hand.

"My crash was even more dramatic than I had planned it to be. My new pink handlebars had paint scratched off them, where, I noted with satisfaction, there would be rust. They twisted the wrong way now and would have to be repaired. The white basket had fallen off. What I hadn't counted on was the small, sharp piece of broken glass that I hit with my chin when I landed and the blood that seemed to be everywhere. I didn't cry because my chin didn't hurt much and because my plan had worked."

"What was your plan?" Henry said.

"I think I wanted to give my mother the chance to run out of the house and say to our father, 'Goodness me, that bike is far too big for a six-year-old! George, I don't know what you could have been thinking.' She brought ice cubes and a clean dish towel for my chin. I didn't plan on the stitches I had to get, but honestly I thought they made the whole incident that much more satisfying for my mother. Be- fore taking me to the hospital, she shooed our father away. Suddenly she said, 'You're not supposed to be here until to- morrow.'

" 'Six stitches.' I kept hearing her say that over and over again to her friends on the phone or in the grocery store or to neighbors out in front of our house. 'And of course she'll have that scar for the rest of her life.' "

"She was right," Henry said.

I said, "True, but I got to keep the bike a long time too."

Henry held me around the middle and put his head against me "I'm going to miss this," he said. "And this." He kissed my shoulder. "And this, and this, and this." He kissed my neck, a breast, a knee. He looked up at me. "I bought the ticket before I knew you," he said for the third time tonight. "That was way back before I lost my job, before anything."

"It's OK," I said. "It's only a week, then you'll be back. And everything will be just like this again."

I went to the side of the bed where I had dropped all my clothes and started putting them on. "Hey," Henry said. "Don't do that. Where are you going?"

"I have a present for you. It's in the car."

I went out to the parking lot to get Henry's Christmas present out of the trunk and brought it inside. Henry tore off the wrapping paper. It was a box I made out of some scraps of good wood I had in the garage. I had used dovetail joints again and bought nice hinges and a pretty lock and key to make it look special. "You *made* this?" he said. "*Made* it, all by yourself?" He really liked it, I could tell, and wasn't just acting to make me feel appreciated. He opened the box, closed it, turned it over, opened it again.

Then he looked up at me, stricken, tears in his eyes. For one horrible second, I thought there was going to be bad news. He said, "Mimi, I'm in love with you." I laughed, and he cried, wiping his eyes on the sheet. "Let me give you your present," he said.

He gave me a box, too, a coincidence. It was black lacquer inlaid with mother-of-pearl. I inhaled. "Pretty," I said. I lifted the lid, and it played "I Want to Hold Your Hand." I hadn't realized it was a music box, and the song was so unexpected, so sweet and well meaning—just like Henry—that I felt a stab of emotion between my ribs. After years of avoiding Beatles songs, I made myself listen to the whole thing straight through. I did it for Henry because he didn't know about my constellation of memories that would be triggered by this one simple song. I listened, remembering everything, good and bad, and found that I could stand it. Every once in a while, I planned in my head, I'll wind up this box, open the lid, and listen to the song. Not often, but sometimes. Then I kissed Henry on the mouth and said, "Thank you. Thank you, thank you, thank you." He seemed to know that I didn't mean just for the box but for the way everything was different now, better all over.

"While I'm gone," he said, "I'll call you every day. And I won't really be gone but right here with you all the time, my heart, anyway. My heart will be here with you."

CHAPTER 10

The Money Thing

Patty came in on a Saturday to mail some Christmas presents. "I already wrapped them," she said, "but would you box them for me and send them UPS? Here are the addresses. How's business?"

I started unfolding some boxes. I said, "You know, it's hard to get everything working right at the same time. Before I met Henry, I had a reasonably profitable business and no boyfriend. Now that I have a great boyfriend, the business is falling apart."

"I noticed the new Send It, Inc., is open," Patty said.

I nodded. "We started feeling it right away. Think about it: Their store is close to the best supermarket in the area, the only workout place, and several big office buildings. People are there anyway, and now they can do their mailing in that center too. Have you been in there?"

"I've checked it out a couple of times. Unfortunately, it's nice, and it seems to be busy. They've got six people working in there most of the time." Patty looked at my face. "Sorry.

But you've got a bigger space. I think you could do more with that front area where all the machines are."

"Like what?" I said.

"I don't know."

The two of us looked at the self-service photocopy machines. Nothing came to me. "Last December, we hired two college students, remember, and barely handled our customers. I used to have nightmares about it, the line growing and growing while I was struggling to tape a package shut, get the postage meter to spit out the tape, take the money, make change, make copies, and on and on. This year, it's a different kind of nightmare: no long lines ever. We're getting by easily without hiring anyone extra. We're open late now, until ten. The new place is only open until six, so we thought it might help."

Patty said, "And who is working the late shift?"

"Eve and I are taking turns."

"That sounds awful. Is it helping business?"

"Not really. And it's so hard to get anything else done. I'm working on a desk for my mother's Christmas present, and I'm worried it won't be finished in time. Before he left, Henry did some grocery shopping for me. He went to the bank a couple of times to get me change and make deposits."

"That was nice of him," Patty said.

I shook my head. "I don't want him doing my errands."

Patty shrugged. "Times are hard, and he loves you." I taped the boxes shut. "What about Prince Charming? Is he helping out at all?"

Prince Charming was what Patty called John. "The investigation seems to take up all his time. They're always talking about it on the phone."

"Really?" Patty said. "What do they say?"

"What his lawyer said, what papers he needs," I said. "He

keeps trying to contact former employees of the place he worked to get someone to back up his story. I guess he can't find any of the people he wants."

"What did he do, anyway?" said Patty, leaning forward with interest.

I put her boxes in the UPS stack. "He was manager of a restaurant. Someone made off with a lot of cash. The owners, and I guess several other people, think it was John."

"Did he do it?" Patty said.

"Can we talk about something else? The whole thing gives me the chills."

"Wow," Patty said. "So it's about money. You think you know a person." She shook her head. "But wait a minute. Money. Isn't that kind of like what your dad—"

"Right," I said. I went to the photocopy machine.

"And if I remember correctly, wasn't he this kind of charming, smiling guy, like John? I never met him, of course, but didn't you tell me that?"

"Not exactly like John," I said.

"No," she said, "of course not exactly, no two people are exactly alike. But sort of the same type. I'm right, aren't I? Is Eve aware of the similarities? Have you talked to your mother about all this?"

"All what?"

"The fact that Eve married someone like your dad."

I said, "Are you kidding? It's never a good idea to mention our father to our mother. There are about ten thousand things he did, big and small, that she just can't seem to get over. She cries, she apologizes, she suddenly remembers an appointment she can't miss, then she comes down with a cold. It's not something I like to get started, if I can help it."

"I see what you mean," Patty said.

A young woman came in with an envelope. "Can you check if this has the right amount of postage on it?"

I weighed it. "Fine," I said, and dropped it into our mail bin.

"Thanks," the woman said, and left.

"So what kind of stuff are they looking for in the investigation?"

"Do we have to keep talking about this?" I said. "What did you get your kids for Christmas?"

"I didn't shop yet," she said. "I usually figure it all out at the last minute. What about you? Maybe I'll just get them what you're getting your kids."

"Geez," I said. "I'm afraid to spend any money. Our rent here is going up in February. I guess I told you that. Of course, I was counting on the extra income from Christmas business to help me get by the first few months at the new rent. Now I'm worried I won't have enough for Christmas presents. I'm near my limit on all my credit cards. Melanie asked for a new pair of Rollerblades. Her feet are growing so fast it's scary. Daniel wants his own tape player for his room. They're very specific about the brands they want. I priced both items, and I almost had a heart attack. I'm going to have to ask for a contribution from my mother even to get them cheap imitations of the things they want."

"What are you giving Eve?"

"I ordered a handmade quilt from that woman with the studio near here. This was back in September, which now seems like a lifetime ago. She delivered it the day before yesterday. I had to get money out of my savings account to pay for it. My mother's getting the desk I've been working on."

"Listen, don't get so hung up on this money thing," Patty said.

"How can I not be hung up on it?" I said. "I don't have any."

"Well, I do. I can always lend you some. You don't need to get an ulcer over Christmas presents and rent. You're making it more difficult than it is. There is a way for you to get more money. You just have to trust that it's coming and proceed as if it's already there." She dismissed the whole subject with a wave of her hand. "What kind of stuff are they looking at?"

"Who?" I said.

She said, "With John, I mean. I'm back to John."

"Oh, John. Bank records," I said. "How much money he spent over a certain period of time."

"Now wait a second. Would he keep stolen money in the bank? I would have thought they'd look for something a little more imaginative than that, a coffee can on a windowsill, a tackle box in the garage."

I shrugged. "I wouldn't know. Anyway, I know they're going over bank stuff from here, from where he lived before, and all his credit card accounts. They're talking to people from the restaurant where he used to work, the ones they can find, anyway."

"He does seem to have a lot of money."

"No kidding."

"I feel sorry for Eve," Patty said. "What does he do with himself all day anyway?"

"He stays home and bakes cookies," I said.

"Cookies?"

"Yes," I said. "He can't leave the phone. So he stays home all day and bakes cookies. He's got all these special pans and mixers and stuff. He makes up his own recipes."

We saw Bridget struggling toward the door. She was carrying one whimpering daughter and a bag of manuscript pages with the same arm, and with the other hand she was dragging along her older child. Patty ran to open the door for her. I came around the counter and took the bag. The smallest girl was crying and clutching at Bridget's hair, while the older one said, "I don't want to go here. I don't *want* to *go* here." Bridget had something brown spilled down the front of her T-shirt, and her hair was sticking out every which way.

"What can I do?" I said. "How can I help?"

"I have to get this stuff out today. Could you make me three copies, and I'll come back for them?" she said.

I said, "Sure." Then to the crying child, I said, "What's the matter with my friend today?"

"Rachel's got an ear infection," Bridget said. I went to the big copier with Bridget's manuscript. "It's going to be like this all day, maybe tomorrow too, until the antibiotics start to work. My husband's out of town at a conference, naturally. I'll drive down to the Federal Express office because I can't afford the Saturday charge for pickup." She thought over her strategy. "Let's see, I gave her the Tylenol at—oh, it should start to work any minute now. If I can get this one to sleep, driving around, then I can park by the Fed Ex door, dash in to drop off the packages, and still watch the kids. Luckily, the whole place is windows."

"That'll work," I said, picturing the building and where she could park. "I can have this done for you in about fifteen or twenty minutes."

"Great," she said, and sighed. "I'll start driving around."

Rachel lifted her head momentarily from her mother's shoulder and peeked at me. "Hi, pumpkin," I said. "I hope you feel better soon." She screamed. "Sorry," I said to Bridget, "didn't mean to set her off again."

"Don't take it personally," Bridget said.

Hannah, the older girl, said, "Mommy, you said we could have a candy, and now you're not giving us one!"

I got the candy jar and leaned over the counter with it down at the little girl's level. She chose two pieces. "Here, Rach," she said, handing a mini Tootsie Roll to her sister, who grabbed it and held it tight.

Bridget said, "What do you say, girls?" They both hid

their faces against their mother, who shook her head in resignation. She took them out, saying, "Thanks, Mimi. I'll be back."

Patty shook her head. "I don't know how we did it. Ear infections. The horror of those screams! God, it was impossible to do anything but carry them around all day when they had those. And strep throat!"

"Chicken pox," I said, "and the isolating effect it had on you."

"Bronchitis, roseola," said Patty.

"Croup," I said, "don't forget croup and the shower in the middle of the night."

Patty shuddered.

Eve came in with bags from Christmas shopping. "Hi, Patty."

"Hi. Looks like you had some success," Patty said.

"Not bad," Eve said.

"I've got to go," said Patty. "See you guys."

"Bye," I said. "Thanks."

I set the machine for three copies and started on Bridget's pile. Eve pulled out wrapping paper and started wrapping the presents she had just bought. She didn't say anything, didn't show me the presents or tell me who she had bought them for. I made the copies and put them into Bridget's envelopes, which were in her bag.

I was waiting on someone who wanted to send a fax when I saw Bridget's car come back into the parking lot. "Eve," I said. "Could you take over for me here?" I grabbed Bridget's bag so she wouldn't have to get out of the car.

Both girls were asleep in their car seats, and Bridget rolled down her window. "Thank you, Mimi," she whispered. "You're too good."

"Can I do anything else?" I said. "Do you want me to get

you some lunch or something while you have a chance to eat it?"

"That's so nice of you. Would you just get me a coffee? I've been up since three-thirty, and I'm desperate."

"Sure," I said. "Follow me." I walked to the grocery store while she inched along beside me in the car. I bought the coffee and handed it through the window.

"You are so *nice* to me," she whispered.

"I hope they stay asleep for a while," I said over my shoulder as I started back toward the store.

When I got there, the phone was ringing. "Wrap It Up, Mimi speaking."

"It's me," Henry said on the other end. "What was I thinking? My family? New Jersey? This was a mistake."

"What? You're not having fun?"

"Fun?" he said. "It's so cold here. I sort of forgot about cold. And I'm walking around these indoor malls all day long with my sisters. They always have to get *one more thing* and, of course, they need old Henry along for the ride. You know what they need me for? 'Do you think Mom would like this cardigan, or should I go back to that other store for the blouse?' So there I am in this big *coat* for hours and hours looking at all this *stuff* and I'm *inside*. You know what else I forgot about? Being by myself. I can't do it anymore. When I get back, I'm never going anywhere without you again. Did you get the new Cranberries CD yet? There's a lot of Mimi-ish music on there."

"No, I don't have it yet," I said. "But I'll wait until you get back."

"Good. That's good. I like that. That kind of thing is just what I called for. Am I done yet? Can I come back?"

"No," I said. "You have to open the presents first. Remember? Christmas?"

"Oh, that, yeah."

"Yeah."

"OK, I guess I better go."

"Thanks for calling. Talk to you soon."

"In about five minutes." And then, so his parents wouldn't hear, he whispered, "I love you."

"I love you too," I whispered back.

That night when I was working by myself in the store and had no customers, I called Patty. "Are you sure about this money thing?"

"What money thing?"

"You said 'trust that it's coming and proceed as if it's already there.' Is that what you do?"

"Oh, *that* money thing. I thought you meant about John. Yeah, that's what I do. I pretend that I don't care, and then it comes to me. If I want it too much it avoids me."

"Come on," I said. "Are you serious?"

"Really. If I start worrying that I'm running out of money, all of a sudden, I'm getting shortchanged at the grocery store, accidentally dropping twenty-dollar bills in the toilet, and the kids lose their lunch money. Then once I relax about it and decide I don't care if I have to sell everything and start over from scratch, all of a sudden I sell two houses in a day, find a fifty in a parking lot, and someone offers to buy my car. You have to let go, give up, not care, and it will come to you."

I said, "I guess. I tried it all day, not thinking about money, like you said, not caring if I ever got any again. Every once in a while, it worked. For about thirty seconds at a time, a minute maybe, I could trick myself into thinking money didn't matter."

"There you go," Patty said. "Keep at it, and you'll get really good."

"I'll try," I said. But after I hung up, I realized it would take all my effort, all the concentration I had, not to think about needing money, never to worry about where it was going to come from. It would be a full-time job to master this trick. To put that much time into it, I'd have to be rich. And, of course, if I were rich, I wouldn't need this system at all.

CHAPTER 11

Merry Christmas

On Christmas Eve, I couldn't sleep. I kept worrying about the presents for Melanie and Daniel, thinking that if I couldn't afford to get them what they wanted, I should have gotten them something else entirely. This way, they would be disappointed, and they would remember their lousy presents forever. It would be one of the stories they told about their childhoods, the way I told Henry about the scar on my chin. When I did fall asleep, I had weird dreams. First I dreamed I could hear a lot of people talking but I couldn't make out what they were saying. There were a lot of voices, people telling me things in the dark, the words all jumbled together, and I couldn't make any sense of it. I woke up and had to get a drink of water.

When I fell asleep again, I had a dream about Bill that didn't feel like a dream. We were walking on a cobbled street that seemed to be in Europe somewhere, someplace pretty where nothing worked quite right and everything was out-of-date. Bill said, "Watch out for that one." I looked at the stones, expecting to see an obstacle that might trip me. "No," he said.

"That *guy*," and I looked behind me for a pickpocket. Nobody there. Then one of the kids flushed the toilet, and I woke up. I was disoriented for a minute, surprised to find myself at home in bed, Bill and the cobbled street gone.

Melanie and Daniel had had their Christmas with Richard the night before. He gave them electronic games that had educational value; books; earrings for Melanie; a wallet for Daniel; and his yearly gift to them, a certificate he made himself, redeemable for a trip to Disneyland.

My mother arrived at my house before I was even dressed. When the kids were little, she used to sleep on our sofa bed Christmas Eve because it was too hard for them to wait for her to get there before they opened their presents. Now they were a little more patient. "Merry Christmas, everybody," she said, coming in. "Oh, your tree looks so nice." She bent to plug in the lights. "Look at all these presents for Melanie and Daniel. Goodness me, that's too many. We're going to have to save some of those until next year." She said this every Christmas. Daniel rolled his eyes at me. "Mimi, did you make coffee?" my mother asked.

"No," I said. "I'm waiting for John and Eve."

"When are they coming?"

"Should be any minute now." I looked at my watch. "Or maybe not. It's only a quarter to eight."

"I'll make it," my mother said.

"That's OK, Mom," I said. "You don't have to do that."

"No trouble," she said on her way to the kitchen.

Daniel said, "Can we just do our stockings before they get here?"

I said, "Sure. I guess so."

The kids got their stockings down from the fireplace and held them impatiently, listening to the coffee drip through. When my mother came back with her coffee, she said, "All right, go ahead. Coffee, Mimi?"

"No, thanks," I said.

Melanie pulled a new hairbrush and some tights out of her stocking. Daniel got a box of watercolors, some paintbrushes. They both got rulers and pencils with their names on them, tape and scissors, candy, bubble bath.

We waited a long time for John and Eve, but Melanie and Daniel got impatient again, so we started opening presents without them. Daniel gave my mother a bird feeder he made for her in his after-school art class and Melanie gave her a scarf she had saved up for. They had gone in together on a fancy carpentry book with glossy photographs for me. My mother and I said thank you and kissed them both. Then my mother gave Melanie a pair of leggings and a matching top. She went to her room and put on her new outfit, and returned looking pretty and older in it. Daniel got art supplies in a case. They hugged her and thanked her.

I handed Melanie the box with the skates in it. "These are from Grandma and me," I said. She looked happy, so expectant and sure.

I gave Daniel his box. He smiled at me. "I'm so excited," he said. I wanted to cover my face with my hands while they opened their gifts.

"Oh, wow. Thanks, Mom," Melanie said. "These are neat. They fit too. Where'd you get these? I've never seen this kind." She wasn't going to cry, no matter what. She wasn't going to hurt my feelings.

"Sportmart," I said. "Do you really like them?"

"Yeah, they're fine. Cool." She nodded.

Daniel said, "This is almost like the one I wanted! Thanks, Mom. Excellent." And then he nodded and went silent, examining the buttons.

They both did a good job of trying to cover their disappointment. I tried to convey my anguish to my mother in a look. She returned a Merry Christmas smile.

We took a break to eat something, my mother staying behind to pick up wrapping paper and stuff it into the recycling crate. Without being asked to, Melanie and Daniel put their presents in their rooms. Their good behavior cut into me like a hot knife. Quietly, I spoke to them in the kitchen. "You guys, we can take your stuff back to the stores and get something else. It's OK with me."

"No," Melanie said stoically. "We like our presents. Don't we, Daniel?"

"I do," he said. "Mine's great. It's fine. I don't want to take it back."

"You guys are being good sports," I said. "I really appreciate it."

"Want some cereal, Mom?" Melanie said.

"Yes, please."

"You put on your own milk, though," she said. "I always put on too much."

"But listen," I said. "Both of you. I want you to know that I really tried to get you what you wanted. It just wasn't possible this year. You know the way things are going at the store. So unfortunately, all our money is—"

"It's OK," Melanie said, cutting me off.

"Mom, forget it," Daniel said.

I sighed. "I know when I was a little girl—"

"Mom!" Daniel snapped, startling me. "Stop! It doesn't matter. We like the presents. Now get off the subject!"

"You don't have to yell at me," I said. "I'm just trying to tell you I understand how it feels. And I'm sorry."

They were both silent. They sat down to eat their breakfast. I poured milk on my cereal. I wanted coffee, but there was still a lot left of what my mother made. I hoped she would finish it soon, then I would make sure that I was the one to make a new pot. She came in with the recycling crate full of torn wrapping paper and put it by the back door.

The doorbell rang, and John and Eve came in with packages. "Ho, ho, ho," said John. He walked straight to the kitchen, picked up the coffeepot, sniffed its contents, and poured it into the sink. Whistling "Jingle Bells," he began rinsing the pot, sloshing it out with a sponge. My mother opened her mouth, indignant and amazed.

Eve was putting presents under the tree. The kids went to watch her, sitting close together on the couch. John measured the coffee into the filter and poured in the water. While it dripped through, he got mugs ready on a tray with cream and sugar and spoons. He had a tin of cookies too, which he opened and put on the tray. They were an assortment of iced Christmas shapes: stars, bells, stockings, Christmas trees with ornaments and melting snow. I looked at the coffee and my mouth started to water. "This is yours, Meemers," John said, handing me a mug.

"Mimi," I said. "Please. Thank you." I took a sip. Eve was right: John made great coffee. There were just the right amounts of half-and-half and sugar in it. How did he know?

He was handing a cup to my mother. "Joyce," he said.

"She likes skim milk and Equal," I said, standing up to get my mother a new cup.

"Mm-hm," John said. "That's what I put in it."

"Oh," I said.

"Evie, here's yours, love," John said.

Melanie was eating her second cookie. "Take it easy on the sweets, kids," I said. They ignored me.

Melanie said, "These are so good. Awesome. I can't believe you made these yourself at home. They're so fancy, like they came from some expensive bakery or something. Did you make up the recipe too?"

John nodded.

"Did you used to work in a bakery or something?" Daniel wanted to know.

John shook his head. "No," he said. "That's one thing I haven't done."

"How come you're not fat from all these cookies?" Melanie said.

John shrugged and took a careful sip of his hot coffee—black, no sugar. "I don't eat them. I just bake them. Keeps me out of trouble." Melanie and John smiled at each other.

A shiver went through me. I sat down next to Melanie, took one of her warm hands in mine, and squeezed hard. John offered the cookie tin in my direction. "Maybe in a little while," I said. "I just ate some Cheerios." I looked at my watch and figured out what time it was in New Jersey. Henry could have called me by now, but he probably didn't want to interrupt our Christmas morning. I pictured his face and felt a clutch in my throat.

John handed Daniel a small package. "Merry Christmas, bud," he said. He handed a bigger box to Melanie. "For you."

Daniel's present was a portable CD player with headphones—top of the line—and four CDs. A stunned guffaw came out of him. Melanie opened her box. "Oh, my god," she whispered. "Oh, my god." She looked at me in pain. It was the Rollerblades she wanted in black and magenta, the right brand, the right size with room to grow. There were knee pads, elbow pads, and wrist guards too, all in a shade of magenta that matched the blades perfectly. "Thank you, John," she said quietly, putting the box quickly aside, then looking at it longingly out of the corner of her eye.

Daniel tore open the box his new CD player came in. It already had the batteries installed. He chose a CD. "I can't believe it," he said. "I can't believe it."

Melanie looked at me, agonizing. I was thinking about the bike I got from my father. I said, "Melanie, go get your helmet so you can try out the blades John and Eve gave you."

Melanie said, "Let's give them their present first." She

brought a big box from under the tree and put it between John and Eve on the couch. Before opening it, the two of them paused, smiling, for my mother to take a picture. Eve opened the box. She pulled out the quilt. It had a complicated pattern of triangles in greens and blues all over it in different kinds of fabric. The background was pale blue. There was a lot of hand quilting in swirling curlicues. There were hearts stuffed with extra batting to make them puff out. They both looked at the quilt and then at each other. There was something about it they didn't like. "Thank you, Mimi," Eve said. "Thanks, guys."

John said, "Thank you very much."

"It goes with your curtains and your rug," Melanie said. "Mom took over some swatches and secretly coordinated everything. Look, here are your names and your wedding date. She had it made extra wide so it would hang down on the sides. You know how some quilts are too narrow?"

Eve smiled at her, folding the quilt and putting it back in the box. "Yeah, I see. Your mom put a lot of thought into that." There was a short silence, then Eve said, "Now what? Oh. Mom." She looked at John.

John pulled an envelope out of his pocket and handed it to my mother. "Merry Christmas, Joycie!" he said.

She opened it and pulled out a plane ticket to New York and an itinerary. She cried. "Goodness me! I'm overcome. And what's this? Theater tickets. Hotel, and everything? How did you know I wanted to go to New York?"

"Because you've been talking about it ever since we were little," Eve said, laughing.

John handed me a box. It was big, some sort of clothes. It had just a ribbon around it, so it was easy to get open: a leather jacket. I pulled it out and held it up. Melanie inhaled sharply. "*Mom*," she whispered. "That is so cool."

"Whoa, Mom," Daniel said, "awesome."

I'll never wear this, I thought. Never, ever, ever. "Thank you," I said. "It's beautiful." I tried it on.

Melanie was stunned. "Mom," she said, amazed. "You look *good.*"

That did it. I went to my bedroom, pretending I wanted to look at myself in the mirror, but really it was because I didn't want to burst into tears in front of everybody. Everything piled up inside me, the Rollerblades, the CD player, the ticket to New York, John and Eve's cool reaction to the quilt. I missed Henry. He would understand how I felt. He would hold me and make me laugh, telling a joke that only the two of us would hear. In my head, I could hear his voice saying something I didn't quite catch, and I felt better. I picked up the music box he gave me from my bedside table and wound it up. I opened the lid and listened to "I Want to Hold Your Hand" until the notes slowed to a stop. Then I took the jacket off, blew my nose, splashed water on my face, brushed my hair, came out.

"Let's go outside," I said. "Melanie's going to show us what she can do on those blades."

"Really?" Melanie said. "Mom, are you sure?"

"Let's go," I said again. "We'll go out through the garage and show Grandma her new desk." I got my sunglasses and my keys. At the last second, so I wouldn't seem like a bad sport, I put on the leather jacket. We all went through the kitchen to the garage. I pushed the button to open the garage door.

My mother made a big fuss over the desk I made for her, even though she had known about it for a long time. "I just love the little drawer pulls," she said. "Where did you find those? I'm going to put the phone and a light right here. This is just perfect. Mimi, you're an amazement to me. To think that a child of mine could make something like this, it's— well, it's hard to believe."

Everyone stood around and looked at the desk, as if waiting for it to do something, spin around in a circle or play a melody. I pulled out a drawer and looked at the joints again, closed it, stroked the finish.

"Nice work," said John after a long pause, and we all went out in the driveway.

The sun was blazing, and I started to feel sweaty in my new jacket. Children from our block were trying out new cameras, skateboards, and two-wheelers. Melanie got into her gear and took off fast down the middle of the street. She was so coordinated and sure of herself, twirling, skating backward. It was stupid of me to care who gave her the skates. She had what she wanted, and I should be happy. She skated toward me, smiling, coasted to a stop in front of me to give me a hug. With a shock, I realized that in the Rollerblades she was taller than I was.

Dinner was at my house this year. Usually we had it at my mother's. But she had been doing so much for me lately, staying with the kids and lending me money, helping out all the time, that I wanted to relieve her of at least one responsibility. Everybody was contributing something for the dinner. John went home to get the desserts he had made. Patty was coming with her kids and bringing some vegetables. My mother said she would tell me what to do with the turkey, which I hadn't made very often. I was also in charge of the gravy and the rice.

Melanie went skating with Janine, who had also gotten new blades. Daniel was listening to a CD on the couch and could not be reached. My mother, Eve, and I were all in the kitchen, getting ready. At the sink, washing dishes, Eve said, "So everyone seemed pleased with our presents."

My mother said, "Well, who wouldn't be! Goodness me! A trip to New York! I never in a million years—"

Eve smiled. "John is very generous."

I said, "What was wrong with the quilt? Why didn't you like it?"

"I did. It's very pretty. Thank you. I said thank you, didn't I? I meant to. I hope I did."

"You did," I said. "I just had this feeling you didn't like it."

Eve rinsed a plate. "It isn't that we didn't like it."

"What then?"

"Nothing. It's just that we decided that everything in our house is going to be white. Plain white," she said.

"Oh, great. You could have told me."

"I thought I did," she said. "But John suggested we could use the quilt anyway, with the wrong side facing up. Isn't that a good idea?"

"The wrong side? But the design is on the other side. It's handmade. This woman sewed every single stitch *by hand.*"

"Mimi," our mother said. "Now let's just try to have a nice holiday with everyone—"

"OK, OK," Eve said to me. "We won't do that. Don't get all worked up about it. It's not that big a deal." She rinsed a few more plates. "Did you like the jacket? John picked it out for you."

I said, "Where does he get all the money?" It just slipped out; I couldn't help it. Eve stiffened, and my mother turned sharply to glare at me from the table, where she was making a salad. "I'm just wondering because he always seems to have so much, while the rest of us have very little. I mean, he doesn't work or anything. So how come he's got all this money?"

"Nice, Mimi," Eve said, her voice shaky. "So now you want to check him out too. What—are you working with the police now or something?"

"The police? No, I just asked a simple, basic question that

anyone would ask about her sister's husband: Where does he get his money?"

My mother said, "Eve, you don't have to tell us anything at all, if you don't want to."

"No," Eve said quietly. "I'll tell you. He sold his house in L.A. and didn't buy another one."

"I see," I said.

"Where did you think he got it?" Eve said.

"I didn't know," I said. "That's why I asked."

"You thought he stole it?" Eve said.

"I just didn't know."

"You did, didn't you? Sometimes, Mimi, you are really too much."

"Now listen. The guy appears out of the blue as charming as anything, he spends money like crazy but doesn't work, you marry him fast, then you tell me he's being investigated for something that happened at his old job. You may remember that I was at your house when his lawyer called to say that there were witnesses." Our mother left the room. I hadn't told her the part about the witnesses. "What did you expect me to think? What would you think if he were my husband? He smiles and buys things for me and my kids that I can't afford myself. He rubs my back as if he's my best friend and calls me a nickname I can't stand. That's what I know about John." I stopped, folded my arms. She took a breath to say something. I held up my hand to stop her. "Wait a minute. I left out something. He makes great coffee. *Brilliant* coffee! If there were a Nobel Prize for coffee, he'd be a shoo-in."

She looked at me for a long time, trying not to cry. "Are you finished?" she said. "Somehow you seem to have missed the fact that I am going through a very hard time. I got married, and you cried. You, my own sister, got so depressed right there at the wedding that you burst into tears in front of everybody. On *my* wedding day, everybody was looking at *you*, feeling concerned about *you*. Now how do you think that made me feel?"

I looked at the linoleum. Guilt enveloped me, as inescapably as the radiation following a nuclear blast.

Eve cried, leaning against the counter. Then she said, "I don't know why this should bother me. You've never liked anyone I was with. I should just assume it and not let it get to me."

"That's not true," I said, realizing immediately that it was.

"Most of the time you were right, I guess, but that doesn't make it any easier to take."

"Have you ever liked anybody I was with?" I said.

"We're not talking about that. You haven't given John a chance. And it's been really horrible with all this checking into our financial records, all these lawyers and bastards and creeps telling lies about John. You have no idea what that feels like! And then every time I talk to him on the phone or mention his name, you get all tight and snappy. I don't give you any information because you don't want any. You make it absolutely clear that you don't want to know anything more about John than you have to. You're not being supportive, Mimi. You're not even being kind." She lowered her voice to a whisper. "You're being like Mom, covering her ears whenever a fire or a war or a disease is mentioned. Get with it, Mimi, there are some unpleasant things you need to know about. John is being accused of stealing a lot of money from the restaurant he used to work for. Add to that the fact that I have a sister who doesn't support me, and you might understand, for once, what I've been going through." She paused. Then she said, "You think he's guilty, don't you?"

"Is he? Has he told you whether or not he took the money?"

Something seemed to boil inside her. She drew herself up and opened her mouth as if she were about to spit fire.

"Mimi," she said. "That's the difference between you and me. That's it right there. I would never think to ask that question. He's my *husband!*" She heard her car coming into the driveway—John with his desserts—and she said, "I'm getting out of here. Good-bye and Merry Christmas!"

"Merry Christmas yourself!" I called after her.

Daniel was lying on the couch with his headphones on and didn't even open his eyes. He's got that thing turned up too loud, I thought; he's going to ruin his hearing. Eve slammed the door so hard the house shook. Daniel sat up, ready to run. "What was that?" he said. "Earthquake?"

"That was Aunt Eve leaving," I said. "Turn that thing down."

He didn't.

I went to the kitchen and listened to Eve's car drive off. It had gotten too warm in here. I opened the window behind the sink. I checked the good plates for dust and counted them out, figuring on two fewer dinner guests than I had originally planned for. I took the pie that Henry and I had bought in Julian out of the freezer. We could eat that for dessert. I wished again that Henry had not gone to see his family. I would bet almost anything that if he had been here, I would not have fought with Eve. Blowouts, tantrums, and panic attacks didn't seem to happen when he was around. When he called I would tell him about the fight, and he would seem puzzled: How could we get so angry at each other? he would want to know. Surely things weren't that bad, were they?

John walked in, startling me. He put a pumpkin pie and another plate of cookies on the table. Then he pulled out a kitchen chair and sat down on it backward. "Eve went home," he said. "She told me she's never coming here again. I guess that means I'll need a ride home later. So. What happened?"

I went to the oven to baste the turkey. "We had an argument."

"I got that." He waited for me to go on.

Opening the oven door, a hot blast hit me in the face. I straightened up, checked to make sure my eyebrows were still there, then picked up the plastic baster, sucked up some juice, and squirted the bird.

"My name come up at all?" he said.

I closed the oven door. "Yeah," I said. "You probably already know the whole story, but since you're so interested, here it is. The first time I met you, you reminded me of our father. You know the story, don't you? He was a charmer who was always working all the angles." He nodded, smiling guiltily. "Here's the thing. I'm worried about this investigation and what it will turn up. You know what I'm saying? I don't trust you. I'm sorry. I've tried, but it's just this feeling I've had since the first time I met you."

"Oh, that," he said. "Don't worry about that. It's my face."

"Your face?"

"I have a guilty-looking face. I've always had this problem. In school, I always used to get yelled at for things I didn't do because of the look on my face. Seriously. And you know when you go by the border checkpoints, going north? *You* always get waved through, right? You have the right kind of face; people trust you on sight. Not me. Nine times out of ten, I get pulled over and my car gets searched. Come back from Europe, same thing. They wave *you* through without even checking your customs form, right? Me? I get my bag opened and everything gets looked at. They open my shampoo bottle, check the bag for secret compartments. I'm telling you, it's the way I look. It's the distance between my eyes or their position in relation to the bridge of my nose. The shape of my mouth. I don't know. Something. I could never sell used cars. People don't trust me. So that's part of the reason for this investigation. If something's missing, people always look at me first." He shrugged.

"Where do you get all the money?"

"Money? I made money in my old job. Honestly. Then I sold my house. You can look at my bank statements. Everybody else has. I'm getting rid of that money pretty fast, though, if that makes you feel any better. I'm pretty good at making money, but I don't keep it very long." He looked at me. "What did you think? I stole the money and was showing off? Does that make sense? Meemers, use your head."

"I see what you mean," I said.

"OK, kiddo?" He smiled at me.

"Why don't you work?" I said, not giving up.

"It's hard to get a job when you just got fired and are suspected of embezzling. I'm going to try to get something going on my own. I'm not quite sure what yet."

"Hm," I said.

"What else?" John said. "Let's get it all out there. Come on."

"My name is Mary. People call me Mimi. I don't like to be called Meemers."

He snapped his fingers and pointed at me. "Got it," he said. "You'll get used to me. Have to. I'm going to be around forever."

He looked at me and didn't say anything for a few moments. His eyes were brown, like a young animal's, and wide open. I looked away and squatted in front of a cupboard, looking for a platter, something to put the turkey on when it was done. I found it and yanked it out from under a pile of baking pans.

John said, "You know what? And don't you dare tell your little sister this." I looked at him. He had an expression on his face that I hadn't seen before. "I'm scared," he said. "I'm afraid I'll have to go to jail. I've always been afraid of police, of being locked up and not able to get out. I'm scared to death it's really going to happen."

Looking at his face, he was so convincing that I wasn't sure whether this was another ploy to win me over or a genuine secret, confided in trust.

John smiled. "But you know what they say."

"No, what do they say?"

"It's what you're most afraid of that's most likely to happen," he told me.

"I've never heard that." I shook my head. "Where did you hear that?"

"You've never heard that?" he said. "Oh, yeah. It's in the teachings of the ancient masters."

"Really?" I said. "Which ones?"

John shook his head, looking flustered.

"Is this something you picked up in one of those workshops?" I said. "Don't you think it's kind of pessimistic to think that what you're most afraid of will happen to you?"

John said, "Not necessarily. It's a very positive experience to be able to survive your biggest challenge. When you think about it, it's probably exactly that one thing that scares you so much that you *need* to face. For growth, I mean." He leaned forward and looked at me. "To grow as a person, you need to conquer your fears and get past them. Don't you think that's true?"

"No," I said. "I think if you're afraid of something, there's probably an excellent reason. And you ought to steer clear of it, whatever it is, avoid it, find a good spot to hide."

He shook his head, narrowed his eyes. "But it will always find you. Your own personal monster will seek you out and discover you in your clever little hiding place." He smiled at me.

I shivered and closed the kitchen window.

"I like you, Mimi. I really do."

"Thanks," I said.

"What are you most afraid of?"

"What? Me?" I said. "Afraid of?" I thought a minute. "Mice. Spiders too. That's about it."

"Good for you. That's nice. You don't have any big fears, monsters, like I do," he said. "I wish I could be like you. And then there's the other thing that always happens, that whatever you love the most, whatever you can't stand to let go of, you're going to lose. But that already happened to me, so I'm not worried about that anymore. It was the restaurant. I loved it too much. I held on too tight. It was the most beautiful little place I ever saw. I loved the menus, the dishes, the way the place looked at night with the flowers and the candles and the waiters zipping in and out of the tables, the sound of food sizzling as it hit the hot pans in the kitchen. That place was *mine; I made* it! I was the luckiest man in the world to be able to do that, and I knew it. I put the whole thing together myself, every detail, from the waiters' aprons and the butter plates to the light fixtures in the bathrooms. And then I got to be there every day and stand there and look at it. I could eat that perfect food every single night! You see what I mean? It was a restaurant, for god's sake, not a *person,* or a *mission,* nothing of any real value. I loved it too much, and it's gone." He considered his loss. He looked resigned, accepting. Then he sighed.

I said, "You lost it because you loved it so much? How does that— Why do you think— I mean, isn't it good to love what you do, where you work?"

He brought his hands together in front of him, as if he had caught a small bird, then quickly opened them, looking up, allowing it to fly free. "Pffft," he said, the same way Eve did when we were stuck in traffic and she told me about the trouble John was in. "Gone. Want me to baste the turkey?"

"Sure," I said, "why don't you? I'll get the rice started."

John inspected the apple pie on the counter. "You make this?"

"Henry and I bought it in Julian." The doorbell rang. "That's going to be Patty."

"I'll get it," John said.

Patty and her two kids came in with their dishes at the same time that my mother appeared, yawning. "Would you believe I fell asleep on Melanie's bed? Took a nap in the middle of the day!"

"Merry Christmas, Joyce," Patty said.

"Merry Christmas, dear," said my mother, kissing Patty on the cheek.

Patty said to me, "Where's Eve?"

"She wasn't feeling well," my mother said quickly.

John and I looked at her. I said, "We had a fight, and Eve went home."

"Oh no," Patty said. "Want me to drive over and talk to her? Want me to try to bring her back?"

"I don't think that's going to work," John said. "I'll call her in a little while. She needs some time. Let's get set up here."

Melanie came home sweaty and pleased with herself. Her cheeks were flushed with two pink circles, like a painted doll. "Mom, you should have seen me on these things! They're great! I'm starved. Is dinner almost ready? Hi, Patty. Merry Christmas, everybody!"

I said, "Honey, go take a shower fast and change. You've got about fifteen minutes."

"OK. Where's Aunt Eve?"

"Mom made her mad," Daniel said from the doorway, "and she stormed out of here. You should have heard the door slam. I thought the whole house was going to fall down."

I said, "Daniel, is that what you're wearing?"

"What's wrong with it?" Daniel said, looking down at his jeans and T-shirt.

"Nothing," I said. "It's fine. Melanie, get going."

Melanie said, "What was the fight about?"

I tried to think of a diplomatic answer.

John said, "Your mother doesn't like me, and Eve does." Patty laughed nervously. "But that's OK," he said. "I like your mom, and she'll come around."

I could feel my face reddening. I opened the oven to look at the turkey again. "Oh, god," I said. "I think this is done."

My mother put on oven mittens. "We'll take it out then." I stepped aside as she lifted the turkey pan out of the oven. Patty got out of the way so she could put it on the counter. John handed her the baster, and my mother squirted juice on it again. Then she turned around and looked at us all, addressing us as if we were a class assembled to learn about the preparing of a Christmas turkey. "We'll just let it rest there, fifteen or twenty minutes, doing nothing more until we're ready for it," she said.

Everyone was quiet for a minute, watching the turkey rest.

CHAPTER 12

Oldies

It was almost time to close the store, but not quite. I hadn't had a customer in over half an hour. It was dark; I was hungry. I went in the office and sat there straightening my desk to fill a couple of minutes before I pulled the gates down for the night. Suddenly someone—a man—was behind me; grabbing me around the chest, squeezing the breath out of me. Someone had sneaked into the store. I screamed as loud as I could, struggled free of his hold, jumped to my feet fast, turning sharply, my arms in front of me, ready to punch, scratch, kick, bite.

"It's me! It's me! Mimi, it's me." In front of me, backing away quickly, was Henry with his hands up in front of his face, ready to defend himself.

It took me a second to take this in, to go from thinking I was going to have to fight for my life to realizing that Henry was back from New Jersey a day early. I opened my mouth, but nothing came out for a second. Then I yelled, "What are you doing here? I'm—How did you get in here?"

"Through the door," he said, his hands on his chest. "I

had the shuttle drop me off. You're still open, and I—I just walked in. It's not six o'clock yet. Don't ever do that again! Don't scream like that. You scared me half to death. Feel my heart."

"I scared you?" I said. "Are you kidding? You came in without a sound! I would have picked you up at the airport! Feel *my* heart!"

Henry put his hand on my heart. "Wow," he said. "I wanted to surprise you."

"Well, you did. Holy smokes." I put a hand to his chest and felt his heart pounding fast. I laughed. "Sorry I screamed. I didn't know it was you."

"I'm sorry," he said. "I didn't mean to scare you." He put his arms around me. "I thought you would be happy to see me. Hi, Mimi. I'm back."

"I see that," I said. "Yikes, no kidding. It's going to take me a couple minutes to calm down. My legs are shaking," I said. I kissed him. "I *am* happy to see you. Did you have a good time with your family?"

Henry sat down on my desk and ran his hands through his hair. "I guess so."

"What's the matter?" I said.

"I just need to find a job," he said, sighing.

"You will," I said. "Sometimes it takes a little while."

"Are you sure?" he said. He picked up a rubber band and looped it over four fingers. "This seems like forever."

"It's a few weeks. Nothing," I said. "Nobody gets a job right before Christmas. But the beginning of the year will be a much better time."

"Hm," he said, unconvinced. "I'm going to send out more résumés tomorrow, call some more people." He bit a hangnail.

"That's right," I said. "The more you do, the faster you'll get a job."

"I thought you said it was a matter of luck," he sneered, "timing." He shot the rubber band at the doorknob.

"Did I? Well, I guess luck does have something to do with it. Sometimes." He sighed and seemed to collapse inward a little. "Did your family give you a hard time about getting a job or something? Is that why you're so worried about it?" The longer you know somebody, I thought to myself, the more facets of his personality you discover. I had never seen Henry in this kind of a defeated mood before.

"So what's been happening with the store?" He didn't want to talk about his job search anymore.

"Very slow," I said. "I'm stuck. I just haven't come up with anything that will save us."

"Maybe you should give up, try something else."

"Give *up*?" I said. I looked at him, checking to see if he was serious. "Something *else*?" I said. "Like what?"

"I don't know. Some other kind of store, or maybe you could get a job at one of the other mailing places."

I shook my head. "No. No. I don't think you understand. I'm not going to work for anyone else. This is *my* place. It's important to me to make the store profitable again." My voice broke. "It's going to work. I am going to do this."

"Well, good then. Fine. It wouldn't be for me. But if you like it, then that's what you should do." He shrugged.

"Why wouldn't it be for you?" I said.

"I don't know. It's not, it's just—you know, I went to graduate school because I wanted a career. To me, making copies for people is not a career. I told you, I like big things."

"But we could really get our place going. We could get a great idea and become the number-one mail-and-parcel center in the whole area. With the right approach, the place could really take off."

He smiled.

"It could happen," I said.

He shook his head.

"Listen," I said. I knew it was useless to argue with him while he was in this frame of mind, but I continued, frustrated, defensive. "It may not be what *you* want to do," I said, "but *I* like it. At least *I'm* working." There was a thick silence. He didn't look at me. "Sorry," I said. "I didn't mean that. It's just that you made me mad, putting down what I do that way." I went out to the front of the store, pulled down the gates; it was late enough now.

When I came back, Henry changed the subject. "How are Eve and John?"

"Eve and I had a fight."

"What else is new?"

"We don't fight that much—do we? Anyway, this was a pretty bad one. My fault completely. About John and his problems. She said I never liked any of her boyfriends. I said the same was true of her. She's never liked any of my boyfriends, or husbands, for that matter." Henry looked at me. "I asked her whether or not he did it. Took the money."

Henry put his hand over his face.

"I didn't mean to say it. We were at my house on Christmas, and there was all this tension about presents. It just slipped out. Anyway, she got mad and stormed out. And since then we've hardly spoken."

"This was on Christmas Day? Christmas, Mimi?"

"I know," I said. "I realize it was lousy timing. But we'll get past it. She's my sister. It will work out."

"It just seems as though you could think ahead a little more carefully. I mean, you're not just making your personal life uncomfortable—and on Christmas Day—but you *work* with her too."

"I was aware of that, but thank you so much for reminding me. I didn't plan to fight with her! It just happened! OK?

That's how fights are! They just blow in out of nowhere some-times, like bad weather!"

We didn't speak again while I finished closing. Then I said, "Let's go."

Henry said, "Drop me off at my place, would you? I have an interview tomorrow, and I need to get organized first."

"Sure," I said. "OK. Fine."

I drove him home. We didn't talk on the way. When we pulled up in front of his building, Henry said, "Thanks. See you." He kissed me on the cheek, got his suitcase off the backseat, slammed the car door, and went inside.

The next day, I was supposed to be working with Eve. We would have a chance to talk, I thought, get over our fight. She was late, not that I needed help with the customers. The store was slower than ever, an after-Christmas slump that nearly brought business to a standstill. Just as I was about to call her, John walked in with a plate of foil-wrapped cookies. "Eve's sick," he said. "Stomach flu, something she ate, I don't know. She threw up all night."

"Oh no," I said. "Is she all right now?"

"Sleeping," he said. "I left her some ginger ale and came in to work with you myself."

I tried not to look startled; I tried to take it in stride. I said, "I'm all right. You don't have to stay. There's no business anyway."

"I want to. Have a cookie." He held the plate out to me.

"No, thank you," I said. John looked hurt. "I'm trying to behave since Christmas." He nodded.

Bridget came in with her two kids. She flopped a thick stack of paper on the counter. "Happy New Year," she said wearily. "I need one copy, and see all this stuff in red pencil here and this in blue? That all has to be legible. It's really tricky to get, I know. You remember, we've done this before?"

"Yes," I said. "We have to use a pretty dark setting."

Bridget said, "I don't care if there's gray on the parts that are supposed to be white. This is just going to be my backup copy."

"OK," I said. "I remember."

In a lowered voice, John said, "Can the kids have a cookie?"

"Thanks," Bridget said, smiling at him. "Yes, they may. Kids, you get cookies!"

"Yay!" the two girls said at once. John leaned over the counter with the plate, letting them choose. Bridget took one too.

I set the machine to a dark setting, copied a page with red pencil on it, showed it to Bridget. "Good," she said to me. "Fine." She held up her cookie. "Did you make these?"

"Are you kidding?" I said. "The most I ever do these days is microwave leftover take-outs." I pointed to John. "He's the baker. My brother-in-law, John. Eve's sick, so he came in to help me today. John, this is Bridget. That's Hannah there with the three ponytails and Rachel taking her shoes off."

"Rachel, no," Bridget said, turning around. "Leave them on. Stop. We're going. I'll be back for that, Mimi. Nice to meet you, John."

"My pleasure," John said with that smile of his, and Bridget blushed.

I started the copies. After I finished Bridget's stuff, I showed John how to use all the machines, including the quirks of paper placement and warming up. I let him take the next few customers while I dusted the counters and put away supplies. He was polite and listened carefully to what they wanted. When he had a problem, he asked me, instead of winging it. Soon, he had things pretty well under control. If he had been looking for part-time work, and if we had had enough business, I would have been happy to hire him, except that I still didn't trust him enough to leave him alone in the store. Every time I heard the cash drawer open, I found myself glancing nervously in his direction, watching his hands with the money.

When I saw Bridget pull into the parking lot, I was waiting on a customer. I said to John, "I want to take this out to Bridget so she won't have to get the kids out of the car again."

I meant for him to take my customer for me, but he grabbed the bag from a shelf under the counter. "What kind of car?"

"Blue station wagon over there."

"Got it," he said and ran out the door with her bag.

As I was making change, I watched him leaning down, smiling into the car window. Bill would not have done that. Eve would, and I would. It took a certain personality.

"She's nice," he said when he came back. "She seemed so grateful."

Later John helped a teacher who had two big boxes to pick up, and he did the same for her, trotting out to the parking lot with the stuff, putting it in her trunk.

Late in the morning, Richard called. "Would you do me a huge favor?" he said.

"I don't know," I said. "What's broken?"

"Nothing. I just want you to go shopping with me."

"Shopping?" I said. "Richard. Please, ask me to do something else, unclog your garbage disposal or something. You know I can't stand shopping. Aren't you dating someone you could ask?"

"I was for about five minutes. She was a great shopper too. Good idea. One small problem, though. She's in love with someone else now."

"Sorry."

"Hey, it's not like it's the first time this has happened to me."

"I don't want to go, Richard."

"But this is important. The principal of my school is getting married again. You met him. Anyway, I'm the best man. I don't have anything dressy to wear. I hate shopping too," he said. "That's why I called you. We make such a good team. We'll be done really fast."

I thought about it a minute. I said, "Next month we will have been divorced eight years." I meant that by now he should have stopped asking me to do things for him.

"Wow," he said. "Eight years. Seems like only yesterday. So you'll do it, right?"

"Listen," I told him, "I'll go with you, but we're only going to one store and you have to make up your mind quickly. I'll give you one hour, eight to nine."

"I'll take it," he said.

I didn't know why I said I would go, except that I didn't want to argue and two more customers had just walked into the store. The truth was, I didn't need to go with him. I could have told him over the phone everything I knew about men's clothes: navy blazer, gray flannel pants, blue shirt, some kind of tie. Then if he had to go to another wedding or attend a funeral, he would be all set. If he needed more help than that, he had asked the wrong person.

The day went by slowly. Two men came in a truck to take away one of our self-service copiers. With business as bad as it was, it didn't make sense to lease a copier we hardly used. After they were gone, the front half of the store looked open and unfinished, as if we had just moved in.

John called Eve a few times and went home to see her at lunchtime. Henry didn't call. Maybe this was because he was interviewing all day or maybe he was still mad at me.

Ron from UPS came in. "Good afternoon," he said. "And how is the world treating Mimi today?"

I handed over the packages to him, thinking about the fight I had with Henry. With the thought of what it would be like to lose him, panic came over me like a fever. I said, "Fine, thanks, Ron."

Ron said, "That's what we like to hear," and wheeled the dolly, loaded with boxes, to his truck.

At the end of the day, I took the money out of the register. We had not done a lot of business, so there wasn't much there. Despite the small amount of cash, I sent John to the front to pull the gates down while I opened the safe.

After our father's disappearance, I made sure its effect on me was permanent. Even when I was still little, I taught myself to be watchful, an expert detector of liars. I could always tell from the way people spoke—the pauses they took, the speed of their words—whether they were telling the truth. I was always the first to know when someone was going to turn out to be a traitor. This was the combined blessing and curse my father left me with: the ability to see a deception coming from far off in the distance and the inability to convince other people of what I saw. Eve didn't have this; she was probably too young when our father left us for the experience to instruct her the way it had me. While I was protected from deception, I could never warn Eve away from someone I knew was going to hurt her.

I dropped the money into the dark hole in the floor, put the cover back on, closed it up, and covered it over with carpet. The parking lot was practically empty when John and I said good night out on the sidewalk and went to our cars.

I was emptying cartons of Chinese food into dishes at my house that night. My mother was having dinner with the kids and me before I went shopping with Richard. "So," she said, smiling, "you and John got along."

"Well," I said, "nothing's changed between us, but it's not as if we're going to fight and bicker all day in the store, in front of customers. I mean, what would be the point?"

"Good," said my mother. "I'm glad you've put your differences aside. That's what I like to hear."

"I didn't say that. I—"

My mother didn't let me explain it again. "What does everyone want to drink?"

"The usual. Milk for us, water for Mom," Melanie said. "John's nice, Grandma. But Mom is never going to admit it."

"And he gives good presents," I said.

"Oh, thanks, Mom," Melanie said. "And I'm just this shallow person who only cares about what I get. Thanks for thinking so much of me. You know why his presents are so good? It's not just that they cost a lot, but because he thinks about what a person really wants. But the presents are not the only reason I like him. He's nice. Henry's nice too, Mom. I'm not saying I like him better than Henry or anything. They're both nice."

"*Nice*," I said. "I never said he wasn't nice. Ted Bundy was probably nice. Nice is not the issue."

My mother gasped. "Ted Bundy!" she said. "Honestly, Mimi—"

"What do you mean? Nice is everything," Melanie said, interrupting. "What else is there? What do you want?"

"Honesty, straightforwardness, openness," I said. "Little things like that that seem to be important only to me."

"Oh, Mom," Daniel said. "That's what 'nice' means. Besides, he makes really good cookies. Did you ever taste the ones with the powdered sugar on them? And the little chocolate sprinkles. Mmm. I love those."

"Mom has never tasted John's cookies," Melanie said. "She's afraid they might be great, and then she would have to admit that John did something right."

"Mimi—" said my mother, taking a deep breath for a big lecture.

"Grandma, forget it," Melanie said. "Don't even try. You can't reach her when she gets like this."

"Now you listen to me, young lady," I said.

" 'Young lady,' " Melanie sneered. "That's what Mrs. Kornman used to call us in second grade when we did something wrong." She narrowed her eyes. "And don't you dare ask me what I did wrong in second grade. Sometimes you need to just back off. You know that, Mom?"

No one spoke for a minute. Then Daniel said, "Who was Ted Bundy, anyway? Oh, I know. A vice president, right?" He smiled at us.

My mother let out a little exclamation, then clicked her tongue in shock and disapproval.

"Just kidding, Grandma," Daniel said, laughing. "Just wanted to make sure you were paying attention."

What was I thinking, bringing up the name of a serial killer in front of Melanie and Daniel? We ate our dinner with very little conversation. I had the feeling they were all waiting for me to go out. I took my plate to the sink and said, "Listen, I have to go, or I'm going to be late. I'll be back in about an hour. Homework's done?" No answer. "Do it, then. And don't forget baths, and get out your clothes for tomorrow so we don't have to rush in the morning."

"Yeah, yeah, yeah," said Daniel.

Melanie just glared.

"I have my pager, if you need me," I said. I didn't explain where I was going, why, or with whom; they were all so mad at me that no one wanted to know.

I picked up Richard at his place. I didn't even have to get out of the car. He was waiting for me. It was raining a little, and he ran down the front walk and got into the car.

"Hi," I said. "Where are we going?"

"Nordstrom?" he said.

"Fine," I said. "Whatever you want."

Richard said, "So what did you want to talk to me about?"

"I didn't say I wanted to talk to you about anything."

"Come on. You agreed to come so easily. It took far less than the usual twenty minutes of whining to get you to do this with me. What is it? Soccer again? Money? I could lend you some until things pick up at the store."

I shook my head. "No, it's not soccer or money."

"So what is it?" he said. "You wanted to talk to me about something."

I shook my head. "Nothing."

"The schoolwork's OK?" I nodded. "Nobody's having nightmares or eating problems or giving in to peer pressure?"

"Not that I know of. I just, you know—"

"I do know! Now I do." He snapped his fingers. "You and Henry broke up! I knew it! Well, listen, he was *much* too young for you, and an ambitious climber. He was a little weasel. He gave me the creeps the first time I saw him."

"A climber? A weasel? Henry? Come on. He's the best person I've met in ages. And we're not breaking up. That's really unfair." We were near the mall. I said, "This was a mistake. Richard, you make me so mad. Here I am doing you a favor, and you say mean things about someone I'm seeing. If you don't like him, just keep it to yourself. I didn't ask for your opinion of Henry. Where are your manners?"

"Sorry," he said. But he was looking out the window at the rain, just waiting for me to stop being mad so that we could get on with the shopping.

I pulled into a parking space near the store. I turned off the car and yanked up the parking brake. Then I just sat there and didn't make a move to get out.

A minute went by. Richard said, "All right. I shouldn't

have said that. I'll keep my feelings about your lovers to myself from now on."

"Lover!" I said. "I only have one!"

"I'll try to do better," he said quietly, as if he meant it. "I promise."

"OK," I said. "That's more like it. Thank you." I rested my head on the steering wheel and closed my eyes.

Richard said, "Mimi? You OK? What's wrong? We don't have to do this. Are you tired?"

"No," I said. "Do you think it's true that whatever you're most afraid of will happen to you?"

"What?" he said.

"John told me that."

"There's something in the Bible about that. He probably got it from a workshop or something. You know how people use a key phrase or two to support their own interpretation of whatever is happening to them." Softly, Richard said, "Is there something you're worried about? Something you're afraid of?"

"I don't know. Do you?"

Richard thought. "Do I know what you're afraid of? Let's see." He patted my back, rubbed it for a minute. It felt good. I didn't want to open my eyes. "You're afraid of charmers like your dad."

I straightened up and opened my door. "Now that we're here," I said, "let's get this over with."

"Was I right?" he said. "I've known you a long time, Mimi. Did I hit it?"

"Everybody knows that much about me," I said. "Someone who has known me for fifteen minutes could have come up with that one. Can we just do this shopping?"

Richard came around to my side of the car, took my hand, squeezed it. "Yes, we can," he said.

Just as we got to the entrance to the store, I wiggled my hand free of his. "Menswear is over there," I said.

A saleswoman found us right away, and Richard told her what he was looking for. She started rounding up jackets and pants, while Richard and I picked out some shirts. Then Richard went in to try on the clothes. I sat on a chair and waited. He came out in a navy blue blazer, a blue shirt, and gray flannel pants. He raised his eyebrows at me as if to say—Well, what do you think?

Have I fully explained the reason I don't like oldies? Familiar songs can trigger vivid sense memories of events that happened a long time ago and the ghosts of feelings that have been dead for years: I hear "I Want Candy" by Bow Wow Wow and remember a deli where I worked making sandwiches, the smell of mayonnaise, and the joy and deep fear I felt when I found out I was pregnant. It's just a song, but it brings all that back. It's a trick of memory, a flashback to something that seems real.

Richard looked so good in those clothes that it was like listening to an oldies station and singing along. All of a sudden, I thought of the way he looked going to his first school job when we were just married. I thought, *I have known Richard forever.* And standing right here in front of me was the problem with keeping in touch with my ex-husband: I couldn't forget anything that had happened. I knew him when he wore bell bottoms and tried clove cigarettes. And from the distance of many years, some of it, even the bad parts, the misery and despair, could seem tolerable.

"So?" he said now, prompting me to say something.

"Good," I said. "That's it."

If I weren't careful in situations like this, old details still hanging around in my brain might cause me to have the thought that being married to Richard could have worked, if we had done things a little differently, eliminated some distractions, not given in to certain impulses. Just because he looked nice dressed up, I might think, *What was so wrong, really, all those years ago?* I might overlook the fact that he had left me and the children to go out and sleep with someone else a few times and he was immature then and we argued a lot. Other than that, we had loved each other—I mean, a lot of the time. Nostalgia, that was all this was, a distorted view, like a television show about the fifties with a sound track that could make greasy hair and ankle socks look cute.

I said, "The clothes look fine." I stood up to go.

"Really?" he said. "I don't know. It couldn't be that easy." He looked uncertainly at the saleswoman. "What do you think?"

"Perfect," she said. "We'll hem the pants for you, and you'll be all set. That is, if you're happy. I know your wife is, but you have to be satisfied too."

"*Wife?*" I said. "Are you kidding? I'm not his *wife*."

"Excuse me," she said, flustered. "I'm sorry. I thought—"

"Not to worry," Richard said kindly, touching her sleeve. "Sometimes I'm confused about it myself."

"He is not," I said. "Don't listen to him."

She said, "I'll get someone to pin those cuffs for you." I sat down again. I had forgotten about alterations. She picked up a phone at the sales counter.

"Thanks," Richard said, and sat down next to me to wait. "How's it going with Eve? Is she still mad at you from Christmas?"

"What's with all the questions?" I snapped. "I'll go find you a tie and some socks. Then you'll have everything."

"Well, not quite everything," Richard said. "I mean, what about personal satisfaction and spiritual fulfillment?"

The saleswoman laughed. "I like that," she said, smiling. "That was good." For a second, their eyes met. I pretended to be interested in some belts. "It'll be just a few minutes on the cuffs," she said, and vanished.

After the cuffs were pinned and the other clothes paid for

and in a bag, we walked to the car. Richard said, "That sales-woman gave me her card. Look." He showed it to me. "She wrote her home number on the back."

"Call her," I said.

He looked at the card again. "Beth," he said. "She was pretty. How old do you think she was?"

"Thirty-four," I said.

"Do you think she gives her card out to men all day long?"

I checked myself all over for jealousy: nothing there. "No," I said. "She didn't seem to me like that kind of person. I think she really liked you. She liked the way you looked in those clothes, and she thought your joke was funny."

"I think I'll call her." He put the card carefully into his wallet.

I unlocked the car and drove him home.

Henry was waiting for me, sitting on the couch with my mother, watching a PBS program about neurons and memory. "Where were you?" Henry said, standing up as I walked in. "Are you still mad at me?"

"Shopping," I said. "Are you?"

My mother hurried to gather her things together. She didn't want to hear this. "Melanie's still working on her math," she said. "Daniel went to bed a few minutes ago. No one called. I love you. Bye, bye." She was in a rush to leave before we said anything unpleasant to each other. She gave me a quick hug, picked up her purse and the pile of papers she had been grading, and got out the door as fast as she could.

"Thanks, Mom," I said. I looked at Henry. "How was it?"

He groaned. "First I talked to five different people. It took all morning. I ate lunch with two of them. I talked to three more people. My face started aching from all the smiling. Then the last two guys took me out to dinner. When we were having coffee, one of them told me he thinks they're going to hire someone internally."

I put my arms around him.

"Stupid job," he said. He kissed my neck. "I'm sorry, I'm sorry, I'm sorry," he said into my hair.

"Forget it," I said, and laughed. "Hey, you're tickling me. It was just an argument. You were worried about not having a job. And a lot of the things you said were right." He kissed me.

A wave of relief crashed over me and got mixed up with arousal and longing. His hands were touching my breasts through my T-shirt and bra. The word "Wait" came to my lips like a bubble about to pop.

"Mom?" Melanie was in the doorway. "Hi, Henry. Nice suit. Did you get the job?"

"Hello, Melanie. Thank you," Henry said. "They don't tell you right away. It takes awhile before they let you know for sure. But I don't think so."

"That's too bad," Melanie said. "I'm going to bed now. Mom, could you wake me up early tomorrow? I have a test and I need to study more."

"Five?"

Melanie nodded.

"OK. Night, honey."

"Night."

She hesitated, then stepped forward to touch Henry's lapel. "Nice. What is that?"

Henry looked down at his clothes. "I don't know. It's— must be—some kind of cloth?"

Melanie laughed, and she went to her room.

When she was gone, Henry put his hand over his heart. "God," he whispered. "I'm still not used to having kids around. It's as bad as having your parents walk in on you."

"Worse," I said. "You're not mad at me anymore?"

"I take full responsibility," he said, looking me squarely in the eye. "I was wrong, and I'm sorry. Delete from memory."

"OK," I said. "It's gone."

That was easy, I thought. Was that it? No residual resentments, no leftover hurt feelings that would resurface later on? I was going to ask him something more, but then he was kissing me, a hand under my shirt lightly touching my spine, and I stopped thinking about it, forgot about everything completely.

CHAPTER *13*

Emergency

I was lying in bed, worrying, while Henry breathed softly and rhythmically beside me. Now I didn't have to worry about Henry; we were fine again. It was the store that was keeping me awake. I needed a big idea that would change everything. I reviewed all the strategies that hadn't worked out: coupons, advertising, late hours. Going over these ideas again now seemed to make the inside of my head ache. I had to hit on something big, something unique, that only I would have. I couldn't think of anything.

I turned over onto my other side. I flipped my pillow. My hair kept getting in my face and bothering me. I twisted it into a tight knot and lay down on it. That felt too lumpy. I sat up. I was trying to wake Henry to get him talk to me about the store one more time. But he slept on. I lay down on my back again. Maybe he was right, and I was going to have to give up and try something else. I would have to go to school, learn how to do something completely different. I pictured myself in a classroom full of people twenty years younger than I was, a notebook open in front of me. A few big tears rolled down into my hair. I wiped my eyes on the sleeve of my pajamas. *No,* I thought, no, no, *no.*

I woke from a sound sleep. I thought I heard something, but maybe I dreamed it. Then I heard it again: a loud knock on the door. I jumped out of bed and rushed to the door, my heart thumping hard. I was thinking, My mother! Eve! Something has happened to one of them, and an official has come to inform me. Then I thought, The store's on fire! Maybe someone has had an accident and needs help right away! Images of blood, broken glass, crimson flames licking at scorched metal filled my head.

I flung the door open. There was John, smiling sheepishly. "Sorry," he said. "You were sleeping. I guess you go to bed earlier than we do."

"What time is it?" I said.

"Ten-thirty," he told me. "I thought you'd still be up."

"What happened?" I said, and cleared my throat.

"I made these great cookies," John said, pointing at a plate of cookies he was holding. "I wanted you to try one."

"Cookies?" I said. "You made more cookies." My heart was still pounding hard. I looked at him for a second, trying to take in the fact that nothing was wrong. "Come in," I said.

Henry was there, putting on the bathrobe I never wore. "What happened?" he asked. "Hi, John."

"I made these cookies," John said. "I wanted you guys to try them. You know cooking is a performance art. I needed an audience. I couldn't wait until tomorrow. I think these are the best I've ever made."

"Cookies?" Henry said. "What time is it?"

I was too sleepy and confused to argue. I took a cookie and bit it. It had pieces of chocolate and something crunchy and sweet that I couldn't identify. I took another bite.

John said, "Henry, you have to try one too."

Henry raised a single eyebrow without replying.

I took another bite.

"No, really," he said to Henry. "Try one. Please."

Reluctantly, Henry reached for a cookie. "I don't even eat cookies," he said, choosing the smallest one. He sat down on the couch and took a bite. Daniel appeared in the doorway.

"Have a cookie," John said. "Sorry to wake you up."

Daniel said, "What are you guys doing? What time is it? Henry, that's a girl's bathrobe. And this is a school night." He rubbed his eyes.

I took another cookie.

"Daniel, try one of these," John said.

"Cookies?" Daniel said, incredulous. "It's the *middle of the night!*"

John said, "I couldn't wait for you guys to taste these. I just made them."

Daniel took a cookie and sat down next to Henry. The two of them chewed. "Wow," Daniel said, gobbling the cookie. "Mom, can I have another one?" He took another, ate it in two bites.

Henry reached for another. "I don't usually like cookies," he said. "But these are very good."

Melanie was up. She squinted against the bright light of the living room. "I have a test tomorrow," she complained. "What is this? Why is everyone up so late, eating? What are you having?"

"Cookies," we all said.

"Can I have one?" Melanie took a cookie and sat beside Daniel. "Mmm," she said. "Whoa, John. You didn't really make these with your bare hands, did you? These are so good they should be illegal!"

Where did she get these things she said? Television? School?

She said, "Oh, my god. Give me another one of those. No

wonder you woke everybody up. This was an emergency. These are seriously awesome."

Henry said, "These are the best cookies I've ever tasted."

"Me too," Daniel said. "And I've eaten a lot of cookies."

"No kidding, these are great," Melanie said.

Everyone seemed to stopped chewing at once and look at me.

I thought a minute, choosing my words carefully. "The texture is just right, kind of chewy, but not too soft. Then when you hit—I don't know what these little things are, these little crystallized brown things—the contrasting crunch is very satisfying. The chocolate has a kind of melted quality about it. And they're not too sweet. I like that. Yes," I said to everyone. "These are the best cookies I've ever tasted."

"In your whole life?" Henry said.

"In my whole life," I said.

John smiled broadly, then looked at the floor.

Melanie clapped. "Yay, Mom."

"Possibly the best cookies in the world," I went on. "I mean, frankly I'm amazed that anything could taste this good. Excellent." I shook my head. "No. Superb."

"Yay, John," Daniel said, smiling.

"Really good," Henry said.

We had cleaned the plate, eaten up every cookie he had. John was beaming. "I thought you'd like them," he said quietly. "Well. Guess I'll go."

"Thanks for bringing the cookies over," Daniel said.

We all said good-bye and he was gone.

I couldn't get back to sleep. The problem now might have been the chocolate and sugar late at night. At first the cookies had cheered me up, the way they tasted so good and everyone agreed about them. Now I was back to thinking about the store, and the long, slow days we had been having, wondering where I was going to get the money for the rent and all the other things I needed. If I didn't do something drastic soon, our finances would be a disaster. It would be my fault.

I thought about Henry and Richard and my children and my mother and Eve and John—freestyle worrying that went on and on—until it was after two in the morning. Finally I was so worn out by my own dark thoughts that I started to fall asleep.

As soon as I relaxed, the beginning of a dream starting up somewhere in my head, I thought of something. I had to sit straight up in bed. I had an idea: the cookies. Henry stirred beside me. We could sell John's cookies in the store where the other self-service copier used to be. We wouldn't need much space, about as much as one of those espresso carts they had at a lot of the gas stations and parking lots lately. And coffee. John made such great coffee; everyone said so. We could feature his great coffee and cookies. I kept thinking. Was there anything else I could throw in? Something no one else had? I thought of our customers, of Frances the designer in a hurry all the time, of Bridget and her two kids, struggling to get everybody in and out of the car with all she had to carry. What about a drive-through window? Was that possible? If we had a drive-through window, it would be a whole different store. We could have coffee, cookies, and office services, all with drive-through convenience. You wouldn't even have to get out of your car. Or you could come in and use the store the regular way and also get a cup of excellent coffee and the cookie of your life. Maybe I had room for chairs and a kind of work table where people could put together their packages and drink a cup of coffee.

I didn't go back to sleep. I got out of bed and went to the kitchen and drew a picture of what I wanted the store to look like with all the improvements. At five, I woke Melanie. She sat across from me and studied for her test, while I copied over my drawing.

"You're going to sell cookies in an office store?" Melanie said.

"Yeah," I said. "If John is willing to do it. You know, working in an office is kind of social. People drink coffee together, eat, chat, just hang out. That's probably the best thing about it. But a lot of our customers do their jobs by themselves at home or in a small office all alone."

Melanie looked in her textbook and wrote something on a sheet of notebook paper. "They're lonely," she said without looking up.

"That's it. We give them a lot of what they don't have in their offices, the technical stuff they don't have. But you know what's missing? The cozy stuff—the office birthday parties, the treats, procrastinating with your pals before you start on a big project, hearing people's stories, complaining."

Melanie drew a horizontal line across her paper and divided it with four vertical lines. She labeled the divisions with tiny printed headings I couldn't read upside down. She tilted her head back and squinted, moving her lips, trying to remember what to write without looking in the book.

"Then you have the people who don't have time for all the social stuff," I went on. "They need streamlined service. That's where the drive-through window comes in."

Melanie opened her eyes. "Drive-through window?"

I showed her my diagram. "Luckily, the store is on a corner." I pointed to the paper. "You'll be able to drive up here, drop off your stuff—"

Melanie interrupted, "And get coffee and cookies to go!"

"Exactly. Then you come back and pick up your stuff at the same place. This could be big," I said, my mind racing. "Or it could be a complete disaster."

"Like everything, Mom."

"Right," I said.

Melanie closed her eyes again. "Our country would be nothing if it weren't for people with ideas," she said flatly.

"That's it," I said, trying to draw a table that wouldn't take up too much space.

"If you don't go for it . . ."—she paused to write—"you'll never know."

"Right," I said. It was getting light. I wondered if it was late enough to call John. It wasn't, but I called him anyway and woke him up. "Listen to this," I said. I told him my idea. "The way I picture it," I said, "you could make the cookies at home, then sell them in the store. The coffee would be no problem. You could grind your own and everything at one little counter."

There was a long pause. I waited, worrying about what he was thinking.

"Muffins," he said finally. "I want to do muffins in the morning too. Can I do muffins?"

"Fine," I said. "You got it."

"A bran and a blueberry to start, then we'll add a carrot later?"

"Yes. I like that," I said. I was smiling, holding the phone. Melanie looked up from the table at me and smiled. She was so pretty when she smiled like that, and it had been a long time. "Yeah," I said, winking at her. "Yeah, muffins."

Daniel was up, and I made breakfast. Melanie said, "Mom is going to let John sell cookies and coffee at the store to bring in more business."

Daniel looked at me. "True?"

"True," I said.

"Cool, Mom. That will bring in *millions* of people."

"I don't know about millions," I said. I showed him my drawing.

"Mom, this is going to be great!" he said. "This will be a real winner!"

By the time Henry got up, I had already left a message at the shopping center's management company to ask about the drive-through window.

"I have a great idea," I told Henry as soon as he came into the kitchen. "Listen to this. Finally, I got it. I don't know why I didn't think of this before. It's so obvious."

"What?" he said, smiling. "What is it? Tell me."

I told Henry my idea about John's cookies, the coffee, showed him the diagram and where I wanted to put the new window. "I've already talked to John, and he wants to do it. He wants to sell muffins, too."

Henry looked at my drawing. He took it out of my hand and studied it. "Cookies?" he said. "Muffins?"

"*And* a drive-through window!" Melanie said.

Henry said, "This could work. I don't know, though. There are a lot of places selling good coffee now."

"But not the office stores, and none of the other coffee places has John's cookies," I said. "It's not as if we have to spend a lot of money to get it going."

"Smart," he said, still holding the drawing. "You're offering a service and a product that aren't usually sold together. I like that. A little offbeat, but logical at the same time. Nice work. It's not big, but it's good. Is there any coffee?"

I pointed to the pot. I took the drawing back. "This *is* big," I said. I looked at the paper in my hand. "I think it could be big. You don't think so? I do."

Henry laughed and shook his head. "Cookies and muffins are not big. But I mean, it might work. And, as you say, you're not taking a huge risk with it."

When he took his coffee back to the bedroom, Melanie said, "Well, don't get too excited or anything." She rolled her eyes. "What was all that about? What does he mean, 'big'?"

I said, "Henry prefers to work on a larger scale. The fact that small can be huge doesn't interest him. Look at, I don't know, intermittent windshield wipers and Thermoses and Post-its. Those aren't Henry's kind of thing. Now to me, it's the small things that are holding the world together."

"Yeah," said Melanie, nodding.

"I see," said Daniel, tipping his head to one side, considering. "Nail clippers, key chains, refrigerator magnets."

"Mm-hm," I said. "I thought we could put dictionaries, zip code directories, and phone books on a shelf right here, a reference center." They looked to see where I was pointing.

"So people could look stuff up?" Daniel said.

"That's it," I said. "Like study hall for grown-ups."

"Mom," Daniel said. "Can I tell you something? You're going to be rich."

"Rich?" I said. "Silly, no one gets rich by making copies." I put my arms around him and squeezed him tight.

CHAPTER 14

Good Things,
Bad Things

Right away, I started working on the coffee counter with a showcase for John's cookies and muffins, and it was coming along faster than I expected. I was building it in the empty front part of the store, where it would stay, instead of at home where I could only get to it in the evenings and on weekends. I worked on it at night when the store was closed and during the day between customers. Getting permission for the drive-through window was progressing far more slowly. There was a lot of paperwork to do and phone calls to make. Almost every day, I had to explain what we wanted to do to someone else in the management company who was supposed to be the one to decide about the window. As soon as I stopped talking, the person on the phone always told me the number of someone else I should call.

While we were waiting for a decision on the window, John came in one afternoon with something torn out of the newspaper to show Eve.

"All right!" she said when she saw it. "We're going!" She

looked at me. "I mean, if it's OK with Mimi. I'm going to call right now and see if there's still space."

While she went to the phone, John showed the ad to me. It was for a three-day workshop, starting that Friday. "Hm," I said. "Abundance?"

John smiled at me. "Yeah," he said. "Abundance." He opened his arms expansively. "We've been waiting for this one."

Henry walked in then.

"Thank you," Eve said into the phone. "I'll call you right back." She hung up. "They still have room for us," she said to me, "and I want to go."

"Go where?" Henry said. "Mimi, could you make me some more copies of my résumé?"

"Sure," I said. "Eve and John want to go to a workshop." I said. "It starts Friday, and I'd have the store all by myself for two days." I took the résumé and showed Henry some paper. He nodded.

"But this could be good for all of us," Eve explained to Henry. "It's about abundance."

"Abundance?" Henry said, as if the word were new to him.

"Yes," Eve said. "It's called 'Embracing Abundance.' The idea is that any lack we experience—of love, money, trust, shelter, hope, food, ideas—"

"Justice," John added.

"Employment," Henry put in.

"Right," she said, "any lack is illusory. Everyone has equal access to everything he or she needs or wants at all times. By correctly aligning your thinking, your self-image, and images of your world, you can change your experience of lack to an experience of abundance." She looked at me, waiting to hear whether or not it was all right with me for her to take Friday and Saturday off.

"Go ahead," I said. "We're not busy enough for it to be a problem. Henry, want to work with me here this weekend?"

"Yeah," Henry said. "OK. It will be fun."

"See that?" Eve said. "Employment. Already the workshop is helping."

"No, no, no," I said, shaking my head. "This doesn't count. The store isn't Henry's *scale*. It has to be something *big*." I opened my arms, demonstrating.

"Mimi," Henry said, "you make it sound like—"

"I was kidding," I said. "I was just—"

Eve interrupted. "But seriously, this will help us all. It's the same woman who did the Valentine's Day workshop, where John and I met. Things happen with her." As she nodded, Eve's earrings, two little baby dolls, one in pink and one in blue, did an energetic dance.

Over the weekend, working with Henry, we didn't have many customers, so I was able to finish the counter and start on a table for the corner nearest the coffee counter. I already knew what kind of chairs I was going to buy to go with it. We listened to music all day and rewrote Henry's résumé, sanded the new counter, and took turns leaving the store for fresh air and food.

"Are you sure this is OK with you?" I said to him. "Working here?"

"Would you cut it out?" he said. "I like this. This is not bad at all." He looked at me sideways. "I mean, not forever or anything. I can't always—"

I put my hands on my hips and said, "Nobody's asking you to."

He held up his hand. "But for now, this is just fine. I like it. Small, but good."

Monday morning after the workshop, Eve sat on the stool by the cash register, a cardboard cup of coffee in her hand, talking about what she had learned. "The hard part is believing," she said, "trusting the universe with your dreams." She closed her eyes for a second, then opened them. "Once you've got that licked, you can have everything you need, everything you want. We did some really potent imagining this weekend. You don't know how powerful that is, a room full of people envisioning abundance. It was really strong." I noticed she had new earrings, the word *YES* in tiny gold letters against her right ear lobe. I leaned to see the other ear, to find out if it was different. *YES* was there too.

"Cute earrings," I said. "Very positive."

"That's the idea," she said, and winked at me.

The phone rang, and I answered. Maybe it was a coincidence, but the mnagement company was ready at that moment to say we could have our window. I hung up the phone. "Eve," I said. "We got it. They said *yes* to the window!"

"See?" Eve said. *"See?"* We jumped up and down, clapped for ourselves, and laughed. We put on Annie Lennox and danced around the store. There was no one there; it didn't matter what we did.

The next day, I hired a contractor to install the drive-through window. The store was noisy with all the drilling and pounding, but it only went on for two days. We didn't even have to close. John bought an espresso machine, and I helped him set it up. We made up coupons for a free coffee with every ten-dollar purchase from Wrap It Up. When everything was finished, we hung a "Grand Opening" banner across the front window, and the new store was ready for business.

"Outstanding!" Bridget said the first day she saw all the changes. "It looks like a McDonald's where they have poetry readings. Or an office with a party going on all the time. Drive-through! You guys were thinking of me when you put this in, weren't you?"

"Of course we were," I said.

"It will change my life," she said, laughing, and for a second I thought she was going to cry.

John said, "Is it OK to give Hannah and Rachel cookies?"

"Fine," she said. "Thanks." Then she put her hand over her mouth. "He remembers their names."

"He's amazing," I said. "A man of many talents."

"I'll say," said Bridget. "OK, I need two copies of this, and I'll pick them up at the drive-through window."

John handed out cookies.

I said, "I can do those for you right now, if you want to wait five minutes."

"No, no," she said. "Don't do it yet. I want to drive through." She took a bite of her cookie. "My god," she said to John. "You've really got talent."

John came around his counter, took her hand in both of his, and kissed it. He said, "Thank you." Bridget looked embarrassed and pleased.

"Oh brother," Henry said under his breath, and Eve glared at him.

For the most part, Eve and I were getting along better. Having John in the business with us had changed everything. There was still a little scratchy space between us filled with sparks and static. But we were much better now that we all shared the same goal: making our store work.

By sheer luck, someone from a newspaper that did fluff pieces on local businesses came in to make some copies the first day the drive-thrugh window was open. She noticed the new window and tried one of the cookies. The paper sent a photographer to take a picture of me, Eve, John, and Henry, and ran a story about the new Wrap It Up. Partly due to the article about the new things we offered, our business picked up right away. The drive-through window was a success, and so was the Wrap It Up Café.

Soon we got a couple of big accounts. A woman from an adult education center came in for copies and stayed two hours in the café, rewriting something she was working on at our new table. "I just had to get away from my phone," she said. The next day she came in to set up a contract with us for copying materials for classes.

Part of our increased business was luck. A software company moved into the empty offices across the street and hired us to do ID badges for all its employees. We had a special Polaroid camera for this, but until now had hardly ever used it. This company would also need a lot of copying, of course, and we were closest.

Almost everybody who came in bought coffee or cookies or both. Some people came in just for the café and didn't want any office services at all. Eve and John believed it was the abundance workshop that had brought about these changes. Within the first month, I could pay off a couple of bills I had been postponing for ages and also pay our new, higher rent.

Richard came in one day with a cardboard box full of work from his school. He said, "My principal wants to set up an account with you guys."

"Great," I said. "Thanks."

Richard went over to the new window. "You know," he said. "This is a very good idea." He looked at me. "Yours, right? I can tell."

Eve said, "Yes. The café was her idea too, but John's in charge of the food and coffee."

"It looks really good," Richard said before he left. "I'll pick that stuff up tomorrow at lunch."

"It will be ready," I said.

John ran the café, Eve and I did most of the office services, and Henry stepped in wherever he was needed. We got so busy all the time that we had to hire two more people. First, I hired another mother I knew from Melanie and Daniel's school, Laurie, to work behind the counter weekday mornings and early afternoons. Then I hired a college student named Jake to work afternoons and Saturday mornings. With two more people, I could work in the office sometimes without worrying about what was going on behind the counter. Laurie quickly got to know the regular customers, remembering the way they liked work done and chatting with them when they came in. She treated them as if they were old friends. "I bet you didn't have breakfast, did you, Frances?" she would say. "Sit down while I do this for you and have a cup of coffee. Those muffins of John's are almost too good to be true."

Jake made no small talk at all, and he moved quickly through whatever task we gave him, so we usually put him on drive-through. Even Melanie and Daniel helped out in the store after school sometimes or did their homework there.

With all we had to do, there wasn't enough time to pay attention to everything. While the store thrived, other things became neglected. Laundry and housework were our worst areas. When we finally found time to wash our clothes, they stayed unfolded in the garage—in the dryer or spilling out of several baskets—for five days or so, until everything was dirty again. We didn't have time for housework, either. Lolling under our couch and in the corners of the house were dust balls growing to the size of coyote pups. We didn't have time to shop or cook either, so we lived on take-outs and John's muffins and cookies.

One night, Henry and I, John and Eve, and Melanie and Daniel went out to dinner. We said it was to celebrate the success of the new Wrap It Up, but it was also because there was no food at any of our houses.

"So," Henry said quietly to me when the others were talking about soccer. "You're a success."

"So are you," I said. "We all did it together."

"No, we didn't," he said. "You did it. It's your place. I just followed orders." Henry raised his glass. "To Mimi and her big ideas!"

Everyone raised a glass and sipped. I paid the check.

Then John took us to an ice cream place his friend had just opened and we all stuffed ourselves on ice cream buried in gooey sauces and whipped cream. Because the owner was a friend of John's, everything was free.

Eve and I were closing. John and Henry had already left. I was counting money to put into the safe, and she was pulling down the gates.

"We're short," I told her when I calculated the total.

"How much?" she said.

"Thirty-two dollars," I said.

"Again?" she said.

"What do you mean, 'again'?" I asked.

"The last two nights we've been short. Night before last it was twenty-two dollars, last night it was thirty-six."

I said, "I guess you told me that. What's going on here?"

"I don't know," Eve said. "Mistakes? Most of our help is not used to making change. Do you think we should watch everyone's transactions now?"

"I guess we'll have to."

"Or one of us could work the cash register all the time."

"I think that would really slow everybody down," I said.

"On the other hand, we have to keep this in perspective: The store is making more money than it ever has. We all have enough, so we shouldn't get too worried about a little loss here and there."

"True," I said. "But we can't have our employees stealing from us, either."

We didn't speak for a minute. I thought Eve was going to say I better not be thinking it was John taking the money. And I would answer that of course I wasn't thinking any such thing. It might not be theft at all, I would add quickly, just a lot of little mistakes adding up. But she didn't say anything about John. Instead, she just sighed and said, "I'm going home. See you tomorrow."

After that night, I tried to carefully observe what was going on with the money. For several days, the amounts were so small that it wasn't clear whether the loss was due to error or theft. When we came out even for a week or so, Eve and I almost dismissed the problem altogether.

Then there was one day when I counted the money and found I couldn't overlook the problem anymore. I said to Eve, "We're a hundred dollars short."

"What do you want to do?"

I said, "I haven't seen anyone making wrong change or pocketing money. Have you seen anything?"

Eve said, "No."

"I can't bring myself to fire either Jake or Laurie. I don't suspect either one of them more than the other. I'm not even sure if it's one person doing it. It's actually my fault. I've been too slack, letting my focus go soft somewhere, or this would not have happened."

Eve said, "There's a lot more going on in the store now, too much to keep track of everything. How much do you think is missing total?"

"I went back over all the cash-outs since we opened the new store. I think about two thousand dollars," I said.

"What do you think we should do?"

I said, "We'll get everybody together and talk about it. That way, if there is a thief, at least he'll know we're aware of what's going on."

"Or she."

"Right."

I got everybody together one evening after closing. I didn't tell them what I was going to talk about. We all sat down near the coffee counter. Eve, John, Henry, Laurie, and Jake all looked at me, waiting.

I said, "We have a problem. Our cash doesn't match the amount that the register says we're taking in. We're short almost every day. Does anybody know why that might be?"

John looked me straight in the face without blinking. Laurie and Jake looked at each other. Henry looked at Eve.

Laurie was the first to speak. She said, "Short by how much?"

"Twenty, forty, up to a hundred dollars," I said. "Small amounts almost every day that are adding up to a significant total. I wanted you all to be aware of this. I'm not blaming any one person. Eve and I both know it's easy enough to end up short now and then. But please be very careful about taking in the right amounts and making change. Eve and I will be double-checking everything we do too."

There was a knock on the door late at night. I thought, I don't want to taste cookies now; I will if I have to, but I don't want to. I opened the door. Eve was standing there in her nightgown, tears streaking her face. She grabbed at me. "They're arresting John! He's being charged as a suspect in the restaurant case. The police are coming now, to get him, to pick him up and take him to jail!"

I said, "Let me tell Henry and get my keys."

I ran to the bedroom and shook Henry awake. "John's being arrested. I have to go with Eve." I picked up my jeans from the floor beside the bed, put them on.

Henry stood up, followed me to the front door. He hugged Eve for a second, kissed me. "I'll be here until you get back," he said. "I can make Melanie and Daniel's breakfast if this takes a long time, get them to school. Don't worry."

I drove us to Eve's in my car. She was crying too hard to

drive her car back. "They're taking him to jail," she kept saying. "He has to go to *jail*, Mimi!"

When we pulled into her street, we saw five police cars parked at various wrong angles, blocking traffic or John's getaway, I wasn't sure which. Lights whirled around, went on and off. Neighbors came out on their front steps to see what was going on. John came out of the house in jeans and a white T-shirt, his hands cuffed behind his back. He didn't see us, didn't look up, but walked with his head down to a waiting cruiser, ducked getting in. He looked small sitting in the back of the car, not like a full-grown man at all, not even like himself. He was like a boy separated by accident from the people who cared about him, who would make sure that he came to no harm.

We drove back to my house and stayed up all night. We sat in the living room, while Henry and the children slept. Eve talked to the lawyer a couple of times about bail and what was going to happen next. At six-thirty, Henry got up. "You're here," he said. "What happened?"

"John's in jail!" Eve said, and started crying all over again.

"Anything I can do?" Henry said to me.

"No," I said. "Thanks. You have an interview in L.A. today."

"Yeah," he said, and stood there a moment longer. "You want me to cancel it?"

Eve sat there, holding a Kleenex to her nose, not moving. I shook my head. "You go. We'll manage."

He went to the bedroom to get dressed.

I drove Melanie and Daniel to school. On the way, I explained what had happened during the night.

"John's in jail?" Melanie said. "In *jail*?"

Daniel said, "Mom, did he do it? Did he take the money?"

We had almost reached the drop-off zone in front of the school, but I pulled over before I got there, stopped the car. I looked back at Daniel. I said, "No, he did not take the money."

Neither of them said anything. Then Melanie said, "How do you know? No one really knows, except the person who's guilty."

"I don't believe that John is guilty," I said. "For a long time, I did. I thought the worst of him. But now I realize it was something else that made me dislike him, something that really isn't his fault. You know how you can just like somebody right away and want to be friends? It was the opposite with John and me. He reminded me of somebody I knew a long time ago." I looked out the window at two kids chasing a ball across the playground. "So I just assumed he was going to be like that other person."

"Don't tell me," Melanie said. "Your dad who disappeared with the hospital money."

"Who told you that story?" I said too sharply.

"Grandma," Daniel said quietly.

"She told us the whole thing a long time ago," Melanie said. "About how he lied about Aunt Eve's heart and everything. About how he took money from people and said it was going into a new hospital. What a creep. I feel sorry for you, having a dad like that."

I shook my head. "Eve and I loved our father. It was one of the saddest things that ever happened to us when our dad went away."

Some parents dread explaining to their children where babies come from. Some worry about discussing what happens after a person dies. Not me. I had already covered those topics with my children. For me, those talks weren't as difficult as most people thought. The conversation I had always dreaded was happening right now in my car.

I took a deep breath. I stopped. Melanie and Daniel waited for me to get my thoughts together. "He was funny," I said quietly, thinking how inadequate words were; somebody ought to come up with a better way to transmit ideas. I kept trying. "He used to make Aunt Eve and me laugh like crazy. And he always seemed to know what we were secretly wishing for and find a way to get it. Whenever he came to pick us for the weekend, he would run from his car to our front door because he couldn't wait to see us."

I stopped, remembering the way at the end of the weekend, before he turned us over to our mother again, he would squeeze the two of us tight, not wanting to let us go. Then he would say, "Don't forget about your old dad now. Don't forget me, girls." And we would laugh, thinking he was joking. Now for the first time I knew what he meant. He was asking us to remember the good things he had given us, the things about him that made us feel happy or safe or important, and not just where he had gone wrong, what he had taken away from us, the way he had hurt us forever.

I tried to think of something else that would convince Melanie and Daniel about my father, to win them over with my memory of him. "You know those paper dolls you can cut out of folded-up paper? He could make those. Not only the regular kind, but fancy ones—a string of little train cars all hooked together, things like that. He made us a pretend airplane once out of cardboard boxes. He made great pancakes, and I don't know—," I said. "I can't explain it. You're right, Melanie, he stole a lot of people's money and disappeared." I had to stop and breathe a moment. "But he was our dad, and we loved him."

Melanie shook her head. "I don't see how you could love someone who was that bad. He was a criminal, Mom."

I said, "You're right, he was. He did a bad thing, maybe

lots of bad things I don't even know about. But to us, he wasn't bad. He was mostly good. So for a while, John reminded me of my dad, and all I could think of were all those bad things and the way it hurt Aunt Eve and me when we found out he was gone. Since I was a little girl I have worked hard to forget the things I liked about him. It was a hard job because there were so many. I thought John took that money from the restaurant he worked in, the way my dad took money that didn't belong to him. But I was wrong about John. Now I believe him when he says he didn't do it. And I was wrong to try to forget all those good things about my dad too."

The bell rang, and all the kids on the playground started running to get to their classrooms. "John is telling the truth when he says he didn't steal the money from the restaurant," I said again.

Melanie and Daniel sat there, looking at me. "Mom," Daniel said. "Are you going to get John out of jail?"

"Yes. Right away. Go on now, you're going to be late."

Melanie said, "And you know what will happen if we are?" She looked at me. "Nothing." She opened her door and started to slide out.

"Mom?" Daniel said, and Melanie waited to hear what he was going to say. "Don't you ever wonder where your dad is?"

"All the time," I said. "Every single day."

"Me too," Daniel said. "I wonder where he is too."

Melanie said, "If you loved him so much, why didn't you try to find him?"

I looked at her face. It was a simple enough question, there must be an an answer. "I didn't think he wanted to be found. And ever since he went away like that without telling us, I've been too mad at him to look."

Melanie said, "I would have looked for him. I would. If you really loved him, you should have looked for him."

The second bell rang, and they got out and ran to their classes, turning around briefly to wave at me.

Bailing John out was going to be expensive. We had to wait until the bank opened to do it. First, we opened the store and got it set up to run without us for several hours.

When Laurie came in, I said, "Eve and I will be gone for a couple of hours this morning. Do you think you could be in charge of office services until we get back?"

She said, "What about the café?"

"We'll keep it closed for now."

"OK," she said. "I think I can manage."

"Thank god the store is up and running again," I said to Eve, getting my purse and keys to go to the bank. "We just have to be grateful that we have the money." There was no question about using all the money we had just made in our run of good luck to bail John out. It seemed now that this was what the money had been for all along.

At the bank, an officer was required to clear out our entire account and to make out a special check for the bail. Both our signatures were needed on a withdrawal this large.

Henry came back just long enough to get ready to go to another interview, in New York this time. I went to his apartment. He collected his things for his suitcase, while I talked about John, about the things that had happened when Henry was in L.A. A movie was on in the living room, *The Graduate,* with the sound off. "I just hope his lawyer knows what he's doing," I said. "I just hope it gets resolved quickly. And the right way, of course." I stared at Dustin Hoffman, trying to explain something. "I just hope it doesn't drag on and on," I said. "I'm supposed to ask you, when you're in New York, would you get one of those little snowstorm-in-a-jar things for Daniel? You know, with the Empire State Building and the

Statue of Liberty inside? You shake it and snow falls? He had one once and dropped it. Mention New York, and that's all he can think of."

"Yeah," Henry said. "Sure. That should be easy enough. I'll get one for Melanie too, while I'm at it."

"They're both too old for that sort of thing, of course. But you know they'll love it."

"I'll see if I can find some surprises too," he said.

"You don't have to do that," I said. "Let's not go over-board."

"But I like to go overboard," he said. "I like to."

Then Henry sat down next to me on the couch for a min-ute and held on to me tight. I said, "Hey, what's the matter? Did something happen?"

He shook his head. "I don't like going," he said. "I just don't like leaving you."

"It's a couple of days," I said. "It's not like when you were gone at Christmas. Right?"

"I guess," he said.

"Now if you *get* the job in New York," I said, "then I'll be upset."

"I don't want to think about that," he said. "I'm going to take a shower now so I won't wake you up too early to-morrow."

I wandered restlessly around the room. I still didn't un-derstand how he could stay in this place. There was almost nothing in it. On a bookshelf, I found the box I made him for Christmas. Once again, I rested my hand on the top, picked it up, looked over my work on the joints. I wondered if I could get those better now if I did them again. I wanted to open the lid to look at my work on the inside, but the box was locked. I looked around for the key. At first, I couldn't find it. Without thinking about it much, I ran my hands under the shelves of the bookcase until I found the key taped under one of them. I opened the box and looked inside: money. There was money in piles with rubber bands separating them by denomination. I stared at the cash a few seconds longer. Then I counted it, my heart pounding fast. Two thousand four hundred and sixty dollars. I got sweaty and my heart raced.

Once you have given someone a gift, even if you made the thing yourself with your own two hands, once given, it is no longer yours to handle without permission of its owner. I locked the box, put it back in its place, and taped the key back under the shelf.

CHAPTER 15

Sorry, We're Closed

The families of the boys on the soccer team were gathered on the field, where food tables were set up for a potluck dinner the night of the last game. Melanie said, "Thank god that's over!" Richard was there somewhere too. I was trying to fit in, to smile and behave as if nothing bad had ever happened to me, as if being proud of my children were my whole story. The coach made a speech about sportsmanship and gave an award to each boy. Daniel's award was for "Most Improved Player." His name was the last one called, and he walked slowly to the front of the crowd to receive his prize, a little plastic trophy of a boy kicking a soccer ball, and a coupon for Dairy Queen. He didn't even smile. He came back and handed the things to me. "Here it is, the 'World's Lousiest Player' award," Daniel said to Melanie and me.

"Daniel," I said, "you came a long way. You made four goals. That's what the award is for." He opened my purse and stuffed the trophy inside.

After a while the coach came over to us. "You've got quite a boy here," he said to me.

"Thank you," I said.

"Never gives up," said the coach. "We're looking forward to seeing him back next year."

I smiled at him, and he moved on to Michael Cruz's mother. "You've got quite a boy here," he said. "Never gives up."

People are phonies, I thought to myself; *you can't trust what they say to be the way they really feel.*

Richard was laughing with a group of other fathers. Melanie said, "I'm going to say hi to Dad."

Patty waved me over. I stood beside her in a group of mothers I knew from school and soccer, while Daniel and Mark went to find soda. The women were talking about someone who had bought a new van and sideswiped it on the first day. Then they discussed wallpaper borders. I stood there for several minutes; I had nothing to add. I didn't belong here. Suddenly I couldn't even force myself to listen to what people were saying around me. There was a clump of bushes at the side of the field. I wanted to curl up under them and not know anything. I wanted to lie down in a pile of leaves and pull dead branches over me, close my eyes.

Patty said, "Look!" and put her hand over her mouth in shock. "Ginny cut her hair! Oh, my god! I really didn't think she'd do it." She looked at me, expecting a reaction.

I glanced at the woman. I walked away.

"Mimi?" Patty called after me. "Mimi, are you OK?" I didn't answer.

Melanie and Daniel found me. "We want food," Daniel said. "Can we eat now?"

"Let's do that," I said. "Then we'll go. OK?"

Melanie said, "Dad has a girlfriend."

"Good," I said.

Daniel said, "No way."

"Way," said Melanie. "Her name is Beth, and she works at Nordstrom."

"Cool," Daniel said.

We were at the food table. I picked up some plates and plastic knives and forks. "What do you guys want here?" I said.

They surveyed the table. "Yuck," they said together.

"Come on now," I said. "Do you want tacos?"

"Ew, no," Melanie said. "Look at those gross pieces of onion."

"Lasagna?" I said.

Daniel shook his head. "I'm not eating that."

"Macaroni and cheese?"

"What are those little orange things?" Melanie said.

"What about bread?" I said.

"Is that garlic bread?" Daniel said. "Yuck."

I dropped the plates, forks, and knives back on the table. I had to get out of there. I couldn't stand it anymore. "Let's go," I said. I trudged across the soggy, overwatered field toward the parking lot.

"Mimi!" Richard was calling me. "Mimi, are you leaving already? Where are you going? I didn't even get to talk to you."

I said, "I have to get home."

Something was happening to me. My face around my eyes felt swollen and hot. I kept wanting to shut them. My chest and throat felt clenched and tight. I felt as though everything was closing up on the inside of me.

Richard said, "Melanie, Daniel, do you want to stay and I'll take you home?"

I could hear the kids' footsteps pause for a second in the grass behind me as they considered this. I kept walking. "No," said Daniel. "But thanks. See you Saturday."

Mud got all over my shoes and my socks got wet. I unlocked the car and got in. I had to wait for Melanie and Daniel. They were walking a lot slower than I was, being careful to avoid the mud.

Standing next to the car, they argued about who got to sit in front. For a few minutes, I just sat there, waiting for them to finish. When they didn't seem likely to stop, I turned the key in the ignition and backed up a few inches. They panicked and jumped in the car, Melanie in front and Daniel in back. "Mom!" Melanie said. "What are you doing? Trying to run us over?"

"Nice, Mom," Daniel said. "Really nice."

"I just want to go home," I said. "Can we just get home?"

"God," said Melanie. "We didn't even get any dinner."

The phone was ringing as I unlocked the store Monday morning. I hurried. It kept on while I turned off the alarm. I ran to pick it up, not stopping to switch the sign from CLOSED to OPEN. It was Henry. "Surprise," he said. "I'm in the Netherlands."

"You're what?" I said.

"I'm in Holland. It's a wild story. But I heard about this job from a guy I used to work with, and I just had to go for it."

I stood there a minute not saying anything, my mouth open.

"I interviewed with the guy on the phone from the store in San Diego once, and then—"

"What? When was this? Where was I?"

"You were there. You were waiting on people in front. It was a long time ago. A couple of months. So anyhow, the interview went great; he liked me. All I had to do was get myself here, meet all these other guys, and I was in. They all speak English, but I'm going to learn Dutch. I already know two ways to say thank you: *Bedankt* and *Dank u wel*. Mimi, this place is so neat," Henry said. "You'll really like it here— the canals and the flowers and the buildings! Everything I see is something I want to show you, to give you as a present! You have to come here, Mimi. As soon as you can. You have to come to Amsterdam and be with me."

"You're staying," I said. "Is that what you're telling me?"

"Yeah," he said. "Oh, yeah. I want to stay. This place is fantastic. I can't wait until you see it. You're going to love it."

"Henry," I said. "You know I'm not coming."

There was an empty rushing sound on the phone line when no one was speaking.

"Wait," he said. "No. No, wait. There's an American school here that Melanie and Daniel could go to. The kids there are just like all their friends, regular American kids. I've checked it out with some of the other people who work here. Don't you think it would be great for them to be in another country? In Europe! I mean, don't you? Don't just say no without even thinking about it." He said all this fast, hardly pausing for a breath, then he suddenly stopped. "Mimi," he said quietly. "This is not the end. Is it? Just say you love me. OK? Just say it."

"I love you." I said it simply, cleanly, with the slightest hesitation.

Of course, you know by now that this wasn't the first time in my life someone slipped away from me when I wasn't looking. Did I do this to myself on purpose, just turn my head slightly in the wrong direction at the right moment?

"And by the way," I said to Henry, "about the money—"

"What money?" he said too quickly.

"The money you took from the store," I said.

There was another pause, more rushing, like holding an empty seashell to your ear. "I'm going to pay you back," he said finally. "It won't take me very long. I didn't mean— I borrowed it, just to get myself here."

"No," I said. "It was a gift. A present from me to you."

"OK, OK, OK. You're mad. I understand. Let me just tell you how all this happened. You know that guy Hans I told you about, the guy I worked with in San Diego? His father works for this big multinational here in Amsterdam. So when we both got laid off, he came back here right away. There were two openings he was hoping for. But it wasn't completely sure until six weeks ago that it was going to work out. I did all right on the phone interview, but I still had to get the airfare together to do another interview in person. And of course I needed some money to get myself set up someplace, in case I got the job. I mean, that was pretty tricky. But believe it or not, it all came together just the way we wanted it to. I'm working with Hans just like we were before. And it's great. I'm going to love this job."

"Congratulations," I said. We listened to the seashell sound for several seconds. Then I said, "I would have given you the money, Henry. If you had just asked me, I would have handed over whatever you needed, now that we have it. All you had to do was ask."

He said, "I know that."

"So why did you take it? Why did you have to steal from me like that? You couldn't possibly think that you could take that money from me without my permission and then continue as if nothing had changed."

"I had to," Henry said. "If I told you about the job, something this far away, even something this good, you would have asked me to stay. You would have said, 'Don't go. Look at all we have. Stay with me.' Wouldn't you? You know I'm right. And you know what else?" He laughed. "I would have stayed. I would have stayed right there with you for the rest of my life. And it would have been good, in some ways. Really safe and nice. But at the same time, I would be watching those balloons going up every afternoon and wanting to fly away. Can you understand that, Mimi? Do you see at all what I mean? Am I getting through here?"

"Yeah," I said. "I got it. I trusted you; you robbed me."

"You knew about the money before I left!" he said, sounding as if he might cry. "Don't try to tell me you didn't, because I know you did. You put the key back under the wrong shelf. I know you knew, and you didn't stop me!"

"That's what I mean. It was a gift. My gift to you at the beginning of your new adventure."

John walked into the store then to set up his coffee counter. He waved at me silently because he didn't want to interrupt my phone call. I lifted a hand to greet him and turned away. "I have to go," I said. "I really have to start opening up." For some reason, the way I said this, it sounded as though I was about to embark on a phase of self-improvement, as though I was going to try to be more receptive to new ideas or become more spiritual in my outlook.

"Wait!" he said. "Would you *think* about coming? Would you just consider it?"

"Henry," I said. "I have to go."

"I love you, angel."

"I know that," I said. "I do know that. Good-bye." I hung up, walked to the front of the store, and turned the sign around so the side facing me read "Sorry, We're Closed. . . . Please Call Again."

CHAPTER 16

Things Work Out

Eve was saying, "You didn't know. Mimi, how could you know? No one did. It's just one of those terrible things that happens." She had said this before, repeating it over and over in almost these exact words, since I told her about Henry. I sat motionless on a stool in the store and didn't answer.

Every day now, from the time I woke up until I went to sleep at night, I felt as though a big wad of wet cotton had been implanted in the front of my brain. I was looking at everything through a thick piece of yellowed Plexiglas. When people spoke to me, it was a lot of work to put together a reply. I knew there were a lot of words to choose from, but I had trouble thinking of them. It was easier not to speak, not to say anything at all but to just keep my lips together and nod, shake my head, or shrug.

Melanie and Daniel kept asking me when Henry was coming back. The first several times, I just didn't answer. Finally, I said, "He's not. Henry is gone."

They were quiet. Then Daniel said, "Is that why you're so sad all the time? Is that why you never talk anymore?"

It seemed like work to make my head go up and down in a nod.

There was a flu going around, and I got it. My throat felt shredded, and everything else ached. I was relieved to be able to lie down, close my eyes, and not move. The evening of the first day, I got out of bed long enough to boil two pots of water, one for noodles and one for hot dogs. This was Melanie and Daniel's dinner. The second day, I could barely stand up. My mother was busy with parent conferences, and Eve and John were running the store, so Daniel called Richard, who came over with food for the kids; did some laundry, and checked their homework. He helped me get to the bathroom and made me drink some water, which felt so cold it made me shake. He came back the next day and the next until I had recovered. When I was well, he didn't come anymore.

I couldn't get going again. Instead, I started to do a lot of things that needed to be done and then stopped before I finished. I tried to make Melanie and Daniel's lunches for school. I put potato chips into brown bags, then sat down. Before I knew it, it was time to drive them to school, and I wasn't even dressed. There were two lunch bags in front of me with potato chips in them, but that was all. There wasn't enough time left for them to make their own lunches. Daniel got money out of my purse for them to buy hot lunch at school, which they hated. Melanie called a friend's mother to ask for a ride.

At ten-thirty, Eve called to ask when I was coming to work. She and Laurie were getting backed up and needed some help. I had gotten as far as putting on a bra and T-shirt, but I still had on my pajama pants and nothing on my feet. I couldn't quite recall what I had been doing the last couple of hours since the kids left. The breakfast dishes weren't rinsed, except for a single milk glass that sat alone in the gaping dishwasher. I told Eve, "I'm still sick. I can't work today."

"Oh no," she said. "What am I going to do? I know. I'll call Jake and see if he can come in early. Feel better." She hung up.

Before I knew it, the kids were home from school. At dinnertime, I told them to get money out of my purse for McDonald's. I went to bed in the same mismatched outfit I had worn all day. Something is wrong with me, I thought in the dark. I was afraid. Then I fell asleep.

There were more days like this, I'm not sure how many. On the evening of one of them, Eve and John came over to see us. I was in my room, and they came in, all excited, with Melanie and Daniel following them. Now that I think about it, this wasn't so long after the abundance workshop. But maybe that was just a coincidence.

Eve said, "Tell her, John. Mimi, this is great news."

"You tell her," John said, grinning at Eve.

"It's your news, honey. Go ahead," Eve said.

John smiled at her and didn't say anything.

Melanie said, "Somebody, tell us what happened."

"OK," Eve said. "I will. Here's the story. A busboy, an undocumented immigrant who worked in the restaurant where John used to work, went to the police last night and told them that he had acted as a money courier, picking up large amounts of cash late at night after the restaurant closed."

"Oh my god," Melanie said.

"He says he took the money to one of the restaurant owners at his home," Eve continued. "The other owner didn't know about this. The guy had promised the busboy—"

"His name is Miguel," John said.

"Right," said Eve. "The owner who was stealing the money had promised Miguel a green card for his cooperation and for not talking to anyone about the money." Eve paused a moment to let us take this in. "The restaurant owner, the one who stole money from his own place, had a gambling problem that he had supposedly worked out."

"Years ago," John added. "Way back." Eve waited to see if he was going to say more. "Go on," he told her.

Eve said, "But now they think he had run up some big gambling debts and needed a lot of cash to pay them back. He didn't want anyone to know he was gambling again—"

"Playing the ponies," John put in. "His weakness was the track."

"Yeah," Eve said. "So he promised to let Miguel bring his wife north, his mother, his children, in exchange for getting him this money and not talking about it. He kept his end of the deal all this time. Then two days ago, Miguel was picked up by an INS van on his way to work. He began to talk about the restaurant he worked in and didn't stop until he got to the police. Poor guy had counted on staying in Los Angeles. He thought he was going to be promoted to waiter, make a lot more money. Then, all of a sudden, boom, he was in an INS van on his way south. Anyway, his story is being checked out now. John's lawyer thinks they're going to drop the charges within the next few days. We'll know more tomorrow, I guess. Isn't it great?" She hugged John and kissed him.

Daniel said, "You were right, Mom."

"About what?" Eve said.

"She said John didn't take the money."

"Of course he didn't," Eve snapped.

"Wow," Melanie said to John. "Did you know who it was? Did you know all along it was Miguel working with the gambling guy?"

John said, "No. I had no idea." He laughed. "I never would have thought of Miguel. Never."

Eve said to me, "We've got to get going now. Some friends of John's are taking us out to dinner. We just wanted you to know the good news. Are you feeling any better?"

"Yeah." I worked my face into a smile.

When they were out of the room, I called, "Eve, wait." She came back in by herself. "Eve," I said, "are you mad at me? Do you hate me?"

"Mad at you? Hate you? What do you mean?"

"Yeah," I said. "Because of the way I thought—because of all the time I didn't like John, didn't believe him."

Eve sat down on my bed. She was wearing the YES earrings again. She said, "That seems like a thousand years ago. And I can't be mad now. I'm too happy. Besides, if you really want to know, for a while, I wasn't absolutely sure myself that he didn't do it. It just wasn't as important to me as it was to you."

"I don't know," I said. "I really thought he was guilty until a few weeks ago. I did."

"Everybody did." Eve shrugged. "I'll get over it."

John called to her from the front door. "Evie? You coming?"

"Yeah," Eve said. She gave me a hug and left.

After they were gone, I crawled under the covers again. The good news about John hadn't cheered me up. It was something else I was wrong about, another layer of darkness pressing on me, holding me down.

"Mom, there's no money." Daniel was standing beside me ready for school, holding my wallet. I had overslept. "If we have to buy hot lunch, we need money." There was a look in his eyes, the look he had sitting up in bed in the middle of a nightmare. "There's no food and no money," he repeated, as if he was afraid that I didn't understand words anymore.

I said, "Get money out of your Space Shuttle bank." My voice was flat, metallic, a machine trying to imitate me. "Write me a note. Put down how much I owe you." He didn't argue or whine but turned to go. Then with all the strength I had, I forced myself to say, "Daniel, call Dad."

"OK," he said hoarsely. "Now?"

"Right now," I said. Then I fell asleep again and didn't even hear them leave for school.

I dreamed about Bill. It didn't seem like a dream. It seemed as though he was back with me, right there in the bedroom. His hair was different, and he had on a pair of brand-new jeans. Of course, I thought, he wouldn't let himself turn into some out-of-date dork, just because he's dead. He looked as if he were doing very well where he was; he looked happy. "What you need to do is sit up," he said. "That would be the first thing. Then I'd say take a shower and get dressed. By that time, I bet you'll be able to figure out the rest yourself." I smiled, tried to move closer to see what kind of shoes he was wearing these days, and he was gone.

"Mimi, Mimi. Come on now, wake up," said a whisper.

I opened my eyes. Richard was there. "Hi," I said. I closed my eyes.

"Hi," he said, gently pushing back my hair.

"Am I sick?" I said because of the tender way he touched me.

"You're depressed."

"Oh."

"Yes," he said, "and you have to get up now."

"I'm too tired."

"Sorry." He was pulling me up. I sat, opened my eyes, saw a messy room. He held me against him a long time. I smelled deodorant, laundry soap, his car. Then he let go of me to open the curtains. The sun was way too bright. He came back, held me. "OK, in the shower," he said after a while. And in my head, in my sad brain, it seemed that Bill and Richard had gotten together while I was asleep and talked over what to do with me, how to get me moving again. As if I had no choice, I got up and walked to the bathroom, feeling oddly light.

When I was clean and dressed, Richard tried to get me to eat some breakfast I didn't want. I forced in a few mouthfuls. It was like pretending to eat the play food the kids used to serve me when they were little, going through the motions with plastic ice cream and bacon, a baby bottle of pretend orange juice that magically emptied and refilled. "Mm," I said to Richard, putting a lump of egg in my mouth, swallowing it without chewing. After another bite, I rested my face in my hands and sat still for a long time. Richard took the plate away. "I'm so tired," I said.

"It will pass," he said calmly.

"Why is this happening?"

"You're disappointed."

"Disappointed?" I said, getting mad. "Disappointed? Is that what you call it? I am devastated, destroyed. Everything I thought was true turned out to be a big lie."

"Yeah," he said. "I see that. Call it what you want. It's bad. I'm not saying that it's insignificant. But I am saying it will pass. Here's what I think happened. Someone betrayed you. You were attached to him, he left you, you miss him."

"Attached to him?" I laughed, though nothing was funny.

"All right, you were in love with him." He said this reluctantly, as though I were really asking for a lot.

"That's right, and I made a colossal mistake," I said. "The mistake of my life." I started to cry.

"Mimi, Mimi, Mimi," he said, coming to my side of the table, squatting to get his face close to mine. "Henry was a handsome, sweet, charming, smart guy. OK, he was a thief. But a *nice* thief. You loved him. You still do. Before him, there was Bill who was kind and knew how to fix things. He got sick and died. Before that you had me. Great taste in music, strong potential in the fatherhood department, but frequently incompetent about cars and pipes and banking, and once, a long time ago, I cheated on you. You still love me though, right?" I nodded and cried. "It's just the way things happen, Mimi. Everyone you meet is going to have some big, hopeless defect. Sometimes more than one. Sometimes you can live with it, sometimes you can't." I leaned forward, holding on tight to his shirt. "I know," he said, stroking the back of my T-shirt. "I know it's bad. But we're tough guys, and we're going to keep right on going, aren't we? Aren't we? Not because we want to, of course. Because we have to. We have no choice. Come on now. We are. Agree with me." I nodded my head, just because I knew he wanted me to, heard my hair crunch against his. "That's right. There's my girl. You're going to be all right now. Look out, everybody, here comes Mimi."

I said, "Every time I get everything organized and start to get settled, it all crumbles and falls apart." I stopped to sob. "And here I am standing in this mess, this rubble, and I have to start all over again."

Richard nodded. "Yeah."

"What do you mean, 'yeah'?"

"I mean, I agree. That's how it is for me too. I get things to work, they fall apart, I start over." He shrugged. "The cycle of life. Again and again and again." He smiled at me, as if this were amusing.

I sniffed, reached for a napkin for my nose. "How's Beth?"

"Good," he said. "She's good. But she's not the one. Not even one of the ones. I can already tell."

"Sorry," I said.

"Hey," he said and patted my back. "Not your fault."

He started to pull away, to stand up, but I held on tighter, not ready to let him go. He said, "I've got to move. My legs are falling asleep." We both sat on the floor, me holding on,

Richard with his arms around me, wiggling his legs back to life. Then suddenly he stopped and kissed me on the mouth. We froze for a moment, stunned, waiting to see what would happen next.

I had another dream about Bill. We were sitting next to a swimming pool in the place where he lived. He was wearing a bathing suit. It was a resort of some kind or a luxury condo complex. He said, "Let me tell you what I've learned since I've been here. Are you listening? It's this: Things work out. Got that? That's it, the whole thing. I'll say it again. Things work out." He pointed at me and winked.

I wanted to argue with him, citing everything that had gone wrong lately. I was going to say, "What about Henry taking our money? I was in love with him. What about the way Eve and I didn't get along for such a long time? What about John being accused of something he didn't do and almost everyone, including me, thinking he did it?" I wanted to say all this to Bill, but he had done something to my mouth so that I couldn't open it.

"I know what you want to say," he said. He shook his head. "Don't bother. I'm right. Things work out." He stood up and jumped into the pool.

"You're wrong," I was going to yell at him when he resurfaced. "I know you're dead, and you think you know everything now. But you don't. You don't know what you're talking about! Everything is a mess, a depressing jumble of disasters, disappointments, and mixed feelings." Before I had a chance to say this, Melanie came into my bedroom to ask if she could borrow a sweatshirt of mine. I opened my eyes. Bill wasn't there.

CHAPTER 17

Now, This Moment

It was a big wedding, far more elaborate than my other two. We had chosen an old hotel downtown with a ballroom that had chandeliers and grand pianos and paneled ceilings. I was wearing my mother's dress, updated and fitted for me with a lot of the frillier details removed. It was now an ivory off-the-shoulder gown. I didn't have a veil, but I wore a wreath on my head made of baby's breath and pink rosebuds. Eve, now eight-and-a-half months pregnant, was the matron of honor, and Melanie and Patty were the bridesmaids. Richard was wearing the clothes we had bought together at Nordstrom almost two years before. He was underdressed, but he said he couldn't find a suit that he would ever wear again. The best man was the principal of Richard's school, and the ushers were Daniel and John. My mother had started crying early in the morning, and now at quarter to two, fifteen minutes before the ceremony, her face was blotchy and puffy, her makeup all but gone. "Mom," I said. "Why don't you go get a drink of cold water? Rinse your face again." She stood up to go to the bathroom. "Here, take some more tissues. That toilet paper will make your nose red."

"I just don't know what's wrong with me," she said, laughing through more tears.

"You're happy," Melanie said flatly. She was wearing a pink dress. Eve had braided pink ribbons through her hair. But Melanie kept complaining. "These shoes are, like, murdering my feet." She looked down. "I bet they look like raw hamburger in here. I'm scared to take these things off because I might spill blood all over the place."

"I'm sorry," I said. "Eleven-and-a-halfs were the biggest ones Aunt Eve and I could find. I know they're too small. As soon as the ceremony is over, you can go barefoot. It's only for a little while. Think of what you're wearing not as clothes, but as a costume for a role you're playing."

"You mean maybe if I pretend I'm someone else, I won't feel like such a geek?" She looked in the mirror. "*Pink*. Mom, I'm way too old for pink."

"Too old?" Eve said. "I beg your pardon. What about Patty and me?" We all looked at Eve, who had grown so big that she had to have her dress altered at the last minute. The seamstress, who had started the dresses two months earlier, had miscalculated Eve's potential for growth by a long shot. "Besides," Eve went on, "it's the bride's right to choose any bridesmaids' dresses she wants." She stood up and stroked the cloth over her big belly. "This is our uniform. It separates us from all the rest of the people out there. We belong to a special club of the people closest to your mom. I'm proud to be in pink."

Behind me, Melanie sighed with such force that I had to brush my hair again.

Patty said to Melanie, "Your hair is so long and thick. I'd give anything to have hair like that." She patted her own spiky hair, adjusted her earrings.

"Melanie, I've never seen you look so lovely," said my mother, coming back from the bathroom."

"Gee, thanks, Grandma," Melanie said. "Aunt Eve put so much hairspray on me it feels like I'm wearing a helmet. All I need is a mouth guard, a face mask, and a pair of skates and I'm all ready for ice hockey."

I put on lipstick.

"Oh, can I use some of that?" Melanie said.

I handed it to her.

"When I get married," Melanie said, "I'm not going to go through all this. I'm just going to make sure I have shoes that don't kill, put on makeup, and go. I don't care about the fancy clothes, the cake, the honeymoon, any of that stuff."

"What about presents?" I said, putting on mascara.

Melanie considered. "Presents are fine," she said. "I'll take the presents."

We were all quiet for a while, concentrating on preparing our faces. Melanie said, "Mom, did you think it was going to turn out this way? Did you think you and Dad would end up together again?"

"No," I said.

"I certainly didn't," said my mother. "Not in my wildest dreams." She dabbed at her eyes with a tissue. "Isn't it wonderful?"

"Neither did I," Patty said. "Did you see this coming, Eve?"

"Absolutely not," Eve said. "I almost fainted when she told me, didn't I, Mimi?"

"I saw it coming," Melanie said. "I did. I knew it all along. I could have told them a long time ago that they were going to get back together. People never listen to me. But I didn't count on this dress or these gross shoes." We all put on makeup, looked at ourselves, put on more.

You probably want to know how Richard and I got back together. At first, we saw each other secretly, as if we were married to other people and having an affair. I didn't lie, but I said things like, "I'm going to Pacific Beach for dinner. Here's the number," or "I'm meeting someone downtown. I have my pager." We tried to find places where we wouldn't run into anyone we knew. He would call me at work to say, "I was thinking about you. I wanted to hear your voice." And I would answer, "Thank you. Same here." Eve would prick up her ears and look at me. "Who was that?" she would ask when I hung up. "Hm?" I would say. "What?"

It was fun, having a secret. We would go to restaurants, order, and then talk and talk and talk, ignoring the food, so that by the time we paused long enough to eat, it had gotten cold. It was hard to think straight. Again. This time, though, I wasn't as giddy and silly as I had been with Henry. In comparison, the relationship felt solid, substantial, the accumulation of all our years of experience bringing us back together now, at this moment.

I was a little worried in the beginning about how the sex was going to go. Frankly, it had never been the best thing about being with Richard when we were younger. This time it was much better than before. All those years of practicing with other people had really paid off. Everything we had done up to now seemed to lead us right here.

We had almost decided to tell people what was going on when Melanie let me know she had already figured it out. One night she was with me in my bathroom while I got dressed to go out. She said, "Aren't you going to wear the earrings Dad gave you last week?" She dug around in my sock drawer and pulled out the gold studs in a box I had hidden there. "Here," she said. "They're pretty. I tried them on when you were making dinner last night."

Since we were in my bathroom, I had to watch myself blush. "How did you know?" I asked her.

"I'm smart," she said. She shrugged. "I figure out the things people don't tell me. It's my job."

Daniel was in the doorway. I said, "As a matter of fact, we were thinking of having Dad move in here with us."

I braced myself for shouts and cheers and noisy, happy jumping up and down. They didn't do that. They didn't say anything at all, but just looked at each other for a few seconds, then back at me.

Melanie said, "To *our* house? You're kidding, right?"

Daniel said, "Where are we going to go on weekends?"

I sat down on the bed with them and said, "You won't have to go anywhere, honey, because we will all be here together. We'll be a family again."

Daniel said, "I thought we were already a family. I thought you said Dad would always be our dad, no matter where he lived.

"All right, I did say that. And it's true that we have always been a family. But now we'll be a family in one house again."

"Where are we going to swim?" Daniel persisted. "Dad has a pool, and we don't."

"Uh," I said. "At Patty's?"

Of course, Daniel didn't remember all of us living in one house, and Melanie had been very small when Richard left. I should have expected that the idea would take some getting used to. I guess I had thought it was going to be like some Disney movie, where the children plot to get their divorced parents back together and rejoice when it happens. The two of them kept staring at me skeptically. Daniel said, "Are you going to marry Dad, Mom?"

"Pardon?" I said. I heard what he asked me; I was stalling.

"If you guys get married again, do we get to go to the wedding?" he wanted to know. "Last time, we didn't get to go."

"Because we weren't *born,* goofball," Melanie said.

"I know," Daniel said. "I know that."

I said, "If Dad and I get married again, you will certainly be invited." And then I laughed at the thought of marrying Richard for the second time.

Soon after, Richard moved in.

Since Richard and I got back together, a lot of other things changed fast. You already know about John. The charges were dropped a few days after the busboy came forward with his story. I thought John was unbelievably good-natured about what he had lost in the process of being a scapegoat—a house, a career, friends. "I got a chance to start over fresh," he said. "I've got a brand-new life." He seemed almost cheerful about the way being a suspect in an ugly crime of theft and betrayal had forced him to reexamine everything. "Why should I mind?" he said, when I asked him if he wasn't bitter, resentful about the way he had been treated. "It was pretty hideous while it was going on, sure. But look where it got me. This is so much better. I'm happy now." He pulled Eve close and kissed her neck. Miguel visited him on his way back to Mexico. He told John it wasn't right the way some people told lies and made promises they didn't intend to keep. And John agreed with him.

Our store became so successful that we had to hire several more people until we had six people working all the time. We bought more machines, including a laminator and one that could make personalized T-shirts and coffee mugs from almost any image. Over the next year, we opened three more stores. One, in the Coastal Palms center, was open until midnight. There, we took over the Send It, Inc., space. Following its rapid expansion, the company suddenly went bankrupt. While that particular outlet had done well, apparently the company had opened too many too fast.

These days, Eve and I spent most of our work time driving

around to our four stores, checking on things, working out problems. Each store had a manager who supervised both the café and office services and reported to us. My pager was always going off—in the grocery store, at the movies, at school functions. It felt strange, after all the struggles and hard work, not to be making copies and wrapping packages anymore. But I guess this was success: you work your way up until you're no longer doing your job but managing other people doing it. Even with our expanded responsibilities, we had more time now to develop other interests.

John didn't bake his own cookies and muffins anymore either. Before we opened the second store, he had to find a bakery that could handle the larger orders he couldn't do by himself. Now he was using the contacts he had made in our original store to develop a strong side business, catering office parties and meetings.

Eve had rented a studio where she could work on her dolls. She was doing expensive commissioned ones that were available in stores in New York, Chicago, Dallas, and San Francisco, a single shop in each city. She had also sold a cheaper doll, Bridget, a working mother, to be manufactured by one of the toy giants. Accessories included a briefcase containing a portable computer, a cellular phone, a pacifier, a diaper, a plastic half-eaten cracker, and two smaller girl dolls whose Velcro hands could cling to any part of Bridget's body.

I submitted the design for my cassette and CD racks with the angled slots to a catalog company. I had a whole list of places to go to with my idea, but the first company bought it. They were marketing it for use in boats and RVs. My next design was going to be a secret treasure box, a pretty wooden piece with a lock for storing photographs, letters, mementos.

If you have some unique skill that you excel at, it will support you. I believe that. John, Eve, and I now gave a percentage of our profits to San Diego homeless shelters. This was John's idea. "Abundance is for everyone," he reminded us. We found an accountant to keep track of everything coming in and going out.

Naturally, Richard and I had to work out some of the problems that came up when we started living together again. After the first week, I told him I didn't like the way he expected me to be in charge of dinner. He looked a little startled, but then he agreed that it wasn't fair. In the time that he had been living away from us, he had learned to cook. He enjoyed making meals, while I had just about stopped serving anything that didn't come from some other kitchen in either an aluminum container or a cardboard box. Richard took over dinner, and I did breakfast and the kids' lunches. Another difficulty was that our water heater couldn't handle four showers in the morning, so Richard and Daniel started taking theirs at night, until we got organized enough to buy a new one. The problems this time were minor, mere technical snags, a matter of mechanics that took just a little tinkering before everything began to run more smoothly than it ever had before.

When we started talking about a wedding, we both got excited and carried away by the planning. Like me, Richard felt we had missed out when we didn't have a big wedding the first time. "These rituals exist for a reason," he pointed out. The guest list kept growing and growing until it seemed we had invited everyone we ever knew. Eve helped me make the hundreds of decisions about colors and fabrics and hors d'oeuvres and place cards that occasionally threatened to overwhelm me.

"This is going to be a great wedding," Eve was saying now. "Everyone you know is so happy for you. I can't believe it's finally *time!* After all the work and planning, the big moment is here!" She lowered her voice now and looked straight into my face. "I have such good feelings about this, Mimi. A beautiful new episode is about to begin." She shivered with excitement and hugged me.

Patty said, "I think everybody feels that way, that you and Richard are so right, so good together. Just thinking about what you've been through to get here makes me proud to know you." Patty smiled and huggged me.

A few minutes before it was time to start the wedding, the judge came to see me. She was about seventy and had white hair. I had insisted that the person who married us should be older than we were. She said, "How are you doing, dear?" and put a hand on my shoulder to steady me, leaning down to look at my face. "Oh!" she said, surprised. "You look as cool as a cucumber!"

"Everything's working out perfectly," I said, and smiled.

"That's the way. You'd be amazed at how many brides are nervous wrecks before the ceremony—lost rings, changes of heart, hysterics—"

"Diarrhea, vomiting," Melanie added.

"Melanie," I said.

"You name it," the judge said.

Melanie put on another layer of lipstick, wiped it off with a tissue, and put on some more.

"Really?" I said. "I thought that kind of thing only happened in movies. Don't worry," I assured her. "I'm very level. As I mentioned, this is my third wedding, the second one with Richard. It's not as if there's much left that could surprise me. I know exactly what I'm doing."

"Good girl," she said. "That's what I like to hear. I'll see you in a few minutes, then."

My mother hugged me, kissed me on the cheek, and went

to take her place in the first row. Patty, Eve, Melanie, and I gathered at the door. In a minute, Daniel came to get us. "Ready or not," he said.

"Here we come," we all answered.

There was music on, a tape of our favorite songs that Richard had made for the guests to listen to before the "Wedding March" started. He had chosen the last one especially for me, he said, a song we both loved, one that meant a lot to us. It was a secret. I waited, listening. Then the introduction to "My Love Is You" by David Byrne started up. A warm feeling came over me. The song summed up exactly what Richard had told me he felt about me, about relationships in general. I listened to every word.

> some men desire a princess
> and others lust for a temptress
> well i don't need one of those
> 'cause
> my love is you
> my love is you
>
> some men replace their mamas
> and some want a young baiana
> i have no use for those 'cause
> my love is you
> and my love is you
>
> sometimes dear
> you tell me i'm an asshole
> sometimes you're an asshole too
> even though we're filled with imperfections
> i don't think any less of you

i'm primitive and selfish
i'm childlike and i'm helpless
well i got that because of
my love for you

my love is you
my love is you

I was quietly singing along as I waited beside Daniel, who was giving me away. He gave my arm a squeeze. We peeked through a louvered door, watching the roomful of dressed-up people chatting happily in their seats, waiting for the "Wedding March" to start.

Music started, but it was another song. The David Byrne one turned out to be the second to last, not the last one after all. The song Richard chose for me to hear right before we got married was "I Want to Hold Your Hand." In fourth grade, Richard and I both became Beatles fans as soon as we heard this song, which was why he said it was something that meant a lot to us both. The vocals started, those perfect, exuberant harmonies captured so long ago. I thought I could hear an edge of chained wildness in those voices too, something that might at any moment break free and tear everything apart.

Finally the "Wedding March" started, and the judge motioned everyone to stand up. Melanie had gotten past her sore feet and her aversion to pink long enough to turn around and smile at me. She looked like an elaborate illustration for a fairy tale, a young maiden about to blossom into a queen. She started down the aisle, leading the procession of attendants. My mother was crying without restraint, a wad of Kleenex clutched in one hand. "I love you," she mouthed at Melanie and Eve as they passed. Calmly, Richard took his place, smiling at the judge, the guests.

I felt Daniel start to move forward, but for a second I was rooted in place. "Mom," he said. "Let's go. We're supposed to go now."

Standing there, I thought, *It's now, this moment, I am going to do it.* I took my arm out of Daniel's and said, "Just a second, honey." I grabbed a handful of white taffeta on each side of my dress and hiked up the skirt so that I could move fast. I marched up the aisle by myself and whispered sharply to Richard, "You know I can't stand oldies. How *could* you?"

Richard drew his head back and frowned. "That wasn't an oldie," he hissed back. "It's a Beatles song, a classic. There's a difference."

I stood there for a second, my eyes darting madly around the room at the flowers, the people, everything so prettily arranged. "I can't do this," I told Richard. "This is all wrong." I said it a little too loudly. I heard a gasp from behind me. It was Eve. I turned around and said to her, "I just can't!"

She said, "Mimi, we all—"

At the same time, Melanie said, *"Mom—"*

People started to murmur and whisper to one another. The judge pursed her lips, annoyed at the confusion.

I turned back to Richard. I said, "Richard, I don't want to do this. Let's not." I was shaking my head. "It's all wrong. OK, OK, we get along fine now and everything. Sure, we don't fight anymore. But there's something big that just isn't here. You know I mean, don't you? You *must.*"

He stared at me. He was thinking it over, processing. Then he whispered, "Passion?" I nodded. "Is that it?" He nodded too. "Ha!" he whispered, joyfully, relieved. "Holy shit! I didn't sleep a wink all night, couldn't put my finger on the problem. But you're right. You've nailed it! This is a mistake. Now don't panic. We're in charge here. This is our show." But his face had gone white, and his fingers were clammy when they touched my bare shoulder. "Do you want to say it, or shall I?"

"On the count of three," I said, "turn around and we'll wing it. One, two, three." We turned. As if on cue, someone faded the music. I spoke first. "We've decided not to go through with this."

Richard said, "As you all know, we've already tried being married to each other once, a long time ago, and it didn't work." He laughed and looked baffled. "What were we thinking?" He looked around the room, disoriented, as if he were just waking up from a long sleep.

I took over again. "We've come a long way to get here today. We love each other, we love our kids. And all of you have been absolutely, uh—" I paused. I couldn't think where I wanted to go with this.

"Relentless in your support," Richard filled in. "Now we don't want to ruin it by doing something we're going to regret."

Daniel peeked out from behind the louvered door. "Mom?" he said.

I reached out a hand to him, and he came to join us. Melanie came forward, put her head on my shoulder, and burst into tears.

"Now, now," I said. "Don't be sad. This is a good thing."

Melanie said, "I know. I'm crying because I'm happy. I could have told you it was a dumb idea. But no one listens to me."

I know what you're thinking. You're thinking of all those movies you've seen where people back out of weddings at the last possible moment. So was I. It may have been those very movies that allowed me to feel that it might be possible to shake myself loose of something as big, expensive, and inconvenient as a wedding this late in the day. I was thinking, I didn't know people could actually get away with this in real life! And here I was pulling it off.

We dismissed the judge, changed out of our wedding clothes, and had the party anyway. The mood wasn't disappointment or embarrassment or melancholy, as you might expect. It was relief. I couldn't stop smiling. Daniel said, "Is everything going to be normal now? When is Dad going back to his own apartment?"

My mother said, "As long as you're happy, sweetheart."

Eve said, "Thank god you came to your senses in time! I mean, really Mimi. Richard!" John put his arm around her large waist, and she snuggled against him.

There was a lot of dancing to a long tape Richard and I had worked on together: Elvis Costello, the Cranberries, Suzanne Vega, the Smiths, Morrissey, the Cure, David Byrne, James, Counting Crows, and on and on. I danced with Richard, Daniel, John, Eve, Richard again, Melanie, my mother, Patty, Richard. I think I may have danced with everyone there.

We couldn't get our money back for the trip to Maui we had planned. Instead, we bought another ticket. Before they went to bed that night, Melanie and Daniel collected their bathing suits, shorts, and cameras and stuffed them into suitcases. The next morning, I took Richard and the kids to the airport.

When the flight was being called, Daniel said, "Mom, are you sure you don't want to come with us?"

"Don't be silly," I said. "Have a good time. Bring me a hula skirt and some sand. And call me, you guys."

I went home and worked in my garage on a chair I was making, but it was hard to focus with everything so quiet. I drove to the shopping center and rented a movie. But when

I got home and put it on, I found I had already seen it. I ate some ice cream and took a bath. Then I couldn't think of what else to do with myself, so I took a nap. I almost never take naps, but this one time I did. I had another one of those dreams about Bill. This time he was sitting on my dresser, his legs hanging down to the third drawer, his arms folded across his chest. He said, "See what I mean?" as if we were in the middle of a conversation.

"About what?"

"It's exactly the way I said it would be: Things work out. Remember?"

"Sure I do, but I mean, I just spent several thousand—"

"Oh, money," he said scornfully, cutting me off. "When you're sitting where I am, you'll see what a petty concept money is. And I have something else important to tell you: What you're about to do is a mistake."

"What?" I said. "What are you talking about?"

"Now, Mimi. You're going to have to trust me on this one. Don't do it."

"Hold it," I said, putting up my hand. "Are you saying you know what's going to happen next?"

"Yes."

"And you plan to tell me what I should do?"

"Well, yeah."

"Please don't. What about 'things work out'? Didn't you just say that? So what does it matter to you what I do?"

"Sure, sure," he said. "Things work out. Yeah, I mean, *ultimately.*"

"But you're going to help them work out faster?"

"I'm going to save you a lot of trouble."

"Thanks," I said. "Really. But I have to—"

"No, you don't," he said, cutting me off.

"You know, you're always interrupting me," I said. "That's so irritating."

"Excuse me," he said. "What did you want to say? I'm listening." He pretended to button his mouth closed.

"I appreciate your coming. I'm glad, because for a while I was worried that you didn't exist anymore." Bill snorted at this ridiculous notion. "But now, don't tell me what to do. I don't want to know what's going to happen. Besides, I probably wouldn't take your advice anyway."

He said, "I don't think you understand. One of the advantages to being dead is that you get this incredibly enhanced perspective on everything. It's like—" He thought about it for a few seconds. "It's like you get a new computer with an enormous screen, unlimited memory, and free access to every on-line network that has been or will be created, all at once."

"That's great—" I said.

"So I can tell you things," he said. "Things that I can see and you can't."

"Don't." I shook my head. Then I was quiet for a minute, just staring him down, waiting.

"All right," he said. He lifted his hands and let them drop with a slap against his thighs. "I give up."

I said, "I'm grateful for what you're trying to do—"

"I'm *trying* to help you."

"Thank you," I said. "Now stop. Enough."

"OK," he said. "Have it your way."

"I will. You know, Bill—" I stopped. I didn't want to hurt his feelings. "I don't think you should keep coming around like this."

He was hurt. "But you wanted me to."

"I did. I know I did. And it's helped a lot to be able to see you."

"But now leave you alone, right?"

"Right."

"OK," he said. "If that's what you want."

"I don't mean you should disappear forever—," I said, reaching out my hand, as if I could grab him and hold on.

"Forever," he said, smiling. "Mimi, nothing is forever. You know that."

"Just for right now," I said. "Let me just manage on my own."

"I guess I can live with that," he said, and laughed at his joke.

The doorbell rang then and woke me up. It was someone who wanted to sell me a subscription to a newspaper I was already getting. As soon as I closed the door again, I went to the kitchen. I drank some water and looked at my watch. Then I searched through a pile of paper in the kitchen drawer for a phone number I was sure I had saved but didn't know where. I had to look through my desk, my purse, my bedside table. I finally found it in my bathroom drawer. I dialed. The phone rang and rang. When I was about to hang up, someone lifted the receiver. "Hello?" said a sleepy voice from very far away.

"Henry?" I said.

"Mimi?" he said. *"Mimi? Is that you?"*

After hearing about all that had happened since he left, all the changes in our work, John getting out of trouble, the wedding I didn't go through with, the whole story, Henry had one question: "Mimi," he said, "do you have a passport?"

If you're going to tell me not to go, you won't be the first. Don't worry. I haven't forgotten what Henry did. And I won't. But I'm not thinking about it every minute, either. What I'm thinking about now is the feel of his fingers at the small of my back, the sound of his voice whispering to me in the dark, his grinning face when he looked up—from eating or talking or tying his shoelaces—and caught me looking at him. I'm thinking about the way he insisted on staying in the car when we were listening to a song he liked, holding my wrist, neither of us getting out until the last note was over. Those are the things I'd rather not be without anymore, not all the time, not if I can help it.